THE ADVENTURES OF DOUGLAS BRAGG

MADISON JONES

The **Adventures** *of* **Douglas Bragg**

A NOVEL

THE UNIVERSITY OF TENNESSEE PRESS / KNOXVILLE

LIBRARY OF CONGRESS CATALOGING-IN-PUBLICATION DATA

Jones, Madison, 1925–
The adventures of Douglas Bragg: a novel / Madison Jones. — 1st ed.
p.   cm.
ISBN-13: 978-1-57233-636-0 (acid-free paper)
ISBN-10: 1-57233-636-6 (acid-free paper)
1. College graduates—Fiction.
2. Tennessee—Fiction.
3. Southern States—Fiction. I. Title.

PS3560.O517A63 2008
813'.54—dc22   2008010776

To Shailah, once again

THE ADVENTURES OF DOUGLAS BRAGG

EVERY YEAR ON MY BIRTHDAY I never fail to recall, and rehearse again and again, episodes in my life that had their beginning in the fall of 1960, when I was twenty-four. I guess I could say that I went forth to see the world as I never had really seen it, from the ground up, a world that had to be more interesting than this one. At the time, this meant a hitchhiking trip aimed at no particular destination other than what fortune might have in store for me. Though I am sure that many details of my experiences have escaped my memory, it doesn't seem that way. So many rehearsals, I suppose, are what have kept these events as whole and alive for me as if they had happened yesterday.

The preface to my trip needs a little explaining. After my graduation from college, I spent nearly two full years to no avail, going nowhere. During that time I had held, and within a couple of months lost or quit, half a dozen jobs, the last being a job at the city dog pound. In fact this was the one job I almost liked, and I lost it only because of somebody else's fault. This time, though, my mother was not displeased. She looked hard at me and came up with words she had used maybe dozens of times before. "You, an able young college graduate, cleaning up after animals at a dog pound. What on earth is the matter with you, Douglas?"

"I don't know," I mumbled, not wanting another unpleasant scene and maybe even tears. As usual, she shook her well-groomed head, displayed a knitted brow, and turned away with a sigh.

My mother was an affectionate woman, especially toward me, and I kept regretting that I never seemed quite able to return her affection in kind. It was different in the case of my father, Harold Bragg, though the word *affection* is not precisely the one that describes my feelings toward him. He was a wonderfully clever man, a lawyer, with a wit that could slip up on you and, very likely, deliver a cut that you wouldn't notice till a little afterwards. So it often happened with my mother, who was plenty intelligent but of a trustful nature that made her an easy target. It is anything but a compliment to me that on such occasions I was regularly amused to see her belated and often angry response. I believe it is about right to say that my father's gifts, his cleverness and his verbal dexterity more than anything else, were what so attracted me. I wanted to be like him in those things. Even when my mother divorced him and I learned the reason (he was cheating on her, big-time), my admiration for him was not permanently dampened. I rarely saw him after the divorce, and never after Mother and I moved from Nashville to Birmingham. But I would hear things about him and his reputation as the slickest of slick lawyers whose services were greatly in demand. Perversely, this made me proud. And I think that somehow, even back then, at age fifteen, I sensed that the unbroken distance between him and me was the cause and lasting preserver of my admiration for him.

In Birmingham, my mother's hometown, she got a job as a secretary, and along with the alimony, we were well-enough off. But being well-off turned out to have its cost. In the extended family there was the question of what to do with an ancient and impoverished great-uncle. So, being well-off and having no man in the house, we were chosen to take him in. It was to my mother's deep regret. There was not only the trouble of feeding him and keeping him clean and upright, there was the fact that he talked all the time. My mother soon learned to stop up her ears, but I, on the contrary, kept mine wide open. To me, he was an interesting old man. He had an inexhaustible trove of stories from long ago, and I never missed a chance to urge him on. In some degree he took my father's place.

It took more than eight years and hard going for my mother, but Uncle Jack's presence, not by death, finally came to an end. My mother had finally and decisively announced that the strain was just too much. So, with the families' reluctant compliance, but against his wishes and mine, she put him away in a home for old folks.

The Adventures of Douglas Bragg

I well remember the day it happened. I was, once again, unemployed, and this added still more to my distress at his departure. The house seemed, and went on seeming, as desolate as a tomb, with no life in it but my scattered memories of old Uncle Jack. He would be seated in his big chair with both hands on the cane between his knees, his nearly bald head with its chaplet of tufted white hair bent a little forward, his voice taking me back to a time when the world was as different from this one as daylight is from dark. No end to his memories. He told me about horse races and cockfights and revival meetings and town bullies and coon hunts and outrageous practical jokes, and on and on in a voice only a little coarsened by phlegm in his throat. But of all the subjects in his repertoire, the one he most talked about was, as he called it, the War Between the States. He had a lot of books about the War, but it was like he had got his knowledge not from books but from being on hand at the time, which was impossible. He was better than any book. There were moments in his narrations when his excitement seemed like it just might lift him right out of his chair . . . and me along with him. My mother hated it all. She partly blamed him for my being *the way I was* . . . by reinforcement at least.

Anyhow *the way I was* more and more blatantly displayed itself, especially in the evenings when my mother came in from work and found me either pacing about the rooms or else sitting dazedly sprawled in an armchair in front of her early version of a TV set. I can't blame her for her response on these occasions, a response that day by day came closer to violent expressions of outrage. This couldn't be allowed to go on and therefore was the cause of my abrupt departure. Late one night I made my preparations, and leaving behind a reassuring note on the kitchen table, I was well gone before she woke up.

— — —

In early afternoon of that same day, I found myself abandoned on a state highway some forty miles north of home. Hitchhiking then as now was hard work, no matter how innocent-looking the hitchhiker. The initial stroke of luck that had taken me this far seemed like it would never be repeated, and two hours of walking in unseasonably hot fall weather with a stuffed canvas bag in one or the other sweaty hand had me rethinking my nebulous intentions. Even my thumb was tired, and the little breezes whipped up by occasional cars rocketing past seemed

The Adventures of Douglas Bragg

— — —

only to make things worse. Fields and woods and a farmhouse once in a while, nothing else. It had come to seem downright hopeless when, after rounding a long curve, I approached what was to be my second stroke of luck . . . if you could call it that.

The car, a Studebaker with a dented rear fender, was parked on the highway shoulder at the foot of a rock bank. It was jacked up, and a man whose name turned out to be Roland Belt was crouched down changing a rear tire. He was tightening the lugs as I approached. He looked up, giving me a sweaty and very puzzled glance, as if my appearance on the scene required some explaining. Amiably I said, "Hot day for a flat."

"I can't understand it," he said and gave another vigorous pull at the lug wrench. Obviously I was not the real cause of his bewilderment; the tire was what had his attention. The size of the fellow was impressive, the muscular shoulders under his tense white shirt, the flushed neck straining his sweaty collar.

"You must have run over a nail," I said helpfully.

"I can't understand it," he repeated, addressing either himself or the punctured tire lying beside him. In a brooding voice he added, "Guaranteed for thirty thousand miles. Twelve hundred, and *poof*. Not even twelve hundred. . . . And no nail in it, either. Look for yourself."

I looked at the tire and didn't see a nail. "I sure don't see one."

"You won't, either. I don't care how long you look." He had lifted his big, flushed handsome face and was regarding me with an expression that clearly asked, "What do you think of *that?*"

I couldn't bring myself to say what a shame I thought it was, so I just said, "Well, anyway they'll have to give you another one free."

"It's one of those new puncture-proof Evalasts," he said as though he had not heard me. "It was absolutely guaranteed." I felt he was waiting, and since I very much wanted a ride, I said, "I know how you feel. With a guarantee like that."

"That's what gets me. Things like this shake a fellow's confidence in things." For another few seconds he sat there on his haunches gazing like Hamlet at his punctured tire. "Well." He gave a sigh and then picked up the hubcap and deftly with the heel of his hand hammered it into place on the wheel. He got to his feet and in only a moment had the wheel back on the ground and the jack laid out neatly in the open trunk. I was ready with the punctured tire, which he took with one hand and set with easy grace in the slot made for it. I was standing there at the ready with my bag when he got the trunk shut, but now he was looking

The Adventures of Douglas Bragg

4

as if, in his preoccupation, he had forgotten about me. For fear he had, I said, "I wonder if I could have a ride with you?"

"Huh? Oh, sure. Glad to have you."

But after we were in the car, he only sat mopping his face with his handkerchief and conducting what I judged by his lip movements to be a soliloquy. At length, still talking to himself, he set to rights the rather soiled green tie he was wearing. Then he seemed to be considering, though vaguely, the problem presented by the fact that his cuffs were turned back, exposing thick wrists that were covered with fine blond hairs. I noticed his profile. Very good, with its jutting, heroic jaw. He would do fine posing for an ad, I thought . . . if he could keep his mind on it.

"That's what gets you," he suddenly said.

Surprised, I said, "What does?"

"It gets me to thinking I can't trust them. A guarantee is a sacred trust."

"You mean about the tire? Oh, well, that's one in a million. Just an accident. Bound to be a bad one sometimes."

"I know," he said. "I knew that. There's a bad one in a lot once in a while. Nobody can help that. But there's been a lot of things. Just last week . . ." Apparently a thought had interrupted him, and a furrow appeared in his smooth, ruddy brow. "I'd hate to think I couldn't trust them. Why, the world's built on . . ." Thought failed him. He shook his head.

"I'm getting disillusioned."

"Don't worry. You just had bad luck," I said.

"Maybe." He paused a second. "Why, look here. If I didn't think I could trust the Health Home people, why I'd . . . it'd make your head swim how quick I'd quit. But I believe in Health Home. I . . ."

"What's Health Home?" I interrupted.

"Huh? What's Health Home?" He looked at me as if I had said something very callous. "You never heard of Health Home, Incorporated? Makers of Endurol."

"Yes, I believe I have," I said quickly, to redeem myself.

"If you haven't, you will," he said. "It's way-out the fastest-growing food supplement on the market. Haven't you seen our ads?"

It struck me that he must be pulling my leg, but another direct look into his level blue eyes assured me that he was not. Without blushing I said, "Yes, I believe I have . . . now that you mention it."

The Adventures of Douglas Bragg

– – –

5

"You must have. We're nationally advertised. We used to be just mainly in the East, but now we've spread all over. You remember Geritol? That was it for a while. Then it was Hadacol and then Naturalan, everything was. But you don't hear about any of them now. Now it's Endurol, more and more. For a whole new generation. You know why?"

"Why," I said with increasing astonishment.

"Because it's the best." He left me a moment in which to recover from this blockbuster. "It's not one of those flash-in-the-pan things. It's one of the permanent things. You know why?"

I figured now that nothing would be too much, and I said, "Because it's the best."

"Right. We've found a way to put in *all* the basic minerals. Not just iron and calcium and the other things you *always* find. Endurol has *all* of them. And we've done it without getting the syrupy taste most food supplements have." The gaze he held me with was not to be described as bright, but, rather, subdued, like the light you find in chapels.

"That's sure an improvement," I said.

"Here." His sudden movement directed my eye to the pasteboard cartons piled on his rear seat, cartons labeled "Endurol" in large letters, and in small ones, "Health Home, Inc." His hand lifted one of the carton lids, exposing bottles full of a pale brown liquid and two or three that looked empty. The one he took out was half full. "I want you to try this."

I was thirsty (especially sitting here like a fool in the hot sun) but not this thirsty. A car flashed past us with a rushing sound, and I wished to God I was in it.

"I want you to see for yourself." He placed the half-filled bottle on the dashboard, where in the sunlight the liquid took on a horrid yellowish hue. Reaching under the seat, he said, "It goes fine by itself, but I like it best with just a little water." He produced a thermos bottle, unscrewed the cup from the top, pulled the cork, and poured a couple of fingers of delicious-looking water into the cup.

"I wonder if I couldn't have a little drink of water first," I quickly said.

"Oh, you'll be surprised," he said, aware of nothing in my voice. "It's not sweet and it's not bitter. And it's not thick," he added, accenting his distaste for thickness. He took the bottle and poured maybe two or three ounces into the cup. "Here."

I sat holding it, staring at the dismal contents.

The Adventures of Douglas Bragg

"Go ahead. You'll see."

I lifted the cup and in two determined gulps downed it all. A hot aftertaste made my gullet tingle and my eyes water a little, but the stuff was not as bad as I had expected. He was waiting, the most vivid anticipation in his face. I gave a small cough and said, "Pretty good. Must have a lot of alcohol in it."

"It's got some. But mostly that's the mineral taste. I told you the truth, didn't I?"

"Yeah. It's very good."

He may have been a little disappointed at my response. He took the cup in silence and mixed one for himself and downed it, and afterward said, "Ah." Then, to my deep satisfaction, he pressed the starter and set the car into motion up the incline.

Maybe the feebleness of my response had wounded him, because for some little time he stared at the road and said nothing. We were passing some houses now, indicating a town somewhere ahead, which gave me almost as much satisfaction as his silence. I held my face in the air from the open window.

His silence did not last long. In front of a joint beside the highway there was a sign that said 'Bar-B-Que,' and this set his jaw working again. "You know, I haven't had a thing to eat all day and I feel just fine."

I looked at him, at his handsome profile, his jutting jaw. There was something very benevolent in the gaze he held on the road ahead. I said, "Because of the Endurol, you mean?"

"Yep." He nodded. "I don't even feel thirsty. Even after fixing that tire." A cloud came over his face, but he threw it off. "You'd be surprised how it'll nourish you, just by itself. I've saved myself from buying a lot of meals . . . a whole lot of meals."

I looked at him again. Certainly he appeared to be in the pink of health. I looked at his big bone-crushing hands on the steering wheel.

"It's the minerals," he said. "You want some more?"

"No thanks," I said. But at his request I fixed one for him, which, to my regret, finished off the water. It also emptied the Endurol bottle. He reached behind him for another one.

After he drank (taking it straight now) and gave his little heave, he fell quiet for a minute or two, still driving with a benevolent look on his face.

"You know, it cured my knee."

"Your knee?" I said.

The Adventures of Douglas Bragg

"Sure. I had a bad knee. It's why I quit college."

"Oh," I said. "Where did you go to college?"

"West Tennessee Reserve. I went two years. Then my knee got bad and I quit."

"I guess that was a handicap at college," I said.

"I got where I couldn't turn sharp right. I could only turn left. It ruined me."

"You mean you couldn't get to class rooms that were to your right?"

"No, of course not. On the field, I mean. What good is a tackle that can't turn right. I was ruined. But I'm all right now. I'm happy." He took another swig.

This swig did not make me happy, because I had begun to detect a certain irregularity in his driving. After this I kept looking ahead in vain for the town that the houses behind us had seemed to promise. Before taking still another swig, he remembered his manners and courteously offered me the bottle. I courteously refused, but this kept on for three or four more offers, and I finally gave in. It was plain old thirst, abetted by a monologue that threatened to dry up my brains, that finally overwhelmed me. I took another swallow. It really did seem to relieve me a little, and after a moment I took a couple more.

"Goes good, doesn't it?" he said with an amiably idiotic grin.

I was bringing out the words "Yes. Sure does," when an uncontrollable wheeze took me in mid-utterance.

"Too bad we don't have some water," he said. "It's better with a little water."

"Couldn't we stop and get some?" I croaked.

"No place along here. We'll be in Bellsboro pretty soon. Then we'll get some," he said merrily, and exactly as if I were my old attentive self, launched into his monologue again. I held my face into the wind, with mouth open, and tried not to listen. But this was impossible. He had a loud confident voice and, moreover, a topic, or rather a clutch of subtopics, that inspired him. His discourse reminded me of freshman themes written by my fellow students, with first one and then another aspect of some undefined idea prevailing. Endurol was prominent, but not more so than himself and his mother. In fact he was on his way right now for a little visit with his mother, who lived in Bellsboro. She too, it appeared, was a lover of Endurol, and I got a mental picture of the two of them toasting each other with brimful glasses drunkenly held on

The Adventures of Douglas Bragg

high. In any case, he was a little drunk now, I figured, and maybe had been more or less so all day. Not that he drove especially fast or lacked substantial control of the car. The trouble was that he drove at exactly the same rate, about fifty-five, all the time, whether the road was straight or crooked. It was pretty crooked in places and fifty-five was racing speed on some of those curves. These we took with tires squealing and the car leaning at an uncomfortable angle and me holding my breath.

"Some dangerous curves along here," I said, releasing my breath after an especially harrowing moment.

"A lot of wrecks along here," he said. "People go too fast. Speed limit for cars on this highway is fifty-five. You see them going sixty-five, seventy-five. You notice me? I never go over fifty-five. I got in the habit driving with Mother. It's just like she said. The laws are to protect us. The laws are our friends. They keep us from hurting ourselves."

"I hadn't thought of that, " I said.

He looked pleased. "That's right. They protect us from ourselves. You ought to know my mother, she's a wonderful woman. Taught me everything I know. Lot of people after they grow up don't listen to their mother anymore, but I listen to mine. She's a wise woman. When we get to Bellsboro, I want you to meet her."

"How far is Bellsboro?" I said.

"Oh, just about ten miles now. We go through Lupton, then it's four. Four, four, four more miles," he chanted. "There's no place like home."

"How many more curves are there?" I said, for we had just then, with crying tires and force enough to thrust me against the door, gone into another one. We came out of it all right, and I had had time to get back into a comfortable position and take a good deep breath, when he said thoughtfully, "Three, I think. After we pass Lupton."

"I mean real curves."

He named them off, with descriptions, and I weighed the thought of taking my leave at Lupton.

But I didn't say so, and pretty soon I saw below us what I took to be Lupton, a crossroads with two or three stores. "Couldn't we stop there and get a drink? You're getting low on gas, too, aren't you?" I added, after a glance at his gauge.

"Oh, no. I get home with a gallon to spare. I got it all figured. I get twenty-four and one half miles per gallon. If I keep her at fifty-five. That's cruising speed for a Studebaker and this is a Studebaker. You save

The Adventures of Douglas Bragg

gas if you stay at cruising. I always try to keep her at cruising. Except when I have to stop or something."

I watched Lupton approaching exactly at cruising speed. "Anyway a drink of water would taste mighty good."

He nodded soberly. "Sure would. I always try to keep my little thermos with water in it, but I got caught out this time. It makes you appreciate water when you haven't got any. You ever think where we'd be without water?"

"Where?" I groaned.

He paid no attention. "You stop and think about all the things water does and . . ."

But I was regretfully thinking about Lupton's general store that was passing us by, just at sixty.

"Of course," he was saying now, "it goes down fine even without water."

Whereupon he picked up the bottle lying on the seat beside him. It turned out to be empty, and I had to put it back in the carton and get him a fresh one and open it for him. After this I sat back and, determinedly shutting my eyes, waited for those six curves we had to get through.

The first one seemed a long time coming. It seemed to me it took a full minute to accomplish, with me holding tight to the seat, but it did not even slow his tongue down. The second curve was not so bad, and after that there was a pretty good stretch of straight level road. But then we climbed another hill, and from the crest I saw below us the curve-of-them-all coming up, a nearly perfect one hundred and eighty degrees. I shut my eyes again and may even have uttered a few mechanical words of prayer. The car began to lean. It leaned farther still, with tires whining, but I held my lids clenched tight and hunched farther down in the seat. At last I felt us coming out of it. But when I did open my eyes, it was just in time to see that we were not going to quite miss the car coming toward us up the hill. There was a jolt, a rending sound, and our car made a violent swerve. He quickly got it righted again.

"Oh Lord," I heard him say.

A backward glance at the car now at a stop some distance behind us assured me that my impression was not mistaken. "It's a patrol car," I said.

"Oh Lord."

For an inert moment we merely coasted. Then suddenly he jammed the throttle all the way to the floor.

The Adventures of Douglas Bragg

"You'd better stop," I said, looking back, unable to see the patrol car any more. Then I realized that he had not heard me. He was busy saying, "Oh Lord, they'll arrest me, they'll arrest me," and holding the gas pedal tight to the floor.

"You really had better stop."

"They'll *arrest* me," he wailed, his pale tragic face staring straight ahead.

"You can't outrun them. It'll be a lot worse."

Abruptly he relented. He hit his brake so hard that it pitched me against the dashboard, and then, when the car had slowed barely enough, he wheeled it sharp right into a nearly overgrown dirt lane. We jolted to a stop. For one immobile instant he stared ahead as if he saw something monstrous in the thicket there. What happened the next instant may have been simply an accident, some mix-up as to what he did with his feet. In any case the car started forward with a lurch that snapped my head back. But if it was a mistake, he must have felt that it had committed him beyond repair, for he gunned the car right on down the lane, mauling through brush and saplings that all but obscured the old wheel tracks.

"It's your funeral," I called out, but I don't think he heard me.

He braked suddenly to a stop, with the whole car buried in an undergrowth of bushes and shuddering saplings. He gave a moan. When he twisted around to look behind him, his engine bucked and choked out. But the thicket made the highway invisible. Seconds later I could only hear when the patrol car went whining past. In the stillness that followed, I said, "They didn't see you."

"They'll *arrest* me!" he said and looked at me with his big, heroic jaw hanging. It was a look of incredulous and really horrified astonishment, a white-eyed look.

"You should have stopped."

"What'll I do?"

"Nothing you can do. Unless you mean to give yourself up. Which I advise." But this only made his eyes go whiter still and the Adam's apple twitch in his bull neck.

"Well, then, you'd better just sit tight . . . till dark, anyway," I said.

"But Mother's waiting for me," he groaned.

"All right. Go ahead, then."

He sat there as tense as a banjo string, staring straight before him into the solid tangle of foliage. I started to leave him, but did not. I

The Adventures of Douglas Bragg

— — —

started to leave him a couple of other times, to his alarm, in the course of the two hours before dark, but I never did. For one thing, I was curious to see his mother. Every few minutes he would bring her up again in a strained voice, but always with an expression that broke like dawn across his troubled face. "Look. You can go home with me. You can meet my mother. She's a wonderful woman. She's a great cook, too, you ought to taste . . ." By now my hunger was another argument. Anyway, I didn't see how it could hurt me if he did get caught.

He would not wait for it to get black dark. In twilight we were out on the highway again, driving along in a car that, as I now realized, was not only dents and creases on one whole side, but also festooned with green leaves and branches like a float in a parade. We were close to Bellsboro, and very soon, to my relief, we turned off the highway onto a side road. But even now, though the road was bad, he had not forgotten that fifty-five was cruising. We jolted along, careening sometimes, while he glared out over the wheel like a dazed Hercules. We passed a few small houses, then hit pavement, and suddenly he slowed down. I urged him slower still as we turned a corner and followed a street between rows of aging though still respectable frame houses and maple trees and dusky figures of men seated in front porch swings. Now practically slinking along, we turned another corner. It was the third house on our left.

It was a square, clapboard house, once white, with wooden steps mounting to the front porch and a small shaded yard. But here at our destination, in the very process of approaching the driveway, my friend's newfound restraint broke down. Instead of discreetly, he finished the turn with a crying of tires and went plummeting the eighty or ninety feet to where the driveway ended in a garage just at the rear of the house. In fact it seemed to me that we entered the garage at the accustomed fifty-five, but somehow he got the car stopped shy of the back wall. Even before the car had quit pitching, he was out of it and already struggling with one sagged and rickety garage door. "Help me," he croaked.

It took only a moment, though one of the doors came off its hinges entirely and we had to lean it in place. Then, "Quick," he said, and with five or six athletic bounds, leaving me well behind him, he landed at the top of the back steps and burst the screen door open into the little cubicle of a back porch.

"Roland." It was a rather shrill female voice. "Roland, that is no way to enter a house."

"Mother," he said in a breathless voice, "I . . ."

The Adventures of Douglas Bragg

"Did you break the screen?" Apparently his panic had made no impression on her. Now I was only a little way behind and could clearly see the small prim-looking, gray-haired lady standing just inside the lighted kitchen door. I also saw that in spite of Roland's panic, he had turned back to see whether the screen door was broken.

"No'm," he muttered. "But Mother, I had . . ."

"You are late, Roland. I've been waiting an hour for you."

I think he had his mouth open again when once more she broke in, at the same time pointing a stiff little index finger at me where I stood at the bottom step.

"Who is that? Is he with you, Roland?"

"Yes'm, he's . . ."

"Then introduce him."

Roland turned and looked at me as if he had never seen me before. "I don't know his name," he said feebly.

"Bragg," I said. "Douglas Bragg."

But already she was looking back at Roland. I do not know how she managed the impression of looking down at him when he was a head and shoulders the taller. She said, "How can he be with you when you don't know his name?"

"I gave him a ride," he said, "on the road. I forgot to ask him what his name was. He would have told me if I had asked him. Wouldn't you?" he said, appealing to me.

"Sure," I said.

"A perfect *stranger?*" she said with indignation.

"He's not anymore. I know him now."

"Indeed."

Into the small hiatus she finally had left him, he blurted. "I'm in trouble, Mother. Let's go inside."

"Because of Mr. Gregg?" she said, turning upon me eyes in which a glint was visible.

"Bragg," I said.

"No, Mother. He's with me. It's the police."

"Why doesn't he have on a uniform, then?"

"No, Mother. Let's go inside, please." Roland seemed to be going into a kind of a jig.

"All right. But it doesn't make any sense to me," and she turned back into the kitchen with her son right behind her. What was I supposed to do? Surely I had a right to assume that my being left out was a mere

The Adventures of Douglas Bragg

— — —

13

oversight due to the stress of the occasion. Besides, there would be water in the kitchen, not to mention whatever it was I smelled cooking. So after a minute I entered the porch and stepped across to the kitchen door.

It was an ordinary good-sized kitchen, showing signs of supper in preparation, with nothing to distinguish it except a mynah bird in a cage that hung from a hook in the ceiling near the far door. Roland had managed to get his mother seated in a chair beside the little kitchen table and was standing gigantically over her, excitedly explaining things into her up-turned, sharp-nosed, and very complacent face. Just at first I got the impression that he was communicating entirely by gesticulation, but then I heard his voice:

"They just came flying around that curve. It wasn't head-on, or I would have been killed." I noticed how, at this, his mother's gaze ran anxiously up and down his frame, apparently to make sure he was not dead. "I only sideswiped them," he added. "And then they chased me," he further added in a falling tone.

She looked away from Roland; she looked toward the mynah bird, and her face assumed a determined expression. "I think *they* sideswiped *you*," she declared. At that moment she spotted me in the door and added, "Didn't they, Mr. Brock?"

"Bragg," I said with emphasis.

"Didn't they?"

"I guess you could say that," I replied.

"Of course you could. I do say it." I noticed the fine, small nostrils that flared a little with emotion.

For the past brief space Roland had been standing there with his mouth open, apparently struck by the wisdom of this observation. Now, suddenly, his face and his voice both took on an expression of passion. "But they'll say it was *me*."

"Well, it won't be the truth," Mother said firmly. "You can't believe a thing those police say. They spend their whole lives with nobody but criminals."

I figured later that it was the word 'believe' that had spurred the mynah bird. At any rate he gave a squawk and then proceeded in a voice like a tin horn to deliver a bar of "Believe Me If All Those Endearing Young Charms."

Roland looked at the bird, gaping, a smile beginning to shape his mouth. "You've taught him a new one, haven't you? Mother, you're a wonder."

The Adventures of Douglas Bragg

— — —

14

"He can sing more of it than that," she said complacently.

Suddenly, without the least space for transition back to anxiety, Roland said, "But they chased me, Mother. I cut off in a side road, so they couldn't see me."

"That's just like the police. You did the right thing."

"But what if they find my car. They'll arrest me, they'll . . ."

"I wouldn't worry about it a second. You just stay right here a day or two and they'll forget all about it."

"My car's all bent in, though."

"That's all right, you can have it fixed. Just leave it right there in the garage while you're here."

For a moment longer anxiety still maintained the one or two painful-looking wrinkles that somewhat disfigured his virile brow. The next instant they were fading, then were gone, and only the least hint of a troubled spirit lingered about him. Then he ridded himself of even that. "And you don't think I've done anything wrong, Mother?"

"That is just like you, Roland," Mother said, a note of admiration suddenly evident "Always worried about doing something wrong. Not many young men in this day and time are like that."

"It's your teaching, Mother," Roland said, the spirit beginning to brighten in his face.

Mother, with a small deprecating smile, dismissed the compliment. "So don't you worry. It was not your fault. You are no more responsible than . . . than Mr. Brooks here." She gave me a glance so brief that it could not have distinguished my face from any other, then reached out and patted her son's bone-crushing hand. I did not bother again to make the correction; I was more interested in the proposition that I was just as responsible as Roland was. But Roland, apparently, had swallowed it, quills and all. The fact that he still made no vocal response was not because he was having trouble getting it down; it was clearly admiration that stifled him. Even his Adam's apple gave a grateful little jerk. Beyond question there were words of heartfelt praise and gratitude in the offing, but Mother forestalled them by suddenly springing to her feet. "Oh, it's six-thirty," she said, waving a finger at the platter-shaped clock on the wall. "We'll have to hurry."

She was out of the room in an instant, having passed from my sight at a sort of jog-trot, with Roland in hot pursuit. Again I was not invited, so I took the occasion to step quickly across to the sink and down two or three glasses of water. Just as I set the glass down, I heard a sort of

The Adventures of Douglas Bragg

– – –

wailing sound: a voice, evidently a woman's, calling out maybe from the bottom of a well. It was the TV set, of course, and a repetition of the sound brought to my ear the word *En-du-rol,* each of the three syllables differently pitched in an eerie female voice.

I walked to the door in time to pick up the little drama before things got complicated, for the TV screen was clearly visible to me between the motionless figures of mother and son. There was no indication of what had caused the eerie voice. Instead there was a badly groomed, irritable-looking man snarling at his frightened little daughter who had just now spilled something on the tablecloth. The brute immediately apologized, however, assumed an expression of despondency, and proceeded to explain to his shaken wife that it was just that he felt so tired and nervous all the time. It was not that he did not get a balanced diet, his wife swore on her wifely honor; and judging by her earnestness, I had no reason to doubt it. After this, things developed just as I had expected. White-jacketed Dr. Edwards appeared with a bottle of you-know-what. He delivered a forceful little speech on its merits, not omitting to mention that he took it, himself, and the tired nervous man agreed to try it. So, in the end, domestic bliss restored, the nervous man not only smiled at his daughter's sloppiness but presented a head of well-groomed hair. And the sourceless voice like a maiden wailing for her demon lover called a last time upon the name of Endurol. Immediately afterwards the news came on, and I heard the set switched off as I retired into the kitchen.

Obviously they had forgotten about me, but now, all of us together in the kitchen again, it seemed that even my fleshly presence was not going to recall me to their minds. That ad had entirely cleared the horizon, and they were discussing it in about the tone of old grads after a winning game. Roland had unqualified praise. Mother, however, had one or two qualifications. She did not think, for instance, that the ad was at all successful in showing how much flesh the nervous man would have gained and how much his newly acquired vigor would have advanced him in his job. "And another thing," she said, looking around from a fragrant baking dish that she had just taken out of the oven. "If I was doing it, I would show how good it tastes. I would have the little girl taking some, because children are very sensitive to taste."

"Mother, you think of everything," Roland said.

Certainly, before she was through, she thought of enough things to keep the ad running about thirty minutes, but of course I did not say this. Not that it likely would have mattered. I got the impression that maybe even my voice would have been inaudible to them. And after Mother had brushed past me a time or two, I began to get the feeling that she could not see me, either. So I just backed up against the wall and stayed there, still entertaining the hope that she nevertheless did intend to feed me.

In spite of the intensity of the conversation, food appeared. It looked like enough for a kennel of bird dogs, but still there had been no move to add a third place setting at the dining room table that was visible through the far door. Finally I tried clearing my throat rather loudly, but this produced no effect. Mother was saying, "You're a very lucky boy. I wouldn't ever hear of your severing connections with a fine firm like Health Home, Incorporated."

"I wouldn't even think about it," Roland said. "I know I'm lucky."

It was not only that I was hungry; I had had quite enough of the subject, too. Raising my voice, I said, "I hope they didn't get your license number."

Everything stopped. They both looked at me, Mother unpleasantly. "Let's not talk about that, Mr. Banks," she said. "It was not Roland's fault."

"But Mother, they might . . ."

"Don't be silly, Roland. Think how many license numbers there are in the world. How could they know yours?" With this she picked up a steaming bowl of potatoes and marched into the dining room. I do not know whether she had dispelled all of his uneasiness, but he did not pursue the subject further. Anyhow the remark turned the trick for me by calling Roland's attention my way. The result was that I, under the name of Mr. Book this time, received a not very cordial invitation to supper, which I snapped up.

But after we were seated at the table, with Mother at the end and I across from Roland and all those smoking bowls of beans and asparagus and corn on the cob spread out in front of us, there was still a long preface to be got through. Roland had to read from the Bible, a whole chapter, it seemed, from Leviticus or Numbers or something. Anyway there was talk about Jehovah squashing his enemies. It was a miserable job of reading, with Roland humped over the book like an outsized fourth-grader, taking second and even third shots at fully half the four-syllable words. I watched Mother's face, too. There was a light from heaven out of her rather narrow greenish-gray eyes, and her mouth, which had by nature a stiff-looking upper lip, had stiffened into an expression of particularly benevolent complacency. When I heard what I thought was the end of the chapter bumbling into view, I trained my eyes on the bowl of lovely green asparagus, and for this reason I failed to observe what more was in the offing.

The elaborate clearing of a throat, Mother's, brought me around. Heads were bent. Mother was launching a prayer, and I clenched my teeth. The prayer was entirely extempore. It was also ex cathedra in its tone of authority, for she called down blessings with a great deal of insistence. I have never seen such a long prayer cover so little territory. In fact it was nearly all confined to blessings upon Roland, his work, and his person. I got his whole medical history from that prayer, including the whole story of the hurt knee he had mentioned. In case the Lord had forgotten the details, Mother reminded Him. "Which he hurt playing ball at college and which gave him so much pain," she prayed in a voice of feeling. "Let it not ever give him any more trouble and have to be put in a cast and interfere with his work." (How? I wondered.) In his career Roland had had whooping cough, German measles, one mump (it was demanded of God that Roland never get the other one) a sprained ankle, headache, flu, dyspepsia, and a painful bout with hiccups. And now, piles. Lord, have them go away. Also there were blessings for Health Home, Incorporated, which already had had the good fortune to be associated with Roland, and it was to be hoped that Health Home realized what they had. Finally there were congratulations to the Lord Himself for having created Roland in the first place and having given him so many attributes and such a good Christian upbringing. Not a word for me anywhere. Not even a word for the president. But I was glad enough to have us omitted just to get the business over with.

The food had cooled off a good deal, but this did not inhibit me. I think maybe my gluttony would not have been tolerated except that Roland himself was anything but abstemious. In fact he gave evidence of both the will and capacity to outstrip me in a walk. He was under the handicap, however, that Mother kept talking to him and so he had to leave at least space enough in his mouth for grunts to pass through. There were even some times when he had to empty his mouth almost entirely in order to make articulate responses. Like: "You don't need iron pills when you've got Endurol, Mother. It's a complete food supplement."

Here Mother stood corrected; apparently even she sometimes nodded. But she was back at the switch in no time. In the process of moving the butter plate closer to her starving son, she said, "You know how I worry about your health, Roland, with you working so hard. Did you ever think where you would be without your health?"

The right answer was of course obvious, but Roland did not see it. He said merely something like "Ulmph." And no wonder, for he had just thrust a whole potato into his mouth. But the noise was translated as a sign of intelligence.

"That's how your father died," she said, arching her brow to strengthen the point.

The fact that Roland was masticating with such fervor did a good deal to vitiate the look of sobriety his face had assumed.

"I did everything I could. I kept warning him. I said to him time and time again, 'Eulis, you are losing your health. Then what will you do?' But he just went right on. And I was exactly right. He just wasted away and died at only thirty-five."

The solemn interval that ensued was broken only by the sound of Roland's massive jaw mutedly grinding a pone of cornbread. Mother then proceeded to launch a new subject, that of a rival food supplement named Vito. It seemed that Vito was not only a poisonous product; it was sold by immoral people, including that nasty Bickley boy from right here in Bellsboro. This nasty Bickley boy apparently had something dark in his past, something so dark in fact that it raised Mother's eyebrows higher than I would have thought possible. "Those people ought to know about him," she said, meaning the poisoners who made Vito. "Even they wouldn't put up with *him.*"

Roland seemed to ponder this. He washed out his esophagus with half a glass of milk, but then all he could think of to say was, "Nobody would."

"I really think that it is my moral duty to write them a letter," Mother said firmly.

By now I was not paying much attention; I was considering whether to clean up the last few stalks of asparagus in the serving bowl. Deciding in the affirmative and thinking myself unobserved, I spooned them onto my plate and was preparing to pitch in when I saw Mother glaring at me as if to say, "For all you know, Roland wanted that." What she did say was, "Didn't Roland tell me you were a hitchhiker, Mr. Brooks?"

"Well, not by profession," I said, letting my fork come to rest. "I was just on my way to somewhere and he gave me a ride."

"Roland never hitchhikes," she said. "Even when he was a boy, he never hitchhiked."

"Oh," I said.

"So many hitchhikers are criminals." She was looking at me very straight.

"Well, I'm not a criminal," I said as agreeably as I was able.

"But you could have been a criminal, couldn't you?"

There was no answer to this that I could see except, "Yes ma'am."

"You see, Roland," she said, turning back to him, "that's why you should never pick up a hitchhiker."

Roland, having finished off everything in the serving dishes, was licking the grease off his chops, but he interrupted the process to say, "Aw, Mother, he was a pal. He stuck with me when the police . . ." Roland broke off and his face darkened.

"We will not have any talk about police," Mother said, "It was not your fault, Roland. Now, we will have our pie."

As soon as she was out of the room, Roland said, "Don't get Mother wrong. She's really glad to have you."

"I can see that, " I said.

"You can't understand Mother from one meeting. You've got to know her. She's a wonderful person."

"I can see that, too."

"Can't you tell she's wise just from hearing her talk this little bit? You wouldn't believe how wise she really is."

I had started to produce a nod of some gravity when the mynah bird just inside the kitchen door behind me gave a prefatory squawk and again opened up with "Believe Me If All Those Endearing Young Charms."

"Now just listen to that," Roland said when the bird shut up in the middle of the second bar. "She taught him that." He gazed affectionately through the door.

I was just about to say that that was something when suddenly the telephone in the kitchen rang and the mynah bird, apparently loosened up now, yelled, "Help!"

Moments later I was aware that Roland had stiffened. Next, I could guess why, though so far Mother's voice at the telephone had said only "Yes" and "Oh." Now an interval of silence had fallen, in which the strained and pallid face of Roland glared past me toward the kitchen door. Mother's voice, which even I could recognize as somewhat taut, then said, "No. He's not here. He's off on a trip." And then, "No, I'm not expecting him at all." She was putting her foot in pretty deep, I thought. "It's . . . it's kind of blue," she said. "But it's more kind of green, really." Which was also a lie. With a groan Roland said, "Oh Lord." He appeared to be sinking downward in his chair. From the kitchen came a final "Yes, I will," and the click of the receiver on the hook.

"Goodbye," the mynah bird said.

"Mother," Roland called with a dying fall in his voice. "What if they look in the garage?"

"So long," the mynah bird said . . . aptly, I thought. It seemed much enlivened by the crisis.

"They will not." I could feel Mother in the door behind me standing as solidly as if already she was turning back the police.

"But how can you stop them? They got guns and things." Roland now sat like a man whose chair was threatening to throw him.

"I will not let those police in my yard." From the corner of my eye I got a glimpse of the finger she had raised.

"Have they got my license number?"

"Only the first three numbers. So you don't have to worry."

"Oh Lord." Roland's head rolled forward onto his chest. "And they know it's all bent in, too."

There was an unexpected moment of nothing except the coarse squawks that the mynah bird was making. Mother said, "You just stay right here in this house. They'll forget all about it in a few days." But now, to my surprise, there was a clear note of uncertainty in her voice. Even her step when she turned back into the kitchen seemed to lack its accustomed firmness. But I gathered that for Roland this moment was downright shattering. For maybe the first time in his life his Mother's wisdom had struck him as less than compelling. He sat with his head down like a mourner, shaking it vaguely from side to side and saying, to me, I guess, "I know they'll find it. They'll arrest me. And put me in jail. And I'll . . ." He looked up. Mother had suddenly returned from the kitchen, treading quite firmly again. "Mother, they'll put me in jail. Health Home'll *fire* me."

Mother calmly set the pie down on the table. "We will just put the car in somebody else's garage. Then the police won't find it."

Roland's gloomy expression brightened. It brightened still more and became a smile. But then, almost suddenly, the brightness melted in a gloom even denser than before. I fancied again, from the way he did not look quite at her when he spoke, that this further evidence of Mother's fallibility had struck him a second blow. "Whose?" he said.

Apparently Mother had not yet given this any thought. Her upper lip visibly stiffened. "Why," she said, "lots of people. Lots of people on this street have garages. The Cockorans."

Roland looked down. "They wouldn't do it," he said thickly. "Nobody would."

"Why not? I can't think of a soul on this street that doesn't admire you."

"They just wouldn't. Nobody would if they knew why," he mumbled. "Would they?" he said, appealing to me.

"They would be liable to get in trouble with the law," I said with muted relish. "They would . . ."

"It was not Roland's fault," Mother suddenly flared at me. "Any more than it was yours."

"Well, it sure wasn't my fault," I replied, guardedly in rebellion now. "Anyhow that's not what *they'll* say. And they're not going to like it."

The hostility in Mother's gaze lasted a few moments, then faded amid facial evidences of heavy thinking.

"What am I going to do?" Roland moaned.

"Your best chance is probably to make a getaway right now," I said. The problem had begun to interest me, especially since it could not cost me anything. "No, that wouldn't work," I corrected. "They'll be looking out for you on the roads."

"You can hide the car," Mother declared with finality.

"But *where*, Mother?"

"In the woods someplace."

"Aw, they'd find it. Or catch me driving it there. . . . Wouldn't they?" He looked at me again.

It had become a little like a game, and in the gaming spirit I said, "Maybe you could take it somewhere and leave it and then report it stolen from you. Back on the highway, before you hit the cop." But once I had got it out, it did not sound very airtight. Even Roland saw this. Right in the middle of Mother's reiterated correction of my way of putting things, to the effect that it was the cop who had hit him, Roland said, "But what about me? I wouldn't be here now. . . . Aw, nothing's any good," he groaned. "I'm done for."

The Adventures of Douglas Bragg
— — —

"Never say die, Roland."

"Look," I said, my idea blooming. I was beginning to feel the way writers of TV dramas must feel. "You could walk on back down the highway toward Birmingham a few miles . . . to Lupton, maybe. You could report it there. Tell them you had been walking ever since your car was stolen."

"Nobody'd believe that," Roland said gloomily.

"Everybody knows how honest you are, Roland," Mother said.

"Why not?" I said, excited even if a good deal less confident than I sounded. "Tell them a guy held you up when you stopped to change a tire. You've even got the flat to prove it," I added with a flash of elation. "And you had to walk all that way to Lupton, eight or ten miles. You can embroider it some." At least I could have.

Roland continued to look gloomily skeptical, but Mother's face had a definite light upon it. Her eyes on me had a look as keen as a blade. I said, "You can leave the car where we were this afternoon. It'll look like the thief got scared and ditched it."

"Roland," Mother said.

Roland looked dumbly up at her.

"You might as well get hanged for a sheep as a goat," I said, thinking, as I watched him digest the metaphor, that this was about true, too.

"Roland," Mother said, "that's just what we'll do."

"Aw, Mother," Roland groaned. "Besides, that'd be telling a lie."

"That's all right, it would just be a white lie. Those police were going to lie about you."

"Well, you'd better get started," I said, more excited than ever. "They might be on the way here right now."

"Run on right now, Roland. You can't wait any longer." She even poked his arm with her fingers for emphasis.

Roland sighed heavily, but he got to his feet.

My excitement made me reckless. "Come on," I said, "I'll go with you."

Which encouraged Roland. He rounded the table and followed me through the kitchen.

"Hurry, Roland," Mother said, bringing up the rear. "And call me from Lupton."

The Adventures of Douglas Bragg

— — —

It was about eleven-thirty when I entered the Bellsboro town square and stood looking around for somewhere to go for the night. The place was typical. In the middle of the square was a red-brick courthouse with entrances on each of the four sides, with a cupola and four-faced clock, and confronting the building from across the wide, lighted streets were solid walls of dingy, brick storefronts. Except for a few parked cars and a few drifting human figures, the square was empty. On my own I quickly found the hotel (for such it was called) close to a corner of the square and waked the proprietor from his sleep in front of a raging TV set. The room he took me to was fairly grubby, but nevertheless I settled down for the night.

As tired as I was, I still felt excited over my little drama, which kept me wallowing around that lumpy mattress for an hour or two. The car, with steering wheel and window ledges wiped clean of fingerprints, was sitting there in the thicket. And by now Roland should have reached, or at least be pretty close to, Lupton. If only he kept his head and remembered the details I had concocted for him on the way to leave the car. But was this likely? His air of gloomy resignation, not to mention his jumpiness, had hardly been encouraging. His one moment of animation had come when, with beads of sweat faintly glistening on his forehead, he had turned to me in the gloom and said, "But it's *crazy!*" Of all the weaknesses in my drama, clearly he was the greatest. I pondered the matter from my window overlooking the lighted, desolate square, and while I pondered, I saw a patrol car enter at a routine pace and stop in front of what seemed to be a pool hall beyond the opposite corner from me. I got back in bed and unexpectedly fell asleep.

Judging from the morning sunlight and the traffic sounds, I also slept much longer than I had expected to. I got out of bed and hurriedly started dressing. The play, if it had gotten under way at all, ought to be in Act III by now and the question was how to get into the theater. I had just finished tying my shoes when a startling thud, repeated three or four times, reverberated in my room. It was my door that was getting clobbered. I bounded to my feet and, already envisioning the idiotic face of Roland there, snatched the door open.

It was not Roland. In fact it was not anything like Roland. In the first place there were two of them, a tall and a short one; and in the second place both wore badges and tall Western-style hats and guns on their hips. Also there was nothing vacant in the gazes, a blue one and a hazel one, that they had fastened on me. My immediate thought was that they had caught Roland red-handed and wanted me for a witness. Or maybe for an accomplice? This second thought was a good deal less comforting. As the seconds ticked by under their silent scrutiny, I became still less at ease.

"Fits, don't he," the smaller one twanged.

"He don't miss it," the other said. And then to me, "Get your stuff and come on."

"What for?" I said, quite automatically. It was what arrested people always said.

"Car stealing, most likely," the same one said. "Now get your stuff right quick."

"Car stealing?"

"That's right. And more, too. Now get it," he added in a voice suddenly tough.

Both of them followed me into the room and, while I was picking up my dirty socks, started to look around. They looked in my bag first, then under the bed and in the closet and the dresser drawers.

"What are you looking for?" I said.

"Gun."

"Gun, the devil." Immediately something began to trouble me, but I did not have time to get it straight. Seconds later they had me out of the room and down the flight of stairs and standing flanked by the two of them at the desk to pay my bill. Which indicated at least that they were law-abiding cops.

"Stole a car, huh?" the clerk said, adjusting silver-rimmed glasses for a better look at me.

"The hell I did," I said, ill-advisedly.

"Shut up," the big cop said and gave me a nasty little thump in the ribs behind.

Out on the square, so as to draw all eyes, they held me by both arms and walked me like a puppet to a patrol car. They even gave a little crank to the siren as they pulled out. Both bad signs, I thought, because they indicated that business was slow. As we turned the first corner, I risked another utterance. "Why me?"

There was no response at all. In fact, a moment later, the big cop seated beside me in the rear seat said, "Look at that." He was referring to a broad-bottomed young lady crossing at the light just ahead.

"That's that Rachel Watkins," the driver said.

"Uuh," my big cop said, as if he had been hit just a very light blow in the solar plexus.

We turned at the far corner of the square and stopped in front of a dull brick building with narrow windows. I was escorted just as before, this time into a room with chewed-up benches against the walls and a couple of desks and a uniformed though hatless cop at one of them, playing checkers by himself. He looked at me, looked me up and down a time or two. "Found him, huh?"

"Just about in time, too," my big cop said.

I did not much like the sound of that and was about to open my mouth when the one at the desk stood up and, followed by my cop, went out through a door to my left. My remaining companion ordered me to 'set down' on the bench beside him, which I did, and thereupon he got up and set himself down on the opposite bench. Lying beside him was a copy of *Classic Comics,* which he picked up.

"Can I ask a question now?"

"Just set still," he said and turned a page. "You'll find out quick enough."

I was pretty sure it was not going to be quick, and my thoughts ran right back to what had gotten dislodged when they snatched me out of my hotel room. It had to do with a gun. What gun? Wheels had begun to turn, and I don't know what could have stopped them in mid-revolution except my own instinctive trust that certain things were just not possible. Anyway my mind quickly switched off this track, and pretty soon I found myself contemplating my watchdog's flat-top haircut and knit brow and his copy of *Girls Galore* with a specimen picture on the cover.

The cop in uniform came back in and without even a glance at me sat down to his checkers game again. I got up and got a drink from the watercooler, then stood in front of a fan revolving in the corner near the door, and still I never drew a glance. The room had yellow walls, reminding me of something like a public health office. The fan droned on, and voices and sounds of traffic intruded from the street. I began to have the feeling that I could walk right out and still never get a glance, and this a little comforted me.

At length I heard a clang of metal, distant but all the same startling. The next noise, though unconnected with the first, nevertheless snatched my gaze toward its source. It seemed to me that a whole crowd of people was coming through the door to my left. The first was Mother, in a bright blue sunbonnet that shaded her face like an awning. To one side and behind her, Roland towered. Then came a dried-up loose-lipped cop . . . the sheriff, I guessed . . . and finally my big cop. I was not yet much taken aback. It was only when they had all got in the room and I noticed the sweat on Roland's face and the way he, unlike the others, kept refusing to look at me, that I got my first good sniff of the air.

"That him?" the loose-lipped sheriff said to Roland.

Roland's gaze (he was still in back of his mother, collared and tied as ever) climbed about as high as my belt buckle and fastened there.

"Tell the policeman, Roland," Mother said. She had turned her head to look up at him from under the awning of her bonnet.

"Yeah," Roland barely mumbled.

"Take a good look," the sheriff said. "Be plumb sure about it."

Roland's gaze reached my chin, and broke. There was sweat running down his neck; his collar was darkening fast.

"Tell him, Roland," Mother said impatiently. She held in both hands, though demurely, a big loaded black purse that looked as if it might be first-rate for clobbering heads.

"That's him," Roland croaked.

"The one that held the gun on you and took your car?" the sheriff said.

"What!" I blurted. I lay it to my trusting nature that I required this flat statement before the meaning of it all really hit me.

"Roland has perfectly good eyes," Mother said, to the sheriff, not to me. "He has already said so."

"Well, you got to be sure about these things, you know," the sheriff (or police chief?) said.

"I can tell when Roland is sure," Mother said. "You are sure, aren't you, Roland?" and the awning of her bonnet dipped in affirmation.

"Yeah. He's the one, Mother," Roland said, his eyes flinching away even from her now.

I believe that it took this whole interval since my stroke of revelation for me to draw just the one breath I now used to blast out, "You liar, you lout."

"Shut up!" The big cop had stepped in on me, roughly seizing my arm. But I was seeing red. In fact, when I caught the indignant last little glance that Mother threw me before she turned her back, I saw blood. "You bitch," I yelled. "You . . ."

Here I saw red in quite a different way, for it felt as though something like the business end of a baseball bat had driven my left kidney across to the other side of me. When my vision returned, I was standing crooked over sideways at an angle that required my cop's support if I was to stand at all, watching murky figures file out through a door. When I could see clearly again, the door was shut, and I was being piloted across the room toward a chair by the desk of the checker-playing cop.

Jail, if it is a novelty for you, can be rather interesting at first . . . at least if you do not take your situation any more seriously than I took mine, at the time. I was entirely unable to see how it could be more than a matter of hours before this ridiculous farce was exposed, and so I was at ease on that score. Of course I was outraged, but for a while my interest in the novelty of looking out instead of in pretty well upstaged my other feelings.

My cell was like any other: bars on the front and three concrete-block walls and a barred rear window looking out on an alley full of trash cans. Also, of course, there were double-decker cots fastened to the wall, and a toilet and washbasin crowded into the rear corner opposite the cots. Aside from the novelty of looking out instead of in, the greater part of my interest was furnished by my cell mate. At first, because of my displaced kidney, I had not even noticed him. After that, I had gone off to sleep for an hour or so and waked up feeling a good deal better. There was a ham sandwich and a cold cup of coffee waiting for me on the iron shelf attached to the bars, and for the two or three minutes it took me to down these, I continued facing the other way. Then I turned and saw him.

He was seated on the floor back in the corner, reading a magazine and paying me not the least attention. He was a slight-built man of maybe thirty, with a long narrow face, reddish thin-looking eyelids, and bad teeth that showed because his lips hung open all the time. I watched him turn a couple of pages, evidently to a new article or, maybe, a picture.

"I didn't see you before," I said to him.

He just did glance at me . . . scornfully, I thought . . . with small rabbitlike eyes. He did not look anything resembling dangerous sitting there, and so I tried again. "What are you in for?" I said, thinking this a fellowly remark.

He closed the magazine deliberately. Then he looked at me exactly as if I was some pitiable wretch put there mainly to vex him, and said, "Be better for you you didn't know about it, boy."

I did not know what to say to this, but after a moment I said anyway, "Well, I wouldn't mind knowing if you wouldn't mind telling me."

"All right." He allowed a pregnant pause. "Murder," he said in a low hard voice and looked at me with a narrow-eyed expression that put me in mind of someone I could not recall just then.

I was taken aback. "Oh," was all I could say.

"You know what murder is, don't you, boy? Killing somebody. On purpose. What they call 'premeditate first-degree.'"

"Oh," I repeated and, not knowing what else to say, added, "Did you do it?"

"Sure I did." With this he suddenly glanced around as if he might have blundered. "And I ain't sorry," he added in a whisper.

After a pause I said, "Why did you do it?"

"They double-crossed me."

"You mean there was more than one?"

"There was three," he snapped and showed his bad teeth even more plainly.

By now I was pretty sure my leg was being pulled, but I kept on with it. "How did you do it?"

There was that familiar narrow-eyed expression again. "'lectrocuted them." He let this sink in. "I wired up the door handle and when they touched it, s-s-s, fried fat."

"They sound cooperative," I said. "Looks like the other two would have noticed when the first one got fried."

"They came along at different times," he said in a suddenly level explanatory voice. "It wouldn't have worked if they had all come at once."

I was thinking it was about time to conclude this obvious farce, but then I decided to play along for a little while yet. I said, "I take it you were in some kind of a racket."

"Never mind about that," he murmured and again looked suspiciously around.

After a moment I walked to the cot and sat down. He had followed me with his eyes. To be saying something, I said, "How did you get off into that kind of thing?"

"Oh, you know, one thing leads to another. I was always a criminal, though. When I was just a boy, I pushed my little sister under a freight train. They thought she fell." Whereupon he issued a grotesque horror-movie laugh.

This was when I began to think, with some uneasiness, that the guy was in the wrong kind of a clink. Uncertainly I said, "Why did you do that?"

"Oh, I hated her. You know how kids are. She always got to lick the icing bowl and stuff like that. Mother always played favorites. I fixed her little red wagon."

"And you don't feel bad about it now?"

"Huh. Feel bad. Huh." Here he came out with another of his laughs.

I was preparing to change the subject when an interruption occurred. A cop outside the bars was unlatching the door. Drawing it open, he said, "Let's go, Stanley." Stanley (for this was his name) put the magazine down in a stack of them on the floor beside him and got up.

"Where's he taking you?" I said.

Pausing, Stanley looked at me with a faint half-smile and a devil-may-care toss of his head. "Who knows."

"Get the lead out," the cop bawled. Stanley instantly got in gear and passed out of the cell moving at a pretty good clip.

There was nothing of Stanley's in sight except toilet articles on the washbasin and the stack of magazines on the floor. I thumbed through these last. They were exclusively crime and horror magazines, including one, surely the consummation of them all, named *Horror Crime*. In turning through, I came upon a vaguely familiar face with squinted eyes. It was the face of an actor, I learned from the caption, and I recognized that I had seen it a number of times in crime movies. Then I recognized something more: the face looked a little like Stanley's, and the expression was almost precisely the one that Stanley kept reproducing.

There was a man sitting on a bunk in the cell across the aisle from me. I finally got his rather feeble attention.

"You know the guy in here with me?" I said. "Stanley?"

"Yep."

"You know what he's in for?"

"Yep."

"How about telling me."

"Robbing parking meters. He does it all the time."

"Much obliged," I said, and the man went back to his drowsing.

I did not yet want to break up the fun, and so I did not let on to Stanley when they brought him back. I not only let him carry on, I drew him out. Stanley was not even what is popularly called psycho. He was just playing a game he enjoyed, and I got pretty interested in it myself. He rather overdid things, and sometimes he fell into obvious contradictions, but this I attributed to the abundance of his memories. After all, how many people could get through probably thousands of crime and horror stories and not end up with at least some of their recollections pretty well tangled. On the whole, though, he was quite consistent and, with my encouragement, gave an account of his career which, if hair-raising, was only a little less plausible than most of the stories in his magazines. He even had some esoteric, screwed-up notions about the origins of criminality, including his own, such as love of mothers and hatred of fathers, the reverse of this, bad environment, sexual repression, possessive parents, etc. Crime magazines went the whole route, then as now. In his own case, possessive parents were the cause. (I caught an inconsistency here, but let it pass.) His parents just would not turn him a-loose, as he said, even though he was thirty-one. They would act as if they had, but then just let him ask them for one lousy buck and, whammo, there were the old strings again. He had tried everything to get free: impudence, defiance, domestic vandalism, and one stunt I never would have thought of. He wrote his parents nasty letters about himself, signed with the names of prominent local citizens, all in the hope that this would cause them to reject him. It did no good, however; they responded only by cutting off his allowance and locking him up in the bathroom. (This, by the way, is what furnished me with the germ of the idea that I will tell about presently.) So he tried crime. Surely this would bring about the coveted rejection. Parking meters first. He did not add "last and always." Then on to more serious crimes, until . . . Who was to blame, then? I allowed that I did not know the answer.

"Me?" he said, watching me with a penetrating gaze.

"I certainly wouldn't think so," I said.

"Of course not. All I wanted was my freedom."

"Sure," I said.

"That's what people don't understand about us criminals," he said. "That's why it's a crime wave."

The Adventures of Douglas Bragg

Stanley was also looking ahead, making plans for his future in crime. He had in mind several banks in other towns, but first there were some old scores to settle locally. He particularly had it in for the lady cop who watched over the parking meters and who, I gathered, had caught him in the act of robbing one. He favored for her, as he seemed to for most of his enemies, death by electricity. The idea was to electrocute her on one of her own parking meters, which would be ironical, he said.

"What if you get convicted on those murder charges?" I said.

For answer he gave me a sly look and reached for something among the covers on his cot. It was a pistol made of soap, to be used in his escape. He had been working on it nights. It looked like night work. The barrel drooped, and the whole thing was misshapen. What is more, it was made out of Palmolive, so it was green. Watching my face, he inferred that I was not impressed.

"Of course I'm not through with it," he said apologetically. "It was a whole lot better, but I accidentally dropped it in the toilet. That kind of messed it up. I'm going to fix it, though."

And so the game went on. I am not sure he thought I really believed in it, but I suspect that he would not have cared too much, just as long as I continued to play. The trouble was that my capacity for pretending, unlike his, was limited. By bedtime the game had worn very thin for me, and after an hour's lying there on my cot in the dark compelled to listen, I was entirely burnt out with it. Besides, the novelty of my situation was wearing off pretty fast. Very soon my feeling of outrage had reawakened and with it something new: genuine anxiety. Might not that jackass Roland, literally spurred on by the old bitch, manage to get away with it? What did I have for evidence? Nothing. Until now I had been relying merely on the fact that the whole thing was too absurd . . . but was it? I was a stranger, a vagrant, and Roland was a local boy. Very likely, too, they would find my fingerprints in the car. Add to these the fact that because I was hunched down when we sideswiped them, the cops must have seen only one person in the car, and did not things look bleak? They damned well did. And all my own doing. Roland, after all, was not quite the biggest jackass in the world. And with that crazy old witch on his back, who could know how far he might go? I wanted a lawyer.

I jumped off my cot and began rattling the door and yelling. There were groans from other cells, a thick voice cursing. A door opened, admitting a wedge of light into the cell block, and a shiny bald head appeared in the aperture.

"Shut up that goddamn noise in there."

"I want a lawyer."

"You do, huh? Well, I ain't a lawyer, but I'll give you some advice. Shut your fat mouth and get back in that bunk." Then the door banged shut.

I remembered my lesson from the morning and rather quickly let go of the bars. I heard a whisper out of the dark: "We'll make a break pretty soon. I got it all planned out."

I was feeling brutal, and albeit very quietly, I snarled, "How would you like for me to wash your mouth out with that soap gun."

Stanley was evidently shaken and did not say anything more. I walked to the rear window and stood with my hands on the bars looking out into the dimly lit alley at garbage cans. I must have stood for an hour or two chewing on my rage and frustration.

Things did not look any better in the morning. In fact they looked worse, especially after my brief conversation with the sheriff, who was not of a mind to spend any sympathy on me.

"You'll get a hearing," he said to me through the bars, working his big loose lips.

"When?"

"Next grand jury."

"When's that?"

"Oh, two, three weeks."

"What?" I bawled.

"So settle down."

"I want a lawyer."

"You'll git one."

"I want him now."

"Wouldn't do you no good now." He was already walking away. "So just relax," he said over his shoulder as he passed through the door out of sight.

I was left choking with rage. I expended some of it by glaring at my murderous cell mate Stanley who, evidently feeling that I was rather more dangerous than himself, kept his eyes studiously fastened on his crime magazine. And so I began to pace.

I think I paced back and forth until lunchtime. My mind, after a while, had begun to function pretty smoothly, but it just would not turn up anything. Which was strange, in light of the genius for invention that it had manifested only the night before last.

Lunch was served. I noticed it sitting there on the shelf . . . beans and a hard-boiled egg apiece . . . and then forgot all about it. When I looked again, there was nothing in either tray but eggshells.

"What's the idea of eating mine?" I said rather fiercely to Stanley.

He flinched slightly, and a little bit of a whine sounded in his voice. "You looked like you didn't want it. I was hungry. I been in here four days."

I continued to look angrily at him. "Why in the devil don't you get out on bail? You know damn well your parents would get you out."

"No, they won't. They want me in here so I won't do any more crimes."

"Nuts," I said. "Write them a pitiful letter. You've had plenty of practice at lying."

He looked at me morosely. "I don't think it would work. They don't want me out."

"I don't blame them," I said. And suddenly I was standing very still, because it seemed to me that an idea was coming into focus. In fact within a moment or two it had taken on a fairly definite shape.

"Could you maybe help me write it?" Stanley said dubiously.

"Have you got a pen and paper?" I said, feeling as if a little flame was burning inside my head.

"I'll get them." He hopped off the cot. From down on the floor behind his magazines he produced a pad of writing paper and a greasy ballpoint pen. I snatched them out of his hands and threw myself on my cot.

"Hadn't I better do the writing?" Stanley said. "They know my writing."

"Let me alone," I snarled. After that, lying propped on one elbow, I was oblivious to everything but the fire of creative thought blazing in my mind. It was not more than a few minutes, I think, before I started composing.

"Dear Roland," I wrote. But I soon scratched this out; there would be a rough draft to start with. "Darling Roland." Still not good enough. "My ever-lovin sweetheart Rolly," I wrote and let it stand. "Please don't be mad at your puddin for writing you just a litle letter when you told her not to. Its just I cudnt help thinking and dreming about you. Nawty ones too, like us lying in bed naked tumy to tumy and your big ole arms sqeesin me so tight agenst you til its like Im seein stars. I get so hot down deep in my tummy I nerabout melt away. I hope you do too, think about us like me I mean. O when can we be tumy to tumy agin."

I composed a poem, making it a little more literate, and literary.

> Thy lips are so divine
> Thy arms that me entwine
> I am so thriled that they will soon be mine.
> I want to hug the close to me
> Closer than even two planks can be
> And never let the from me flee.

Adding to the letter just a few more touches of my talented hand I signed it, "Your Hony Love, Ruby," and ended by drawing cupid's lips at the bottom.

I spent a few minutes considering other names, like Garnet and Sapphire, and still others like Zona Lee and Bessie Mae. In the end, though, I settled for the one I had. Very carefully, trying to reproduce my conception of a shopgirl-type hand and adding a few more misspellings, I copied the letter over. To get an envelope and stamp, I had to pay the lousy cop in attendance two bucks. To make sure Mama would peek, I wrote 'PERSONAL' in big letters on both sides of the envelope and addressed it to Roland Belt, Esq. in care of general delivery, Bellsboro, Tennessee. Then I added 'Special Delivery.' But I thought of one thing more, which cost me five bucks, this time. The cop brought me a small bottle of lousy perfume that couldn't have cost two dollars, and I sprinkled some of it on the letter. At least the cop didn't charge me for putting my letter in the mailbox.

I figured on two days, at most. But how was I to endure even one more day, especially locked up with Stanley, whose accounts of his crimes and plans for the future I finally silenced by threats. I found that the crime magazines themselves were to be preferred, and I blanked out a number of hours this way. I do not retain any details from those articles, but I do still have in my head some of the titles: "Mr. Murder"; "Teen-Age Rapist" (he was fourteen, I think); "Horror in Hackensack"; and "Case of the Smothering Mother." (She did things like go to hospitals and shut off child patients' oxygen supplies.) And I could go on, but I won't.

More and more of my time I spent pacing back and forth from bars to barred window. By the end of the second day, my confidence had already slipped a good deal. And when the third day came and crept by a minute at a time and finally passed into night again without having produced anything at all but the same jail routine and, once, a few kids rummaging in the trash cans in the alley, I gave up hope. It had been a foolish hope anyway, I saw now, with all the odds against me from the start.

What could I do now . . . grin and bear it? Who was there I could call on? I thought of my mother. I also thought, instantly afterward, that I would sooner choose a year in the state pen any time. My father? What father? And where was he? Dead or outbound in a rocket, for all I knew. I lay on my cot that night with a weariness that failed to produce any sleep. In fact there were times when rage and frustration stifled me so that I had to get up and go to the window for breath. It was dawn when I went to sleep.

I was shaken out of it, in broad daylight, by the ungentle hand of a cop. "Get up and get your stuff."

Too groggy to think at first, I sat up, fumbled my feet into my shoes, and stood up looking blankly at the familiar face of my big cop.

"Ain't you got some junk? Get it."

I was functioning well enough now to feel a surge of hope. Still, I reflected, for all I knew I was being moved to solitary confinement, and I followed him with a good deal of uncertainty out of the cell and out through the door of the cell block.

"Where am I going?"

"In there," he said and indicated a door, open a crack, in the concrete wall to our right. I heard a voice, a woman's voice, and my heart gave a cautious little bound.

"Go on in," my cop mumbled.

Still cautiously I pushed the door open. There was the sheriff behind his desk directly under a picture of himself on the wall, both looking straight at me. And facing him, backs to me, there they were: Mother in blue straw bonnet, and Roland slumped mountainously forward in a chair at her side. Mother was saying emphatically, "He will just have to be punished . . . ," when, evidently noticing the new direction of the sheriff's gaze, she turned her head and looked up at me from under the awning of her bonnet. I saw a flicker of alarm in the narrow greenish-gray eyes. Apparently she had not anticipated encountering me face-to-face. She snapped her gaze away from me and, looking again at the sheriff, continued, "He's been bad and he will just have to be punished."

But the sheriff was still looking at me, sucking on his big loose underlip. He released it and said, "Set down, friend. This here fellow had swore out a lie on you."

"He ought to be ashamed of himself," Mother snapped.

Then my heart did give a bound for joy. My next reaction was a momentary irrational gratitude directed not only at Roland but even at Mother; for sheer exuberance I plumped myself down in the chair indicated.

"He's done owned up. So you're off the hook."

"It's about time," I said, looking at Roland, feeling that absurd gratitude leave me as suddenly as it had come. Roland never had even glanced at me. His big heroic head hung so far down that I could see only the bottom half of his broad, green tie. But now Mother was looking at me. There was no longer any hint of confusion in her expression, and when I met her with a gaze that must have been anything but submissive, I distinctly saw a marked change take place. Incredibly her new expression was one of indignation. I read it, with mounting indignation of my own, to say that of all the ingrates she had known, I was the basest. The only thing that checked some outburst of my reawakened rage was the sheriff's voice suddenly saying to me, "You want to bring charges against him?"

I clearly heard Mother say, though half under her breath, "Indeed!"

"I just might," I said with force. "Let me think about it a minute."

Then she did look at me. I even saw her faintly discolored lower teeth. I was just conscious of the small but pitiful sniffle that Roland gave, his first response so far. I was a good deal more conscious of a thought that had just now popped into my mind, that maybe this was a time for a little caution. To the sheriff I said, "You've got it all down on paper? Signed, I mean?"

"Yep." The sheriff, who was leaning back in his swivel chair with thumbs inserted under his big leather belt, released a hand to pick up the document lying on his desk. "Want to read it?"

I did, quickly. It was fine, my part in the thing unrecognized. I put the document back and looked squarely at Mother. I felt very cool and collected, like a wasp filing up its stinger. "What brought on Roland's change of heart?"

Roland gave another sniffle, and Mother gave him a hot little glance.

"Roland is a fine boy at heart," she said. "He did a bad thing and now he's ready to take his punishment."

"How come he can't never talk for his self?" the sheriff said.

"Yeah," I said. "Is your conscience hurting you, Roland?"

Roland was clearing his throat, but Mother interrupted. "He feels too bad to talk right now. He wants to go right on to jail and begin his punishment."

"This fellow here ain't said yet if he wants to press charges," the sheriff said. He and Mother both looked at me. Evidently she had begun to understand, and she looked back at Roland and said, "You do, don't you, Roland? To go on and get it over with."

Roland shook his still-bowed head. It was not clear whether he meant yes or no. The sheriff was vexed. "How come you got to do the talking for him all the time?"

"He is my son, isn't he?" Mother said testily.

"Well, it says right here he's twenty-seven years old," the sheriff said, putting a finger on the document before him.

"And what difference does that make?" Mother met his gaze with wide-open challenging eyes.

The sheriff reared back again and slipped a little farther down in his chair.

"Come on, Roland," I suddenly said. "Why'd you do it?"

"But I didn't," Roland blurted, his head popping up to expose eyes full of tearful appeal. "I've been trying to . . ."

"Didn't *what?*" The sheriff roused himself again. "You gave a confession and signed it."

"I don't mean that." Roland shook his head with energy. "I did what it says there, all right I mean I . . ."

"He means he didn't mean to do wrong," Mother broke in. "But he certainly did do wrong. You ought to be ashamed of yourself," she added with an unexpected burst of anger, turning on him a face suddenly flushed.

With one small lunge of desperation he met her nearly eye for eye. "But I didn't, Mother. I swear on the name of the Lord I didn't."

The Adventures of Douglas Bragg

"Don't you swear on the Lord's name." Her face was redder than ever . . . livid, in fact. "And don't you lie to me, either. Shame on you!"

Roland wilted. He turned a drowning man's eye on the sheriff and then on me. The idea came upon me like the Lord's lightning. Looking squarely and openly at him, I gave the biggest and slowest and ugliest wink I could contrive.

The effect on both of them was better than I had anticipated. For the next few seconds I was confronted by two very blank and slack-mouthed faces. Then a flush began to spread upward from Roland's manly neck. In Mother's case, since already there was no deeper hue that could be achieved, the opposite happened: a pallor began to streak and finally to dissolve her color.

"Young man, what did you mean by that wink?"

"I don't know," I said innocently. "I just winked."

"Mr. Smith, I demand to know what you meant by it," she said with force.

"Look," I said. "My name is not Smith. And it's not Brooks or Banks. It's Bragg. B-r-a-g-g. I wish you'd get it straight."

She just grunted "Hunh," as though for me it was a mere boast to claim any name at all, then said, "Officer, I demand to know what he meant by that wink."

"Go ahead and tell her," the sheriff said, obviously interested.

I felt I had my own stride now. "Oh, nothing much really. You know what I mean." I gave a little deprecatory wrinkle to my nose. "Just he's a salesman. You know how those salesmen are. Always got something stashed away somewhere on their route. Some of them got one in every town."

"But I don't," Roland pleaded. I distinctly saw Mother swallow.

"Aw, come on, Roland," I said. "A big ex-football player like you. With a hurt knee. And feeding them Endurol besides. You ought to try that stuff, Sheriff. Man!" And I gave a small suggestive whistle through my teeth.

"Watch your language, son," the sheriff said.

But I was noticing Mother. Confronted with hellfire she could not have gone pale more suddenly. Now indeed I was not about to drop the subject.

"You know how they are, Sheriff. They tell you they're out selling stuff, but really they're off somewhere in a motel blowing in some gal's ear. Or tickling her," I added.

The Adventures of Douglas Bragg

"That's enough, boy," the sheriff said.

But I wasn't thinking about the sheriff. Mother's face had now undergone a change from merely shocked to dangerous, and judging by the way her eyes ran blazing back and forth from me to Roland, it was not clear which of us was the more likely object of possible assault. Evidently Roland thought it was himself; he was leaning away from her, flinching. And for plain good physical reason. Not only was Mother perched stiffly forward on the chair; she held that big skull-busting purse clutched in both hands like a stone. At my distance I felt fairly safe, and I was more than anxious to see Roland's noble head not only bowed but bloody before I pulled the rug out from under Mother. One more good prod ought to do it. But why pull the rug? I thought. Was not this, my Freudian Torture Technique, in its way just as punishing? With this in mind I opened my mouth to proceed, but the sheriff interrupted again. "Can't have that kind of talk around a lady."

"All right," I said. I would pull the rug, then . . . but not too quickly. "But I'm entitled to a little something for my five days. I still don't know why Roland repented."

"We have already told you," Mother snapped.

"Roland hasn't."

"Yeah. Let him talk. For a change," the sheriff said.

Roland had gone back into his slump, but now something about his attitude made me think he was on the verge of spilling the beans. Nothing came of it, however. Mother was too much for him, hovering at his mountainous shoulder like an inflamed little cloud with a bolt of lightning held at poise. In the end he only mumbled, "I just got to feeling bad, is all."

"Just like I told you," Mother said sharply.

"Come on, Roland. Haven't you got a girl? Isn't that it?"

"Naw," he wailed, obliquely directing toward Mother the second of the two syllables he had wrung out of the word.

"That lives somewhere around here?" I said.

He only looked at me from under his brow. Mother looked very straight at me.

"Who goes in for getting squeezed with your big old arms? And also lying tummy to tummy?"

There was no change at all in their response, though now they put me in mind of two people sharing a single vision, and that being the sight of a snake slowly emerging from the woodwork. Apparently the sheriff had spotted something too, because he did not interrupt.

"The poetic kind, too? Writes a mean love poem?"

At first I thought Mother was coming right out of her chair. "Then you are the cause of it," she literally yelled at me.

This was ambiguous. "What do you mean by that?"

"Don't lie to me. I saw the kind you are. The second you walked in my door I saw it. Leading my boy into . . . into . . ."

"Sin?" I said.

"Yes. Sin. Deceiving his mother. With a . . . a. . . ."

"Her name's Ruby."

"Then you admit it!" Here she did come out of her chair, with the abruptness of something on a spring. "I knew it."

"You-all quiet down," the sheriff said, but I know she didn't hear him.

"You knew what?" I said.

"Tempter," she squalled. "Degenerate. My poor little Roland." Here she grew inarticulate for a moment, and I got a glimpse of heads in the doorway I had entered through. Then, "Ruby," she said, as though she was hawking up an insect out of her throat.

"But Mother." Roland's voice came as from down in a pit. "There's not any Ruby."

Mother wheeled and hit him so hard with her purse on the side of his head that it knocked him clear out of his chair.

"Here, Lady!" The sheriff got to his feet. "Set back down in that chair."

But she did not. She was looking down at Roland without even the least appearance of compassion, possibly contemplating another blow. I was delighted and would not have been sorry to see her deliver another just like that one. But the sheriff was not of my mind at all. He seized her purse hand and with considerable firmness set her down in the chair again. "We ain't going to have nothing more like that."

Though short of cold-cocked, Roland was still down. There on his hands and knees he looked like a fighter dazedly hoping for the bell a long time after ten had been counted. "Here, let me help you," the sheriff said, bending to extend a hand. But Roland shook his head, bearlike, and proceeded to crawl the three or four feet to a chair closer to me than to Mother and climb onto it. There he sat looking obliquely toward her like somebody in the aftermath of a lightning strike.

The Adventures of Douglas Bragg

But aftermath or not, Mother's charge was not exhausted. Once again, whether at Roland or me was uncertain, she said with explosive contempt, "Ruby."

I still had not had enough, but I thought the time had come to make it so plain that even she could not miss it. Recalling my most brilliant lines, I said:

"I want to hold thee close to me

Closer than even two planks can be . . ."

She made a sudden movement, accompanied by some half-shaped word in her throat, but instantly the sheriff's hand came down firmly on her shoulder. "Look here," he said, turning an angry face to me now, "I don't know what in hell is going on, but I mean for it to stop."

"All right," I said. She had failed, anyway, to get the real point of my quotation, and more in this line could be nothing but anticlimax. "Just one last thing," I added, and quickly, lest he stop me, I said to Mother, "Roland was telling you the truth. There's not any Ruby. I'm Ruby."

But Mother, still fuming with the old outrage, just stared at me.

"You through?" the sheriff said.

"She'll get it in a minute," I said.

A pause followed, but I still did not see any sign of comprehension rising in her mind. Or did I?

"You mean you did a thing like that, to me?" This, in a measured sorrowful voice from Roland. I turned my head to encounter an expression of hurt just about as real as any I can recall. It was my turn to be astonished.

"And after I gave you a ride and supper and all. Me and Mother."

At first I simply could not come up with any response whatsoever. When it came it was most inadequate. I just said, "You ass," without any force.

But by this time he was turning toward Mother. "Mother, he wrote that letter. And made up that name Ruby. He's a mean person."

There was still no outward response from Mother, but I could tell that now comprehension was dawning on her.

"Okay," the sheriff said to me. "You're through now. Get going. Unless you want to bring charges."

"Skip it," I said, getting up. Mother looked as though paralysis had set in, so I figured the fireworks were now pretty well over. Still, with my hand on the doorknob, I paused for some last words. "Sorry if I seem ungrateful," I said. "After that good dinner and the ride and all."

The Adventures of Douglas Bragg

— — —

They just stared at me, the two of them in silence, like they were watching Judas Iscariot about to make an exit.

"Roland," I continued, "I hope you have a pleasant stay in the pen. Mother, you send him plenty of Endurol. He'll need it out there breaking those rocks. You want me to write Health Home for . . . ?"

I will never know how she managed so much weight with such dexterity, but that big black purse came hurtling through the air like a cannonball. I ducked just in time; it grazed my ear and exploded against the doorjamb inches from my head. There was a great clatter of objects hitting the floor and bounding in all directions: pills, buttons, scissors, coins. I also saw what undoubtedly was my letter, but just at this point the sheriff's voice rising in one long outraged bellow quite dislodged my attention.

The better to enjoy my departure, I gave them all a little bye-bye wave with my fingers. Moments later, pausing only to receive my handbag from a bewildered-looking cop, I was out of there and on my way, a traveling man once more.

![2](shield with number 2)

WITHIN A COUPLE OF WEEKS after leaving Bellsboro, I was beginning to feel disappointed with my life on the road. Actually I had spent the biggest part of that time not on the road but, in order to replenish my store of cash, working in a grocery store in the little town of Ford Creek. I don't know what I kept expecting to happen . . . just something good, like, maybe, getting picked up by a beautiful young woman who would turn out to be the love of my life. This didn't happen, nor did anything else that was good. But something did happen, something bad enough in itself and even worse in its consequence.

First, I was mugged, and not just mugged, but knocked unconscious for many hours. Second, I finally woke up in a place where, though I had no way of foreseeing it, I was to spend a couple of the most wretched months of my life. Lying there in a strange bed in a strange house, I tried to recall how the thing had happened.

At a crossroads somewhere in the distance I had got out of a pickup truck whose loquacious driver had already given me directions. Huddleston, a good-size town where they had places to spend the night, he'd said, wasn't too much of a walk for a boy like me. So I set out. Later, after passing a couple of farms with livestock grazing and many more wooded areas than farms, it happened that I stopped to pull up my socks. This was when I noticed a clattering noise from a dumpster in a cleared space beside the road. To see what was causing it, I went for a look. The dumpster was tall, and to see over the side I had to step up onto the pediment. The maker of that noise was a man digging in the trash. He looked up at me with a grin full of discolored teeth. Holding up the ragged remains of a shoe, he said, "These here ain't even good as mine." Oddly enough, as if in anticipation of what was to come, this was the point at which my recollection of the event began to blur.

Still, I recalled well enough how he had gone about setting me up. To gain my sympathy he had rightly calculated on the strength of his wretched clothes and the abuse laid on him by disloyal friends and also by bad luck. Even though I didn't swallow it hook, line, and sinker, I was sucker enough to start thinking about a small donation, at least.

This was not necessary, however, because he took care of the donation, himself, leaving me, maybe on purpose, exactly one penny. But of course this was after he had clobbered me and left me there naked behind the dumpster. I never was able to figure out how he got hold of the instrument he hit me with.

– – –

I remembered, or seemed to remember, shadowy intervals scattered among the many hours before I regained full consciousness. There had been darkness and bitter cold and once or twice the sound of a passing car. But clearest of all were the spurts of pain when I tried to move my head. Then came intervals of light, during one of which I was being lifted up by somebody I couldn't see. And finally I was in a bed, and there was a room around me. At this point I was able, a little at a time, to figure out what had happened. And now I realized that along with my money he had also taken the bag where I had my extra clothes. A thorough rascal, to say the least. Well, what now?

It took a while for me to get all the way clear in my head, but I had already seen that I was in a small room with one big window and with plastered walls that were stained and cracked all around. This and the fact that my mattress was lumpy and had an unpleasant smell were what told me I was not in a hospital room. Also the people, shadowy figures who came and went once in a while, were definitely not doctors and nurses. There were two women, both fat, a man with a curious whiny voice, and another man or grown boy who I happened to notice had a guitar in hand. Anyway, it was a sure thing that no nurse or doctor could be responsible for the big sloppy bandage on the back of my head.

By nightfall of that day my brains were back in order, and I might have felt like getting up except for the fact that I was now beset with another affliction. I'm sure it came from the cold night I had spent out there on my back by the dumpster. My nose started running, and that turned into sneezing fits, and these into spells of coughing. I mean real coughing, with echoes, like inside a metal drum. Somewhere in the night, breaking into one of my spells, I started hearing the sound of a guitar. It was the boy's, of course, in his room somewhere nearby. My coughing soon stopped, but the sound of his guitar didn't. He must have got caught up with the "beauty" of it because it kept on and on until a male voice from down below bellowed, "Stop that goddamn racket!" It did stop for a while, but then it took up again. The same exchange happened a couple of more times, and I kept waiting for some thunder to follow. It didn't; the "goddamn racket," though now subdued, won out. I soon learned that even if the old man was lord of the manor, his heavy hand didn't reach everywhere and always. In extremes, however, I came to see that the boy was never gutsy enough to really stand up to him.

For a week or so I languished in bed with what I thought was probably pneumonia. My mention of the fact, along with my clear hint about a doctor, made no impression on them. I was left to understand that doctors and hospitals couldn't be trusted and that they, the family, had been doctoring each other successfully all their lives. They had anecdotes to prove it, ones that always involved aspirin, which they also kept feeding me. Anyway, this seemed finally to answer the question as to why all this trouble with me when they could have just taken me to a hospital or something. Anyway, I had reason to be grateful to them. Though poor and ignorant, clearly they were good, well-meaning country people. Or so I thought at the time.

I had reached the first stages of mobility before I understood exactly what kind of a place this was. The one window, an upstairs window, was located so that from a prone position I couldn't see out. But the first time I was able to sit up and move a little forward, the whole scene came into view. I had never seen so many pigs in my whole life. There were pigs rooting around all over the field back there and what looked like a lot more in a long pen on the other side of the field. The sheer number of them out there seemed to indicate that pigs were a profitable business, but when I looked around at my room and at my benefactors when they came in to see about or talk to me, I wondered.

In particular the old man ("Bo" Hogan, he was called) did not appear to be a successful person. The most persuasive evidence, more than his looks, was his voice. That quality like a whine that I had noticed first-off now suggested that here was a man much put-upon and also angry about it: a curious kind of mix between pleading and, maybe, threatening. His clothes, a faded blue cotton shirt, loose fatigue jacket with only one button, and knee-patched overalls looked to be the same ones he wore every day, in and out of the pigpen. It was my guess that he shaved, not very skillfully, maybe once a week, and his stubble was gray only on certain parts of his jaw. That he seemed almost to have no neck at all, as if his ears grew right out of his shoulders, was of course not his fault.

Bo came into my room only a few times while I was still confined to my bed. He never sat down for a real conversation, but he always stayed long enough to recount the details of how I came to be here in this warm bed, taken care of like a real member of the family. "You was some lucky, boy. Lying back there behind that dumpster where nobody couldn't see you. You was on the way to dying, boy. It just did happ'm I caught sight of your foot. And the Lord told me, 'He'p that boy.' And I done it."

This account or some small variation of it, for which I was bound to express my gratitude, was the heart of his little visits. The only other subject, just touched on, accompanied always with a sigh of resignation, was the hard times he was going through.

"And getting harder," he would say, while I nodded my sympathy. To say the least, I was never sorry to see him leave.

Mama, a short fat woman with round watery blue eyes, seemed to be all right. Unlike her husband, she didn't look run-down. I got the impression that here was a woman who had always accepted, and who would always passively accept, whatever came along. She gave me soup and aspirin and a hint of sympathy and never stayed too long. Unfortunately her daughter Mildred, who was built about like her and had the same kind of watery eyes, did stay too long and did it often. Even at first when I was still a little murky in the head, I began to feel that she was trouble. I didn't like the way she sometimes rolled those wide-open eyes for no good reason, any more than I liked the sight of her little pink tongue wetting her lips more often than was necessary. And when, on about my third or fourth day, she sat down on the bed, took my hand into her little fat one and cooed her sympathy at me, I began thinking I had better hurry up and get out of there.

The other family member, J.T. (I learned later that there were two children who some time ago had left home for good), was a full-grown, able-looking boy, and there was no good reason he shouldn't be out there wrestling pigs along with his father. But I never saw him do so. Invariably his excuse was that he needed to practice. He meant, on his guitar, and he was telling the truth. Because he was so close by, there was no way, even with that knotty pillow over my head, for me to quite shut out the sound of his picking and singing along, even throughout the night.

The songs were his own compositions, he would tell me each time he invaded my room. The invasions came to be many and undeterred even by my coughing fits. He would sit on my bed, bent over his guitar, making a face that I assumed was meant to be characteristic of country music stars. He had let his hair, thick and red, grow long enough to hang down over his eyes, which I supposed he thought was another feature popular with these personages. In fact, he told me, he had already been up there to Nashville, where they said he was a "natral" but he needed more practice yet. I agreed with the last part of this.

However, I soon got to where I usually welcomed his invasions. Besides that they helped fill my hours, I developed an amused interest in the lyrics he composed. After each performance, always in what he considered to be the approved nasal style, he would sit waiting, with a grave expression, for my judgment. "Very nice," I would say and let him hang there in expectation of further comment. This was when my interest, and my imagination, would take fire. As it did in the case of "Love That Gal," one of his brand new compositions. It went:

> I do love that Gal I swear
> Love her more than I can bear
> She is sweet as she can be
> Makes me want to climb a tree.

"Very nice," I said, and let him hang a while. "But I feel like it needs a little something." He was all attention, watching my lips. I said,

"Maybe something to show what she looks like. Think of a thing that's sweet."

"Sugar," he said.

"That's too easy."

"Honey," he said. "A honey comb."

"Still too easy. Got to be original. Something different. How about a 'honey tree'?"

"There ain't no such a thing."

"Doesn't matter, it's different. Got a lot of good rhymes, too. Bee. Flee. Me. Key. Knee. We. On and on."

"Sho' does." he said.

"How about:

> I long to get down on my knee
> Right at the foot of my honey tree?"

He looked puzzled. "How come anybody'd want to do that?"

"You know. Like when you think something's awful beautiful. Like maybe at church."

He still looked dubious. "Awright," he finally said. "What's goan come next, though?"

I cast about for a moment. Flee. Me. Bee. Oh, well, I thought. "How about:

> But then I thought I better flee
> So's not to get stung by a honey bee?"

This time he looked downright disapproving. "That ain't no good. Don't fit. Got to be him loving her."

"Doesn't matter, these days. They jump around like that all the time. Look at Buster Bell, how he does." I had used to live in Nashville and so had a smattering of knowledge about such matters.

"You like Buster Bell?" His face had brightened.

"Sure do," I said. Just because it came to me to do it. I added, "I remember when he was writing 'Crying Mama,' how hard he worked on it." For effect I added, "Mostly at night."

J.T.'s mouth fell open. In an awed tone of voice he said, "You know him? His self?"

The Adventures of Douglas Bragg

Why not? I thought, and nodded complacently. But right off, I was sorry, because what I had impulsively imagined would be just fun led straight to the opposite. Not only at that time but on most of his later visits, I was compelled to manufacture new details about my fictional friendship with Buster Bell.

Anyway, it all came down to my spending hours composing more or less ridiculous lyrics for his repertoire. The result was that by the time I was on my feet again, I had him convinced that I was some kind of a genius whose compositions were destined to wow the country music folks.

— — —

Being on my feet again, able to walk around and go downstairs to meals started a new and increasingly unhappy phase in my residence with the Hogans. For one thing the house itself depressed me. I could tell that once upon a time it had been a house that could make claim to some distinction. The roof that extended unevenly out from above the front door must have had, instead of two rough-cut and elongated fence posts as now, a pair of matching columns for support. More than that, the porch floor had been ripped away and the steps from the front-door threshold led straight down to the ground. Paint was needed everywhere on the outside walls, and many a board showed clear signs of rot.

Inside, things were in somewhat better shape, but for a large, two-story house there was just about enough furniture to make maybe three rooms almost comfortable. In what was supposed to be the living room, for instance, there were two rickety straw-bottom chairs and a wooden bench, like a pew. What once must have been the old dining room was the master bedroom now, with the furniture that should have been there long-since residing in the kitchen. It looked as though the house had come through an estate sale that had left nothing behind but rejects. And there was the lighting. On a cloudy day you practically went blind when you stepped out of the kitchen into the hall. The only times I ever saw a light burning there were when Bo was safely out of the house. "Turn that damn light out," he would say. "I ain't made out of money." He is the only man I've ever seen literally bite a penny.

There was still more. A telephone that wouldn't work half the time, and a shoebox-size radio so full of static you could barely hear anything else. But most depressing of all, surely, was the meals.

The Adventures of Douglas Bragg

We sat at the table in the big kitchen, in an almost total absence of conversation, nearly always with nothing substantial to eat except warmed-over collards and white beans and cornpone day after day. Practically the only variation was what he referred to as chicken . . . and sometimes was chicken, if you could count bantams as such. But that wasn't all. Some of that "chicken," as I came to discover, was grown pigeons that he caught in traps in his barn loft. He owned some real chickens, but as soon as their chicks grew big enough to eat, he habitually sold them. Add to all this the slovenly table manners I had to endure, and you have a pretty picture of domestic bliss among the Hogans.

Even so, these things came to be the least of my grievances. By the time I was nearly strong enough to get gone from this place and started mentioning the fact, it was dawning on me that I was up against a not-yet-spoken resistance . . . or at least not directly spoken. Reminders were dropped here and there, always by the boss man himself. Such as, "Sorry them clothes of J.T.'s don't fit you no better. But they beat not having none at all, though. Clothes means money, though, and we ain't got none to spare."

But he was on the way to getting direct about it, and it didn't take him long. A little after supper on a Sunday night, he came up to my room and sat down carefully on the rickety and only chair. On the bed, propped against the headboard, I waited.

"Son," he said, "I'm kind of hoping, now you're well, you'll stay on and he'p me just for a while. Need he'p bad, times like these."

I had already prepared my case, that I didn't know anything about pigs or farm work or any kind of work, much. But Bo just smiled and nodded his head in a grandfatherly way and said what a smart boy I was and how quick I'd catch on. There was a long pause, and I was right in expecting what followed. It was how I'd have sho'ly been six feet under now if it hadn't of been for him and all the loving care him and his family had give me all this time . . . and me not a penny to pay with. And him bad in debt, and nobody to he'p him . . . cause that boy of his wasn't worth killing, wouldn't do nothing 'cept to pick on a guitar all day long. There was another long pause, and this time I couldn't guess what was coming. It came straight at me. "You owes it to me, boy." The hot little core of light that flickered in his eyes vanished instantly, and his lips, that had shut down tight, widened into a smile, a welcoming smile. "I know you goan he'p me. I can see it in your face, boy."

I don't know what was in my face. I know that my mouth was hanging open, with no words to come out, and that he left me believing, I think, that this was an answering smile.

All night long, it seemed, my brains were too busy for sleep. Whenever the thought popped up that I did owe him, it gave way pretty soon to the opposite: that all this caretaking of me was nothing but a design from the start, and that the thing to do was sneak out of here while it was still dark. Then what? The weather, right here in my room as well as outside, had got wintry in the last day or two, and I didn't even have a coat, much less a place to go. All this and, as I couldn't forget, just one penny to my name. So . . . ? All right, I would hang on, working for him only long enough to see my way clear. This was it, and finally reconciled, I pulled the covers up to my chin and lay there inviting sleep.

Maybe I did sleep a little while, but it sure didn't seem that way when, like a jolt inside my head, I heard his voice. He was standing in my door. "Time to go, boy. Already getting daylight."

Daylight! The only light I could see was from that dim bulb out in the hallway behind him. Except for that morning when I set out on my travels, I couldn't remember ever getting up at daylight.

"Got a heap to do."

Already shivering, not quite sure this was really happening, I struggled out from under my blanket. This was the beginning of maybe the worst interval in my life.

Certain things about that first day especially come back to mind. To start with, there were those two big dogs that seemed to live under the back steps. One looked to be some kind of a hound mix, maybe mostly bloodhound, with half of one ear chewed off. The other one, the bulldog, had a head about the size of a two-gallon bucket and was the mangiest and most dangerous-looking. Both of them took a dislike to me on sight, and Bo had to kick the daylights out of the bulldog to keep him off of me. "They be all right," he said. "You just strange to them." But even when they got to know me a lot better, they didn't stop looking at me in that malevolent way. I gathered that this was pleasing to Bo: more than once he went out of his way to mention what a good tracker the hound was. Man or beast, he said, that dog can track them down like you wouldn't believe. It was clearer day by day that Bo was reading my mind.

That first workday, besides wearing me to a frazzle and leaving me with wounds, taught me to hate pigs and all that went with them forever.

The Adventures of Douglas Bragg

A long sagging broken-back barn, or combination barn and shed some distance out from the house, was where Bo kept his equipment and other stuff. The stuff included two skinny irritable mules, a beat-up old, and remarkably small, car, a truck, and a rusty-looking farm tractor. I had heard somewhere that mules were getting to be a thing of the past, but here they were because, as Bo told me, his old tractor wouldn't run but just when it wanted to, and he had got these old mules cheap at an auction. I soon observed that the truck, too, was not dependable.

But these were things that caught my attention only in passing. What was impossible not to focus on was the stink in that barn. It wasn't chicken or mule shit, though these might have been mixed in with it. The real cause was that here was his headquarters for the slop he stored up in buckets and every few days took out to the pigpen. While he harnessed up the mules, it was my pleasure to lift onto the wagon bed about ten five-gallon buckets of the nasty stuff. It looked like so much pond scum with unidentifiable objects floating in it. Two times I spilled some of it on myself, and the stink hung on in my clothes for at least a day or two. The family didn't seem to notice, though. Out of courtesy, maybe.

I couldn't possibly say there was any one moment when my sense of outrage reached its peak, but it could have been that one when, on the night after my first workday, I literally collapsed onto my lumpy and not sweet-smelling bed. This, the whole thing, was not to be believed. I, a young, independent college man with a quite respectable quantity of brains and freedom to choose what I would and wouldn't do, stuck out here in No-place, Tennessee, slogging around in the muck of a pigpen at the beck and call of a crafty moron . . . how could it be for real? But it actually was, and all I had to do to give it substance was recite to myself the events of that god-awful first day.

It had started with the aforementioned slop. Bo had the mules harnessed to the wagon, and he told me to drive them on up to the pigpen, while he went to get something he had left somewhere. (He was always leaving to find something somewhere.) When he saw me just staring at the creatures, he said, "Any fool can drive a team of mules. They won't go, just whack them with the lines." I did, two times, and they went.

They didn't go very far. Well short of halfway across the field, they came to a dead stop. "Come up," I said, feeling authoritative, and when they didn't, I whacked them. Nothing doing. I whacked again, then again, concentrating on the taller mule with a rump like a hat-rack. Still there was nothing to show for it until, strangely, the tall mule turned his head almost clear around and looked me practically straight in the face. It was a look that seemed to say he was going to remember me. I didn't like it and decided not to keep on whacking. I got down from the wagon and walked around and took the mule by the bit. I pulled, but nothing happened. It was like pulling on a big tree limb. I was about to try again when suddenly, as it seemed, I was under attack. It was pigs, all around me and all around the wagon in a chorus of oinking and snorting that made my hair stand up. As fast as I could, kicking pigs as I went, I made progress back toward the wagon. I had almost got there when something (a pig?) hit me hard on the leg just below the knee. I was practically dragging the leg when finally I managed to pull myself up onto the wagon. The leg was aching. A pig? . . . no way. It was that goddamn mule living up to his promise. Who would have thought a mule could kick sideways?

This was just the beginning, and with a sore leg, besides. The pig-pen looked to be a couple of hundred feet long, fenced in mostly with old rusty wire and separated into six or eight individual pens opening onto each other. A mud-colored stream ran the whole length of it, which ensured that the ground on both sides was pure muck. Most of the little pens had pigs in them, large and small ones together, black and white and mixed ones, separated from the other pigs for reasons I couldn't fathom. Apparently Bo could, however. We (Bo had come up from somewhere to join me) hadn't more than got off the wagon before he started cussing. "Goddamn rusty wire," he growled, and added on a few stomach-turning oaths for good measure. I saw pretty quick where the trouble, or part of the trouble, lay. The dividing fence between two of the pens had a big hole in it, and pigs of all kinds and sizes were going in and out. I didn't see why it made any difference, but it did to Bo, and I didn't press him for an explanation. "Got work here, boy," he finally said, and got a roll of barbed wire and some cutters out of the wagon bed. Guess who was elected. A few minutes later, while he went to check for holes elsewhere, I was down on my knees in the muck trying to unwind a strand of formidably stiff barbed wire from the roll.

Anybody who has ever dealt with barbed wire knows it has a life of its own. Cut it and it will strike at you like a snake; bend it and it will most likely coil around your arm, with barbs caught on your sleeve, on other parts of your shirt, or in your flesh. Before I was half through patching that hole, both my hands looked like I had tried to pick up an enraged tomcat.

This was bad enough, but it was made worse by the pigs. They had taken an interest in me. They were oinking all around me, crowding up, goosing, and rooting me in my already tormented backsides. Every time I took a swing or a kick at them, I usually ended up in another baffling tangle of that damn wire. Once, conscious that Bo was standing by, I seized a moment to glance at him. I won't forget that tight little grin. Worse still was what he said: "You learning, boy, you learning." I thought about using some of the wire to strangle him.

There were two more holes after that one, and again, while Bo stood by with sarcastic advice, I did all the work. There was still more to come, though of a different kind. It seemed that now there were pigs in the wrong places. This time I asked him what difference did it make, but he just gave a kind of a snort and said, "Things needs to go in they right places." Which, having already noticed his bumbling ways, I knew to be baloney.

Anyway the job was left to me again. His part was just to stand there and open the gate whenever I captured a pig or got one headed right. For me, it came down to something like mud wrestling, especially when I had to make a dive to catch one of the smaller pigs by the hind leg and drag him squealing bloody murder to where Bo stood yelling instructions at me. "Git that'n, the black and white'n. In the corner."

Mud-smeared from head to foot, I had almost reached the point of outright rebellion when, suddenly, I had a still better reason to rebel. There was a big black sow in the gang, the only one that till now hadn't seemed to get excited. Maybe that last small pig I had grabbed onto was one of hers, because she came right at me with a snort that sounded like a growl. "Kick her in the snout, kick her in the snout," Bo shouted. The hell I would. I took one long leap, then a hurtle that took me over the fence and flat in mud on the other side. Bo stood there looking down at me, and I noticed that he, himself, had stepped back through the gate and shut it behind him. But that didn't stop him from saying, "You ain't a boy's got much brav'ry, has you."

I met his gaze. "I don't aim to be dinner for a damn hog," I said.

He looked offended. "Damn hog nothing. These is finer hogs as they is, boy."

My anger still rising, I said, "I notice you got out of there right quick, yourself."

He didn't answer. Until I got on my feet, he just stood looking at me with the same derisive expression. But he didn't try to get me back in there. Instead he took me to another pen where all the pigs were small, where, he mockingly said, there wouldn't be no danger to me.

Pretty soon after this little event I began to see that my show of spirit had made a difference. I could see him thinking, and from his glances I was sure it was about me. It didn't cause any change in his treatment of me. The next few days were just about like my first one out . . . or would have been except for a single interlude.

We had just got out to the pen that morning when we discovered something that put Bo off his game for a while. One of his sows was lying there dead. He stood looking and looking down at her, bent over and looked in her mouth, and ended up shaking his head. "Can't see one damn thing wrong." He had a grieved look. It occurred me to mumble something about a veterinarian. "I ain't made out of money," he said. "They don't know nothing nohow." Then, with confidence, "Just p'isoned, is all. Something in the slop." He still had that grieved look. It made me think that his pigs, at least, were something he was fond of. We dragged the sow over to the boundary fence and through the gate into the woods and left her there.

Bo soon recovered, and on that day I found out what it was like to drive half-wild pigs from out in an open pasture into a pen. I also learned how it was to sit on top of a squirming, screaming half-grown pig while Bo clipped rings into its dirty snout. Further, after a terrifying close call, I learned not ever to get in a pen with a boar hog that had tushes fit to disembowel a rhinoceros.

The difference in Bo, as I noticed more and more, had to do with how watchful he had got to be. It was just as if the next time he turned his head he might discover that I wasn't there anymore. That was it. He had miscalculated as to how easy it would be to keep me on, and now the question was what to do about it. The proof of this was what he did two days later. Deep in the night, just to see what it would be like when I decided to make my escape, I got out of bed in the dark and crept to the door. I turned the knob and drew the door slightly open. For a split second I thought it was the hinges that made that grinding sound. No way. It was the growl, in unison, of those goddamn killer dogs.

The Adventures of Douglas Bragg

I lay awake in the dark a long time wondering what Bo would, or could do next and, once again (assuming a successful escape) trying to settle on a course of action. I had no answer at all for the first question, but I did for the second one, maybe: an answer I had already been kicking around. At each first glance it looked simple enough. Go to the police, describe my situation, and depend on them to help a poor young fellow. But a harder look always brought Bo back into it. I was as sure as I could get that the bastard wouldn't hesitate at any kind of a lie. I *owed* him. What if, for instance, he saw his way to claim that this meant money, money stolen from him? And him and his family so good to me. I bristled at the thought and went on further multiplying dismal possibilities. So I didn't decide on anything, for a while.

But then, after two more gruesome days with pigs and after running the details back and forth through my mind, I came to a decision. All at once it showed itself to be simple enough, and I wondered why I had waited this long. After all, Bo didn't have any real power over me, especially legal power, being, I supposed, nobody of importance in these parts. The one uncertainty in my plan was J.T. But I believed I could count on him. Besides having always seemed neutral about my situation, he clearly had a lot of admiration for me . . . and, of course, for Buster Bell.

I had seen that the family, no doubt for other than religious reasons, went to church on Sunday . . . all but J.T., that is, who always wiggled out. So, on the very next morning after my decision, I waited until I heard the little car start up and, with two or three backfires like gunshots, move off down to the highway. J.T.'s door was open, and he was sitting on his rumpled bed, guitar at the ready, evidently just on the verge of breaking into song. "J.T.," I said.

He jumped, grinned at me. "Glad to see you. I done come up with another new one. Listen."

"Not right now," I quickly said. "Look. I got to get away from here. Now's a good time. Will you give me a little help?"

His face fell. "I can't be no help." Then, "It's getting cold out there. Fixing to rain, too. Anyway, old man'd raise hell with me. He can get meaner than you know."

"He can't blame you. All I want is some clothes. Even just a halfway decent coat. I can't catch a ride looking like something the cat dragged in. And maybe a shirt," I said, plucking at my filthy one. "And a little money, if you can. Even just a few dollars."

The Adventures of Douglas Bragg

He was looking down, reluctant. "I ain't got no money."

I could tell he was lying.

"Hard to catch a ride out there, besides. And the old man'll be coming after you."

"He'd have to come with his gun." It was time to play my trump card. "Look. I mean to go to Nashville. I'll go see Buster Bell. I know I can get him to help you with the music folks. He's a good fellow."

This made J.T. raise his head, his face with a dawning look.

I said, "I think you're ready to go back up there, you've got a lot better . . . from all your practicing. And get out of this place," I added, looking around at a room quite as bare and dismal as my own. "I'll let Buster know you'll be coming along pretty soon."

He looked straight at me and blinked like a man just now waked up. He almost grinned. "Awright," he said. "I got a pretty fair old shirt extra. And it's a old overcoat hanging under the stairs down there. Part of one sleeve's tore off, but it ain't too bad."

"And a few dollars?" I said. "I'll send them back to you soon as I can get a job."

He blinked again. "Awright."

"One more thing. Those damn dogs."

"I'll bring them in till you get good gone."

Just a few minutes later, wearing a fairly decent shirt and less decent overcoat plus a cap I snitched, I was, in a state of elation, on my way through ragged weeds and grass down to the front fence and onto the highway. Beyond my expectations, he had given me ten dollars. I spent a few seconds wondering where he had got it, till other thoughts crowded my mind. I meant to keep my word about going to Nashville (my childhood home, anyway), getting a job, and paying him back. There was nothing I could do about Buster Bell, though, except regret my lies. As for the route to Nashville, I only knew that in general it was back the way I had come and that it was a hell of a long walk. This last was brought home to me when the first and second cars going my way passed me by without a glance from their drivers.

It was beginning to drizzle a bit, but I went on undaunted and soon came to the memorable dumpster. I paused just long enough to deliver a silent curse at the rascal who had bashed me, and followed it with another one for Bo. And, by the way, what if he did come after me? What could he do, unless he did bring a gun? I dismissed the thought.

The Adventures of Douglas Bragg

— — —

There was mighty little traffic, a truck or a car every once in a while and none of them inclined to pick me up. I wondered if I looked that bad. The off and on drizzle was beginning to get me wet, and every minute took its toll. Here and there I found shelter and rest under cedar trees, which didn't really help. At what I figured was about four o'clock, right after I had rounded a sharp curve, the sound of a car approaching gave me a feeble moment of hope. I got ready to lift my thumb. The thought of Bo popped into mind. Except that the oncoming car was already in view, I would have stepped back into bushes on the roadside. It was not Bo's car. In fact it was a patrol car; in fact it was a sheriff's car, with a sheriff in it. Already slowing to a stop, he had his red lights flashing. I was nailed right there in my tracks.

He was out of his car, confronting me, a tall, lean, sheriff-looking man with no smile on his face. "You named Bragg, ain't you?"

Too choked up, I didn't even answer.

"That coat says you are. Lemme see in your pockets." Without waiting for me to do it, he felt of both my coat and pants pockets and came up with my ten dollars. After a quick glance at them, he said, "Where's the rest of it?"

Able to speak now, I said, "There's not any rest."

"In your shoes, maybe. Take them off."

Leaning against the fender of his car, I did. He looked into them carefully and said, "Sho' do stink. Where's the rest? It's forty more somewhere, 'cause it was fifty you left Bo's house with."

"It was ten," I said, trying to sound firm. I started to explain but didn't, not for now at least. But I did say, "I didn't steal it, though."

"That ain't what Bo says. And I known Bo a long time ."

Oh my god, I thought, wouldn't it be this way! Just my luck again.

"And you under arrest, for grand theft. Put your hands behind you."

So, moments later, there I was, in the back seat of the sheriff's car with handcuffs on. As we road along in silence (on the way to jail, I supposed), I tried to spin things out, with no results. Squeal on J.T.? I was thinking about this when, all too quickly, we passed the dumpster, a sight that in my mind somehow connected with my vision of a cell door swinging shut on me.

I was in for a surprise. In what seemed no more than a couple of minutes past the dumpster the sheriff slowed down and turned and stopped in front of Bo Hogan's gate. What now? The sheriff didn't even bother to turn his head when he said, "Bo's got a little deal for you. You keep on like before, working for him, and he won't bring no charge against you." He added, "Grand Theft means a long pull."

For a minute I couldn't get my thinking straight. J.T.? I finally said, "Working for him how long?"

"He never said. You want to get out or stay with me?"

A pause, and then I slowly got out of the car. The sheriff stayed right there till I got up to the front door.

Bo was waiting. His welcome was the tight little grin on his face, and the words "better get up there and get some rest. Hard day tomorrow."

I passed him by and the women, too, on the way to the stairs. At the top J.T. was waiting. With a grimace he whispered, close to my ear, "Don't snitch on me. I'll tell him it's a lie."

I gave an ambiguous nod and went to my room. A little later, reflecting on his words, I began to feel pretty certain that if money really had been stolen, it was J.T. who did it . . . and who would blame it on me if he was accused.

— — —

So now my hole was a good deal deeper than it had been before, and all my ruminating and dreaming up schemes had brought me right back to the same place: the bottom. I had even lost my only friend (if that's the right word), a loss made clear by the fact that he had quit dropping in on me. Mildred too, who before had not neglected to pay me occasional brief, and disturbing, visits. Now every one of them looked at me with a glimmer of suspicion.

As for the days following my recapture, they continued as before to be full of pig work, with the miserable difference that now they included an interval devoted to killing the creatures. For the occasion we had help, a black family consisting of the husband, called Slats, his wife, and seemingly countless children, who were to share the meat with Bo. (And get the worst of it, I was sure.) I had to endure the business of knocking hogs in the head with the flat of an axe, stringing up carcasses by the hind feet, and cutting throats to let all the blood come gushing out in a jiffy (once, to much laughter, all over me). This, followed by gutting, then dunking in tubs of scalding water to take reluctant hair from hides, followed by boiling fat to make the lard. Then butchering, grinding, seasoning, and stuffing meat into bags like socks. And guts all over the

The Adventures of Douglas Bragg
— — —

place, buckets spilling over with them, that gleeful black children seized and threw at each other and sometimes at me. In the quiet of the smokehouse at last, it was not much short of a pleasure to salt and pack the meat in the ancient hollowed-out logs waiting there.

There were two days of this, which left me wounded, bloody, exhausted, and grim. Long afterwards I still looked back at it, with all the raw flesh and blood and guts and shrill children's voices, as something not unlike drawn-out preparation for a cannibal feast. Add *disgust* to my list of responses to the event, because at that time I had thought the result would be an enlivening of our meals with such as sausage and bacon. It did not. I soon learned that Bo was holding it back for early sale, all of it, right down to the last pig's knuckle.

Just a few days after that event, days not as trying in themselves but still burdened with a case of hangover, I was presented with a new and, to say the least, disturbing problem. It was, in a way of speaking, a *domestic* problem. There had been warnings, evident in Mildred's visits to my room. These, since my *escape,* had stopped. Now, however, out of nowhere a thoroughly amorous Mildred had come onto the scene. In fact amorous is too feeble a description of behavior that was more like attempted rape.

I had just turned off my light (my one light, a dim bulb hanging from the ceiling) and got into bed, when I heard something at the door. I knew it wasn't the dogs, because I was well acquainted with her way of intruding. But this beat everything. Moonlight in the room made it plain. With the door now shut behind her, in one quick movement she let whatever kind of garment or maybe bedsheet she had around her slip to the floor. There she stood, posed for my gratification. It was not a pretty sight. That she held this pose for a little space was a blessing, mainly because it gave me a moment to grab up my covers and hug them tight around me. Then she was leaning over me, settling onto the bed. "I want you to *do* me," she whispered.

I couldn't get hold of any words, but a feeble answer all on its own came out of my mouth. "Do *what?* I stupidly said.

"Do *me.* You know." Then, "Lemme in under with you." She meant the covers. Her big old breasts were hanging right in my face.

There was a moment when I nearly screamed for help. She was tugging at the covers. I held them tight against me.

"Lemme be your sweetie."

"I can't." My strangled voice again.

"Just lemme in and you'll see." At this point she was practically a-straddle of me.

"Your daddy, he . . ."

"He's 'sleep. They all 'sleep. Come on, baby."

My desperation suddenly produced what seemed like an idea. "I can't. Got a headache. Bad."

"I'll make it go 'way."

"I can't, I'm sick." Once again what I said wasn't planned, it was desperation speaking. "Some other time. I'm too sick."

In silence, her groping at the covers came to a stop. I could hear her breath subsiding. "Don't be mean to me," she said in a plaintive tone.

I tried not to, but my croaking voice said something like "Okay, another time."

After a very still minute she rolled off me and the bed and stood up. I shut my eyes against the sight. "Tomorrow night," she whispered. "Then you'll be fit, won't you?"

I don't remember what I said or whether I said anything at all, but the little farewell kissing noises her lips made were indication that she was satisfied. She turned, slowly picked up her garment, and left, closing the door quietly behind her. I drew a long long breath.

After my slow recovery I lay there pondering this mess. What would it come to? "Hell hath no fury . . . ," I thought, thinking of tomorrow night. Either way it went, trouble was sure to follow. Trouble with her, trouble with Bo, trouble with both together . . . a trap to go with the original one. Then it crossed my mind that Bo, louse that he was, just might have a hand, or at least a finger in it. So . . . Tomorrow night? "Sick" wouldn't work again. Sick. My mind paused on a thought.

The pause continued, and my fertile mind began producing names common enough these days. Gonorrhea, I thought; clap, herpes and, finally, syphilis. Given the dire things I had heard about it, this last one seized my interest. Even the folks in these benighted parts, even Mildred, could hardly be completely ignorant on the subject. But if so, well and good, since I with a little ready wit, indeed with embellishments, could step into the breach. So be it, then. I was already composing my script for tomorrow night's occasion when another light came on in my mind.

It was a light that flickered on and off and then grew almost steady. Absurd, I thought . . . but maybe not. Look at who and what I was dealing with. I turned and turned in my bed. Before I went to sleep, if I ever did, I believed I had the general outline of a much larger plan.

The plan seemed more doubtful in the light of day. But nothing would be lost if I stuck to it for a while, inventing as I went. (After all, I was my father's son.) The family were anything but an observant lot, and my show of lassitude in the presence of greasy toast and grits failed to make much of an impression at the breakfast table. Only Mama seemed to notice at all, and at one point she signaled the fact by pushing the serving plate of grits closer to me. The rest, including Mildred, who was too busy sending me furtively amorous glances, went right on feeding themselves with gusto. I would have to be more open about my feeble condition. This I set out to do, all day long at work.

By day's end my little plan had taken a forward leap . . . or so it seemed at first. On reflection, the idea appeared so far-fetched that I completely discarded it. Just for a while, though; it kept on surfacing. I would think about that dead sow back there behind the fence, and the idea would pop up again.

Was it too absurd? Even if Bo was not without good sense, he was nevertheless a fool about his pigs. (I considered that his family came a poor second in his affections.) Even if he couldn't really swallow the notion that pigs could catch it from people, I might be able to get him seriously worried. It seemed a good bet. After all, even I, much less this family of bumpkins, knew little enough about the subject. So maybe pigs could catch it from us. Anyway, this as one detail in my plan could just hang fire till needed, an add-on in reserve. For now my business was to calibrate my steps.

It didn't take Bo long to notice how I was dragging. I moved as slow as I could get away with and kept sitting down, even in wet grass, when I judged the moment strategic. At first he didn't even inquire about the reason. He would just said something like "get up off your ass, boy. He'p me move this tub." A couple of times I made a little show of staggering, as though I was going to fall, and after a while he said, "What the hell's eating you?"

"Just feeling kind of sick," I said. "These little spells come on me sometimes."

His eyes searched me, with doubtful sympathy. "Little touch of something. Keep working, work it out."

This was how I spent the day, setting the stage, holding off till tonight and tomorrow. But mostly, as the day waned, tonight was on my mind.

The Adventures of Douglas Bragg

By suppertime I thought I had a pretty good grip on my plan, but there was still at least one problem. To make me more comfortable with my projected solution, I needed some kind of visual evidence. What I had decided on (whether or not it made any medical sense) seemed to me inspired. In these days I almost always had sores on my hands and arms. One was especially ripe, and it was no trouble, with only a moment of pain, to snatch off the scab and get a little blood. So, up in my room at last, I settled down.

It was a long wait. I kept listening and listening to the noises they made around the house, hoping that each one would be the last. The last was when Bo brought the dogs up to my door and mumbled to them and went away. After that, all was quiet. Later, still with misgivings, I got ready to prepare myself.

There was an interruption. J.T. evidently had decided to renew our friendship, and without ceremony he entered bearing both his guitar and new and revised compositions for my critiques. This time he was especially enthusiastic about a new one he had composed. It was one about a faithful dog (a new departure for him) to which I only half-listened and endorsed with something less than my usual animation. He was not crestfallen and, for once, neglected to introduce Buster Bell into our discussion. For a little while even my plea of feeling sick failed to hasten his exit.

But at last there was quiet everywhere, and after making my arrangements I turned off the light and got in bed. And soon, sure enough, I heard the brief grumbling of the dogs and watched the door swing open, then quietly shut. There she was again, her garment fallen to the floor around her feet, milky pale and outsized and all too substantial in the moonlight. "Here I am, sweetie," she whispered. A second later she was leaning over me. "Now," she said.

My first word got caught in my throat, but I rallied and said, "Wait. I've got something to tell you."

"Lemme in, then you can tell me."

"No, listen," I said in a sepulchral voice. "It's something really serious. I didn't want to have to tell you." She stopped pawing at the covers. Ignoring my sudden doubtfulness I said, "I've got syphilis. Bad."

At first I thought I had drawn a perfect blank.

"You got what?" she said.

"Syphilis. It's a disease. A bad disease. You catch it if you do it with somebody that's got it. You've heard of it, haven't you. "

The Adventures of Douglas Bragg

After a moment, almost inaudibly, she said, "I might of. . . . Like the clap?"

"A whole lot worse." I thought for a second. "Even just being close around them'll give it to you." I thought again. Too much? I took the risk. "They say even animals can catch it, it's so strong."

She was listening, all right. But then she said, if a little uncertainly, "I don't care."

"Yes you would. It finally kills you."

"You ain't dead."

"I will be, though. It keeps coming back, in spells. Worse every time." I paused for the drama's sake. "It makes you bleed . . . down there. I'm bleeding a little now."

This had stopped her. Now was the moment. "Look," I said, and pushing the covers down, exposed my naked self. I could only hope that the moonlight was enough to reveal the color of it, and for a space, seeing how she kept looking, I grew more than a little uneasy. When she moved her hand as though she might reach and touch it, I almost made a grab for the cover. But the hand withdrew and settled against her breast and after that there was silence.

"You see," I murmured. On impulse I said (words I afterwards wished I had swallowed) "Pray for me."

A little later, "I reckon . . ." She didn't finish. She got off the bed and took a clumsy backward step or two. She picked up her garment and turned to the door and went out.

Success, I thought, but not with much elation because now it seemed almost like a dirty trick. But it had to be, and I quickly got over my small misgiving.

There was not much sleep for me that night, either, but I figured this was a good thing because it would most likely add to my sick look. And it did, I thought, when in the morning I paused in front of the cracked and glazed mirror at the bottom of the stairs. But this was only to make a delay. A few more steps would take me to the kitchen door, in view of the family already in place around the table. I drew a deep breath and took the steps.

They were all present except for one; Mildred's chair was empty. With my heart pacing a little, I approached, as usual now to no visible signs of a greeting, and sat down in my place. It would have been a natural thing, but I couldn't make myself inquire about her. "Under the weather," Mama's phrase, was the only thing I heard said, and this assured me that nothing had come to light so far.

Except for my many covert glances toward the hall door, I got through the meal all right, successfully staging my *sick act* once again. In fact, I added on a few skillful touches, slumping a bit, letting my lower lip hang. I could tell that only Mama noticed. But on this occasion, because of what followed, I knew that she had spoken to Bo.

With me feebly trailing along, we had only got as far as the barn when Bo paused and, without turning clear around, held out his open hand to me. There was an aspirin in it. "It ain't nothing like a aspirin to knock a little old fever out." He turned and went on into the barn. I threw the aspirin away.

About two hours later, when I was already, and genuinely, exhausted from capturing pigs, I heard a bell ringing. It took me a few seconds to recall that there was a bell high up on a post outside the back door . . . occasionally used, I had deduced, to signal mealtime and such. It roused Bo from his slump on the pen fence, on the other side of which I was desperately engaged. He turned and headed for the house. I let go of a pig and stood watching his progress, my pulse racing even faster than what my labors had provoked.

This was it, surely. She had come out of hiding, spilling her story a piece at a time, both spilling and holding back, leaving details unspoken. And Bo now almost there. How long would it be?

A good while passed before I even thought to get out of the pen. Once out, I just stood gazing across the pig-strewn pasture at the back of the house, from which Bo, surely soon, would come into view. Finally I sat down on a keg and tried to think how to prepare myself. Nothing doing. I could only stare at the house. I stood up. He was coming.

His approach was deliberate, and well before he arrived, I could see that his gaze was fastened on me. He confronted me from a distance of about ten feet. Before I could hear any words at all, his mouth seemed to be working. "You something, ain't you, boy?' He waited as if for an answer. "Telling all them lies to my daughter. I don't know nothing much about no goddamn *sypherlis*, but I know you ain't got it. Think you can fool me? Stealing my money, too. Next thing, I'll see you in the pen where you oughter be."

I had to get myself together quick. I couldn't quite manage the tone of anger I wanted, but I said, "I never stole a penny off of you." Here the thought of J.T. made me hesitate. I dropped that subject and plunged right on. "And I wasn't lying about my syphilis. I've had it a long time, and it's getting worse. It'll finally kill me . . . if they don't find a cure."

"Shit!" Bo said. "Ain't nothing but a plan to walk out on me. Scaring us with it. Bleeding, you told her. Shit. Ain't no blood about you."

"She ought to know," I said. "She got a good look at it." I was suddenly pleased with myself for being so quick. It made him blink, for reasons I could guess . . . rascal that he was. But he wasn't sidetracked for long.

"Show it to me."

"You think I don't ever wash? It'll come back before long."

"Yeah. I bet," he said with a sneer. "And the biggest lie of all, like hogs can catch it. A hog can give you cholera, but nobody ain't never heard of a man giving it to a hog. Shit."

"That's what they say," I said, feeling a little like maybe I was in the driver's seat.

He made a quick gesture, sweeping it all away with his hand, and said, "Lemme tell you what I say. Try one more of your tricks, and I'll see you in the pen long enough for your teeth to all fall out." He started to turn away, paused, and added, "'Cause they's more of my money missing than any fifty dollars. I just been counting it. Now get back to work." This time he turned away and didn't stop.

Bastard, sonofabitch, louse, rascal: I couldn't think of a word nasty enough for him. I had to cool off a little before I could start thinking about things in our little talk that had struck me. The main one, that I had thought too risky coming from me now, was the matter of that dead hog. But if to any degree I had shaken his certainty about my "sypher-lis," he would likely think about it on his own. A troubling thought came to mind. It lingered a moment, then almost passed. I was betting that in his mind, such as it was, an unlikely explanation for the hog's death would win out against the cost of a veterinarian's fee.

And the stolen money bit. He could have been just plain lying, for obvious reasons, but I suspected now more than ever that J.T. had been stealing from him . . . a trifle at a time, no doubt. I had thought before also that this, if true, might be useful information, but in what way I had not yet explored. But this was soon to come.

Meanwhile, as to my daily routine, things went on almost as before. The only notable difference was, as might be said, domestic. My relations with Bo and Mama (and now less openly Mildred too) already soured since my escape, had deteriorated to a state of not quite spoken hostility. No more Mildred coming to visit me, and certainly not her parents. (J.T., of course, continued to come, but quite discreetly now.) More pointed was the fact that Mama, who had seen to it most of the time, had stopped making up my bed. But most telling of all was my removal from a place at the dinner table. Instead I was seated at a small and already crowded table across the kitchen a bit too near the stove. Which, in fact, pleased me, for two reasons. One was that it removed me from their near presence, sparing me, among other objections, my disgust at the sight of them shoveling in the food. But the second reason was the one that excited my interest. It could only mean that deep down they were afraid of my close presence because maybe, just maybe, I did have some kind of an infectious disease. It was a notion that seemed to square with another of my observations. This one came and went, but it appeared that sometimes when I got close up to Bo, accidentally touched him, it made him nervous. Maybe, and maybe not. It could have been just his dislike, or rather, hatred, of me.

Some days passed in which nothing unlooked-for happened, either in my daily routine or in my busy but unproductive mind. Finally, though, a two-day spell of miserable freezing rain suddenly gave way (brought forth, it seemed) to a perfect springtime day, with birds and a gentle breeze. It was only fancy that led me to make a connection between this and the surge of my imagination. In reality the cause was what happened that morning out at the smokehouse.

The black man there, Slats, was the same one who had participated in the hog killing, according to the agreement that he would share in the meat. He had come this morning, I understood, because Bo, who had made some kind of a deal in town, was planning to haul it off the next day. Slats was standing in back of a little truck that anybody would have bet wouldn't run, in front of the open smokehouse door. Just as I came on the scene, he was taking a side of bacon that Bo handed to him through the doorway. I could tell right off that the atmosphere was more than a little charged, a perception immediately confirmed when Slats loudly said, "That's fo.' And two mo' to go." He put it on the truck bed and turned back saying, "And six hams. And you ain't give me but five pokes of sausage. That's five mo' to go."

From inside the smokehouse Bo's angry voice said, "The hell it is. And it ain't six hams, it's five."

The Adventures of Douglas Bragg
- - -

"It's six. And it's ten pokes."

Bo's flat determined voice said, "It's four hams and five pokes and four sides. And me got it all salted down for you, too. Salt don't come free, neither."

"Yeah," Slats said. "And it ain't had time to get salted good, neither."

"Anyhow I got it wrote down on a paper," Bo said.

"I ain't seen it."

Compared to Bo, Slats was a small man, but neither this nor his blackness held him back. He repeated, "I ain't seen it. And I know it ain't got none of my mark on it."

For just a second Bo hesitated. "I'll show it to you," he said, and came out of the smokehouse. He took a step or two, then turned back and, pulling the door shut, fastened the lock. "Won't take me two minutes," he said and went on. "Yeah," Slats said to his back.

Finally Slats looked at me, his buck teeth very white in his black face. "Trying to cheat me. It ain't the first time. Looks like it the worst time, though," he said, pleased with his rhyme. "I oughter call the law on him. How come you works for him?"

I didn't know what to say. "Can't help it," was what I did say.

"Young fellow like you. Looks plenty able enough."

After a pause something inspired me. "Not as able as I look, I'm afraid."

Slats looked harder at me, figuring. "What's wrong with you?"

"I don't like to talk about it," I said. Sly of me, I thought, just the right thing to say. Maybe law school should be my destination.

Slats was still looking at me when Bo appeared, walking fast, a piece of paper in his hand. Arriving, a triumphant expression on his face, he held it out to Slats. "Here it is," he said, and pointing with a fat finger, added, "And there's your mark, right there at the bottom."

Slats took the paper and began studying it. I wondered if he really could read. He looked up at Bo and said, "That ain't no mark of mine. You the one put it there."

Bo, his voice already lifted, said, "The hell I did!" He didn't add *damn nigger*, which I had half expected.

I turned away and left them there in battle, my mind already beginning to churn.

I was thinking about Slats and how in those minutes before Bo came back from the house, he was studying me. With knitted brow, I seemed to remember, a question on his mind. Had I missed a chance right there? I thought of the dead sow. Disease. Bad meat.

My mind would not let go of it all, and by that evening after supper I had got hold of something that looked like a promising plan. Pigs, I knew, were the money crop on the small farms all around. Spread the word. How? It didn't take much thinking to call Slats back to mind. I knew about where he lived; he had told me at the hog killing, and it wasn't far. So, with my plan confirmed, I settled down to wait. But what about the dogs?

No answer, not for a minute or two. It was the sound of J.T.'s guitar, all of a sudden audible, that prompted a workable answer in my mind. A risk, maybe, considering the uneasiness in my presence that I still detected sometimes. I would take the risk. After all, I had his *stealing* for a weapon, even if it could be a two-edged one.

Quickly, lest Bo come up early with the dogs, with quiet steps I crossed to J.T.'s door. It was open a crack, and I could see him seated on his bed, softly picking his guitar, mumbling words of a song. I noticed something. It was a new, a flashy-looking guitar. The money, I thought. I said, "Can I come in?"

He jumped, looked at me with an uncertain expression. "Okay."

I entered and without ceremony sat down in the only chair. He was still looking at me that way. I said, "Nice-looking guitar."

"Yeah." Then, pretty obviously lying, "I swapped my old one for it. The guy liked the way mine sounded better'n his."

"Good deal," I said with deliberate warmth.

His face brightened. "Pretty, ain't it? Listen how it sounds." He struck off a chord or two. "Ain't that nice? Fires me up to write some more songs. Makes me want to go on up to Nashville right now."

Still holding back, I said, "When are you planning to go?"

"I don't know. Ain't going be long, though."

"Wish to the devil I could go with you."

"Wish you could too," he said, and lowered his gaze back to his guitar. "I've wrote me a new song. Want to hear it.?"

The time had come. "Not right now. Look, J.T., I'm wondering if you'd do me another favor. It's nothing much." He was all attention. I went on, "After a while, when everybody's asleep, get those dogs out of my way so I can go outside." Now he looked distressed. I added, "And bring them back when I come back in. You can keep them up here, in your room. That way, nobody'll hear."

The Adventures of Douglas Bragg
– – –

Looking still more distressed, he finally said, "You up to something, ain't you?"

"Maybe so. We'll see. You wouldn't blame me, would you? All he's put me through."

"Naw," he murmured, gazing down at his guitar. "Long as it don't come back on me."

"It won't. Just the dogs . . . all I'm asking."

"Awright. . . . I don't see how you can, though. Old man'll have that sheriff on your ass in no time. Follow you ever'where you go. He can be one mean old man."

"Okay," I said, and stood up.

"It's just one thing." He had a defensive expression on his face.

I waited.

"Has you really got that . . . that there *sypherlis?*"

To be on the safe side, I gave a solemn nod. "But you have to be up close to me to catch it."

About an hour after I figured everybody but J.T. was asleep, I made my way with utmost caution, with lengthy pauses, down and out through the kitchen door. It was a balmy night, with stars and half a moon making plenty light enough to guide my footsteps. I crossed the pasture, soon trailing a small procession of eager, oinking pigs, to the far boundary line. I climbed the gate and on a barely discernible path entered the clump of woods. The stink, not yet entirely abated, of Bo's dead hog struck my nostrils. A few minutes' walk along the path took me out onto the dirt road that led to Slats's house . . . or cabin, as was probable. I paused, conscious for the first time that up in the night this way, Slats might see fit to greet my call with a shotgun blast. But I went on. It was not far.

At first view of the tin roof that in splashes reflected the sky light, still short of the probable raucous alarm from dogs, I stopped again to try and gather my thoughts. They only stumbled over one another. I went on, and sure enough, there were dogs, half a dozen it seemed, a clamor of bunched and roiling bodies just outside the yard gate. I made ready to call out Slats's name, but he was the one who, in a voice pitched above the clamor, said, "Who dat there?"

"You know me," I answered. "From over at Bo Hogan's place. We talked this morning." Thank God for no neighbors, I thought.

"Yeah. What you want?"

"I want to talk to you."

After a pause his voice prevailed again. "Yeah. Awright." He stepped off the porch and through the gate and, shouting and cussing, waded into his pack of dogs. In only a moment he had them hushed and retreating back into the yard. "Awright," he said. "You can come on up here now."

Up close I could see his bare feet and some ragged semblance of pajamas. "Awright," he repeated. "Something 'bout old Bo?"

Where to start? I said, "It's about that meat . . ."

He stopped me. "Yeah. He cheat me too many times. I goan call the law on him."

"It's not about that. Did you eat any of it yet?"

"Naw. It ain't even got good salted yet. Old rascal can't wait to get his hands on money. He the tightest man in Tennessee."

"It's not about that," I said. Here's where I faltered. Words to the effect that my syphilis might have infected the hogs just wouldn't come off my tongue. Better something he could readily believe, like putting it the other way around. Would it matter? Probably not. And this gave rise to another thought, that a little confusion would be the best thing. I said, "I can't be sure, but I think maybe there's something wrong with those hogs. Something that's making me sick." Then another inspiration likely to thicken the brew. "I'm afraid it might be a disease. Something they call *souphilus*. Or something like that."

Slats just stood there looking hard at me. In that light he couldn't have seen much.

"A little while back he had a sow die. He couldn't see anything wrong with her. He was too tight to have a vet come look at her."

"I seen her," Slats said. "Lying back there where he lef' her in the woods. Wondered 'bout it, myse'f."

"I wasn't sick before," I added, another spontaneous thought. "And me fooling with all that meat. I thought I ought to warn you before you eat any of it." Then, to top things off, "And everybody around here's got hogs."

"Sho' has."

"Of course I might be wrong, I'm not any kind of a doctor. But I got to thinking about it." I was also thinking about what a smooth liar I was, and that at this point I had told enough of them. Then another thought, a necessary one. "I hope you won't tell Bo I told you. You know what he's like."

Sho' do," Slats said. He waited a second. "I'm 'bliged to you."

I left him standing there on his bare feet and went back to the house and, with all the care of a well-practiced thief, climbed the steps to my room.

After the dogs were back in place and J.T. returned to his room, it was only a little while before questions started gnawing at me. My disheartening answer to the bigger question, as to whether or not I had acted too soon, at last became a certainty. *Impetuous, rash, stupid* were words to describe the plain fact I had ignored: that tomorrow would surely be too soon for the word to have got around. So, sometime tomorrow, Bo with money in hand would return triumphant from the butcher's, indifferent as ever to me and all fears of my invented disease.

There were troubles besides. Might not there be some available means for quickly testing the meat? Except for the Black community, would the word get around at all? And might not Bo, by a shrewd guess, go straight for Slats's black throat? For that matter, why not my own? So it went slogging on in my mind through the rest of that dismal night.

But in the morning, still not wholly defeated, I continued with my charade. In fact I added a touch. A little blood from a sore on the back of my hand suggested it to me. I dabbed a little, enough to be seen, just under each of my nostrils. Downstairs in the kitchen, by artful display, I managed to get it noticed. "Here," Mama said, offering a rag. "Need to wipe your nose." I had thought that the others, too, would notice, but there was no indication. And nothing more was said to me till Bo got up from the table. Looking my way now, he said, "Them slops is waiting. Time I was on my way."

The burden of last night's dismal thoughts came heaving back to mind. I sat staring into my plate until I finally realized that I was the only one left in the kitchen. I got up heavily from my chair and went out . . . went out and on my way once more to carry slops to the pigs.

I remember this moment well because it immediately preceded a welcome change of fortune. Its beginning was when, arrested in my tracks, I listened to the grinding mechanical noise that came from the shed out back. It was Bo trying to start his truck, and on and on it went. I stood there with my nerves on edge, dreading that the moment to come might produce the sound of the motor. But moment by moment nothing changed, and hope began to dawn. I heard him, swearing, get out of the truck and lift the creaking hood. Then silence for a while. Then back in the truck, and once again the grinding noise went on.

In the grip of my soaring hopefulness, I had forgot about the slops, but so had he. Stepping out of the shed, he saw me and, in something like an inflated growl, said, "Boy, I know you don't know nothing about a motor, do you?"

I shook my head with emphasis.

"Goddammit!" he said, and went back inside and kicked the truck hard on the fender. He disappeared for a space and came back with tools and got under the hood again.

I thought I had better get out of sight and go about my duties. So, without my accustomed revulsion, I loaded the stinking slops on the wagon, hitched up the mules, and found myself bumping across the field with oinking pigs in train. I meant to be slow, to wait it out, and finally to see in one sweep of my gaze if hope was still alive. I loitered by the pen until maybe an hour had passed. I started the mules, bumped back across field. Then I was close enough; the moment had come. I did not see Bo. The truck was still there in the shed. My spirits gave a leap.

I discovered that he had left for town in the little car, carrying some piece from the truck motor with him. His intention, I later learned, was either to get advice on how to fix it, or, if necessary, pay to have a mechanic fix it, or even, if absolutely necessary, buy a new part. In any case he expected to be back within a couple of hours. Not only did he fail in this, he didn't arrive until after dark, and in a rage. Those fools at the shop, he said, didn't know a goddamn thing. They didn't know how to fix it, and they didn't have a part for an old truck like his in stock. They sent him all the way down to Bartonsville, and the rascals there, after fooling around forever, charged him three times what the part was worth.

It was hell in the house that night. He terrorized the family at the dinner table, even turning his head around to give me a cussing. Every few minuets he blazed up like a heap of gunpowder, accusing each one of us, even Mama, of faults you wouldn't often find among inhabitants of a penitentiary. Relief didn't come until he went out in the dark with a flashlight to install the new part in his truck. I was a lot more hopeful now, at least off and on, but I was also exhausted and went to sleep before he came in.

In the morning, well after the usual time, Bo still hadn't come up to hammer on my door and take the dogs away. Finally I cracked the door enough to see that the dogs were not there. Which told me they hadn't been there all night, or I would have heard, as always. Coming down the stairs, I didn't see or hear anybody. I noticed that Bo's and Mama's bedroom door was shut and then recalled that so were J.T.'s and Mildred's doors upstairs. There was nobody in the kitchen, either. What was more, after glancing around, I couldn't see any signs that breakfast had been served. Where were they all?

A couple of minutes later, after I heard sounds of movement in the bedroom beyond the wall, followed by Bo's sudden appearance at the outside door, I figured it out. They were all in hiding, like rats in a hole. And as soon as I got a good look at Bo's face, I didn't wonder. I barely recognized him. He looked like a man just about to catch on fire, red hot and swollen-looking. I almost stepped back.

His voice was a snarl. "Come the hell out here and he'p me, boy." He turned and went back out and, not even hesitating, I followed him.

It was obvious that for all his labors into the night and again this morning, he had failed to get his truck running. Less obvious was what he was up to now. I was quickly enlightened. In the same threatening voice he said, "Catch up them mules, and quick about it."

Mules? But I didn't hesitate. They were close by in the lot, standing motionless as usual. Dragging both of them by their halters, I got them up to the wagon in record time. He had the harnesses ready, and in a matter of minutes we had them in place, lacking just a buckle or two. It was then, while he was fastening these, that I said what I had been wanting to say all along. "Why don't you just wait till you can get your truck fixed? Wouldn't tomorrow be just as good?"

"Hell naw. Had a 'greement for yesterday. And today's damn Wednesday." He didn't explain, he just seized the big mule by the bit and, starting with a hard jerk, led the team and wagon up to the smokehouse door.

There was the clumsy business of unfolding a big tarpaulin and laying it across the wagon bed, with Bo cussing all the way; then the meat, a ham, or two or three pokes at a time passed out to me for placing in the wagon. About every two minutes he would snatch a big old tarnished silver watch out of his pocket and groan and maybe say, "Time getting short." So I came to understand about Wednesday. Everything closed down at twelve o'clock.

We finally got through and covered the meat, immediately after which Bo all but vaulted up onto the wagon seat. Like an afterthought, to my surprise he said, "Git up here, boy. Might need you." So I did, with reluctance, shoulder to shoulder with him on the board seat.

That was some ride, at a rate of speed I estimated to be about two miles an hour. The ferocious licks Bo put on the mules' butts with the bridle lines didn't do any more good than his blasphemies did. Drivers came up behind us blowing their horns and passed us by with angry or mocking insults like "Don't let them run away with you, Grandpa," and "Slow down, you're breaking the speed limit." All of which made Bo grow stiffer and stiffer from the neck down and just a little short of crimson in the face. I guessed it was a rare thing for most drivers my age to see a wagon and mules on a highway nowadays.

If it was bad out on the highway, it was lot worse in town. Unfortunately our destination was on the far side of town, and the main street passing through had four traffic lights. As if by pure perversity, each one turned red just as we got to it. Then the clamor of all clamors surged up around us: horns blaring, cops yelling, children throwing missiles, including a couple of eggs, at us. Even the imperturbable mules got excited, and the little mule started trying to buck up in his harness . . . to cheers from boys standing by. Both Bo and I hunkered down and went on through it all and came to a crossroads and turned left. Escaped at last.

A big sign reading *Smokey's Smokehouse* stood in front of a square brick building with a concrete ramp across the front. Bo maneuvered the wagon up close and parallel to the ramp, and by the time he got it in place, a tall hook-nosed man (Smokey himself, I supposed) was standing there on the ramp with a sardonic expression on his face. This was the moment when anxiety really tightened up on me. What would he say? Bo spoke first.

"Here I am. With as good a load of hog meat as you ever seen." The little silence that followed made him add, "My truck broke down."

In a sort of offhand way, as if his thoughts were elsewhere, Smokey said, "You was due yesterday."

With assumed cheerfulness Bo said, "Done the best I could. But this here's meat'll make you glad." He leaned back, quickly untied and lifted a corner of the tarp, exposing a couple of big hams.

Smokey looked at them, then shifted his gaze to Bo. I held my breath. There was an interruption.

A good-size truck, new-looking, with a tall canvas hood over the bed had turned in. The driver did a neat job of maneuvering and in no time had his truck backed up to the ramp just steps behind our wagon. Obviously a rival. Bo had turned clear around. The blood was rising in his face. But then he turned back and looked up at Smokey on the ramp. In a voice that fell a bit short of cheerful, he said, "I reckon you got somebody to he'p us tote the meat in?"

Smokey now had a hand on his chin, faintly stroking it with his fingers. Even before I saw his mouth open, my throat went dry. He said, "What's this I'm hearing about your hogs?"

"What?' Bo said. His mouth stayed open for a second or two.

"I'm hearing some of your hogs is dying on you."

Bo had to draw a breath. "No such a thing. It's a damn lie. Never have lost no hogs." He paused, glanced at me. "'Cept just one. Way back a while." Then to me, "Ain't that right, boy?"

It was a tough question, but I summoned up guts enough. "I don't know," I meekly said. For an instant I saw murder in his eyes.

"The talk says it was more'n one," Smokey said. "Did you have that dead one tested?"

Bo's voice was louder this time. "Wer'nt no need. It was something in the slop killed her. P'isoned, that's all."

"I heard that, too . . . about it being more than one." This from the driver of the truck, who was now standing behind us . . . a neat-looking man for a hog farmer, in slacks and a clean blue shirt.

For a moment I thought Bo was going to jump down off the wagon and go for him. Instead, he just shouted, "Who in hell told you that?"

Calmly the man said, "Nate Franklin. Lives out your way."

"Franklin's a goddamn liar. Been wanting to ruin me." Evidently he wanted to say more, but he suddenly got choked up.

All right so far, I was thinking, but it had to get back to me. As it happened, I was immediately gratified. The man said, speaking to me, "I reckon you're the same boy that works for him, aren't you?"

I just nodded. Bo was glaring at me.

"Have you got some kind of a disease?"

Again, with gumption, I nodded. What to say next? I added, "I'm afraid so."

"You think you got it from the hogs?"

I didn't know which way to go. Either way could lead to trouble. A yes would tell Bo I'd been lying all along, while a no would weaken the case against the hogs. I decided. "Naw. I had it already. A long time."

The Adventures of Douglas Bragg

The man said, "The way Nate Franklin took it, I think, it was syphilis . . . which far as I know hogs don't get." He looked at me. "Is that right? Syphilis?"

I nodded definitively.

"You're sure.?"

"Yes," I lied, and plaintively added, "I know from doctors."

"Okay. Then you ought to be somewhere taking care of that. I don't reckon hogs can catch it, but other people sure can, one way or other."

I nodded again and silently thanked him.

"Well," Smokey put in finally, speaking to Bo, "I don't know nothing about no syphilis, but I sho' ain't taking on any meat somebody with a disease been fooling with. You going have to take yours somewheres else." He turned and moved over to the parked truck.

Bo, who had been sitting there tongue-tied, recovered himself enough to spring up from his seat and call, almost bellow to him, "Wait a minute. I'm goan have it tested. Prove it's good. Bring it back to you. Tomorrow."

Smokey didn't even look his way. He lifted a hand and brought it down sharply in a gesture of final rejection.

Nevertheless Bo, back on the wagon seat, went on sitting there in perfect silence, looking stunned, gazing straight ahead. His lips moved a few times, while the flush receded slowly from his face. In those few minutes while we still sat there, I really did begin to feel a little sorry for him.

My sorrow didn't last much longer than it took us to get well under way again . . . through back streets, this time, in hopes to evade harassment. Not that he said even one word out loud, but I couldn't dismiss the feeling that his rigid silence and the hot flush back in his face again were now because of me. Even when we had passed through town (with only a taste of what we had suffered before) and were out on the highway, there was no change. It didn't really bother me. In fact I was feeling pretty good, thinking that I was just about at the end of my imprisonment among the pigs. But at last, when we were not far from his front gate, still without looking at me he said, "You goan pay for this, boy."

I cast about for a strategic answer. I came up only with, "It wasn't my doing."

"Yeah. I got it figured now. You told it all to that no-count nigger Slats. Right there the other day when I left you and him to go get what I'd wrote down."

I was feeling nimble now. "I didn't tell him a thing but that I had syphilis. Because he asked me what was wrong with me."

"Shit!" he said, and gave the big mule a fierce whack with the bridle line. "You got them all thinking that. So you ain't no good to me no more. But I ain't finished with you. I'm goan see you in the pen."

"What for?" I said.

"You know what for. Stealing my money's what for."

"You haven't got a bit of proof."

"Don't need none but what I got. I got me a sheriff."

I hesitated, turned the thought in my mind. We were at the gate, and all on their own the mules were making the turn. Bo said, "I'm goan git that nigger, too."

In my wisdom I had already made preparation for this one. "You must have heard about all the new laws against that kind of thing. People are going to jail for it. Long stretches." By his sudden show of alertness, I could tell he had. I quickly added, untruthfully, "I know of a guy got ten years."

Bo didn't say anything. We went on up the muddy drive and stopped in front of the smokehouse. "Put it all back in," he said, and got down off the wagon and headed for the house.

One way or another, I thought, this was my last chore, and I set to it. It was slow work, in and out of the smokehouse, but all the while I was turning another plan over and over in my mind.

I had got down to the last few pieces of meat when suddenly Bo reappeared. He walked past with one hot glance at me and went to the car. A minute of cranking, and it fired, and he drove away and headed down the drive. To see the sheriff? Not unlikely, I thought. No use to run, though . . . not yet. Because it seemed a conclusive thing to do, I quickly finished with the meat, latched the door, and, walking not too fast, went to the house. Mama and Mildred were in the kitchen, but they didn't speak when I passed through. Hurry now.

Halfway up the stairs, I was suddenly reassured by the sound of J.T.'s guitar. Thank God he was there. His door was shut, but I didn't bother to knock. As always, it seemed, he was sitting on the bed with his guitar, the new flashy one, in hand. My sudden entry made him jump, but he didn't appear to resent it. I shut the door behind me and sat down in the chair. He was looking at me, waiting.

"Look," I said. "I guess you heard what happened?"

The Adventures of Douglas Bragg
— — —

"Couldn't miss hearing it."

"Well, he's likely on his way to see the sheriff, I think. He's going to charge me with stealing his money. Says he's going to get me put in the pen."

I waited. His gaze shifted away. He wet his lips and faintly said, "He can't get away with it, can he?"

"I wish I knew he couldn't. He's got that crooked sheriff in there for him. It's not a chance I'd like to take."

J.T. hesitated again. "I don't think Bill Riggs is all that bad a guy."

"You would if you had been with me when he picked me up out on the highway." I decided not to wait any longer. "Look, J.T. You're the one that stole his money, aren't you? A little at a time. I figured it all along, and, when I saw that guitar you got there, I knew it for sure."

He opened his mouth to speak, shook his head no, but I interrupted. "Come on," I said. "And I never snitched on you."

J.T. looked down, then around the room as if to locate something, plainly a guilty look.

"I wouldn't want to, J.T.," I said, "but I'm not going to go the pen for something I know you did. You can be sure of that."

He seemed to be trying to digest all this, and in the interval I grew more and more uneasy. It was the memory of what he had said that day when the sheriff brought me back. "I'll tell him it's a lie," he had whispered to me, there at the top of the stairs.

He stirred and finally looked at me. "Awright. But what you want me to do . . . tell him I done it?" His eyes came wide open.

I drew a long breath, an uneasy but hopeful breath, and said, "Naw. Not to his face. Leave a note telling him. You've been planning to go to Nashville, anyway. Tell him in your note we'll send the car back. So he won't be coming after us for stealing it. . . . How about the car key?"

"Car ain't none of his, it's mine. Too stingy to buy one for his self. I got the title. And a key, too."

He looked straight at me. I could see he was coming around. But he suddenly paused. "He can still put the law on me about the money."

"It's family business," I said. "Even he won't try to do that." To make assurance surer, I said, "And I promise I'll get you in with Buster Bell."

"Awright," he finally said.

This and a little more wasted urging, and that was it. My plan, as I described it to him, was simple enough . . . except for the scary possibility that Bo, in the meantime, would arrive back here with the sheriff.

Thankfully, for whatever reason, this didn't happen. Just before nightfall, after a tense two hours and more, Bo's arrival alone was announced from down in the kitchen by his uplifted voice and curses. There was no call to supper that night. Once in a while I would hear his voice again, and my name among the cusswords. The final announcement of his presence was when he brought the dogs up and made special noises to be sure I knew they were there. After this, there was silence.

Up in the night, with the dogs locked away in J.T.'s room, with J.T.'s luggage divided between us, we moved like spooks down the stairs and through the kitchen and out. Then came a quite improbable hitch. We had safely reached the shed and the car when suddenly, no matter the explanation, the dogs began to sound off. It was the hound especially, as if he had treed a catamount right there at the back door. That might have been well enough if the car had not been reluctant to start. This grinding interval gave time for lights to come on, including the one outside the door, and, just afterwards, for Bo to appear with something in his hands. But, thankfully, by the time I realized that the thing in his hands was a shotgun, the motor fired, and the car lurched out of the shed. It was barely soon enough. One long breath later, with an enraged Bo at one with the dogs charging at full cry straight down on us, and we wouldn't have been at distance enough to escape the lethal force of his two shotgun blasts. As it happened, the only damage was a few cracks in the car's back window and some shot-size indentations in the metal. And all this as we pulled away was joyful occasion enough for J.T. to bid farewell with several derisive honks of his horn. With nothing to stop us now, we were on the way to Nashville. I was breathing gratitude to my stars, when it occurred to me that I owed these thanks for my devious gifts to my dear devious father.

ONCE WE GOT OUT ON THE HIGHWAY headed for Nashville, clear
of Bo and his pigs, my first thought was "Free at last." But then I started
thinking about that sheriff and noticing how slow this little old car was
going.

"Won't go no faster," J.T. said. "Once we get out the county, he can't
get us, though."

"Okay," I mumbled, my head turned so I could see through the
cracked rear window. There was nothing so far. But just a minute or two
later, something happened. The car slowed, bucked, rolled to a stop.
"Oh my God!" I said.

"It's just the gas line," J.T. said. In a jiffy he was out of the car, bending down, his mouth fastened to the gas tank pipe. I heard him draw
three or four deep breaths to blow with, and then he was putting the gas
cap back on. "It'll go now," he said.

Thank God he was right, but we had lost time. For at least the next
ten minutes, I was trying to turn my head both ways at once, to glance
out the rear window and also to spot the roadside marker for the county
line. But finally there it was, the marker, and the threatening headlights
that had come up behind us innocently passed on by. I drew one of the
deepest breaths ever in my life.

Nashville was still a long way off, and our progress wasn't speeded
any by the repeated necessity for J.T. to get out and blow into the gas

tank. But this, compared to other considerations that had taken hold of me, was a small matter. The big matter, the only one I couldn't dismiss, was the one concerning Buster Bell. After all I had made of him, including the use of him to get me out of Bo's clutches, what could I say to J.T.? My mind was wrestling hard with this one long before we got to Nashville. In fact, in first daylight, we had reached the outskirts before I came up with so much as a skimpy and also doubtful course of action. This was so much true that when he brought up the subject again, I put him off with a promise to telephone Buster as soon as we landed somewhere.

For all my lies to J.T., I had not been in Nashville since I was twelve, when Mother and I moved away. The place was a good deal changed, especially as to the volume of traffic, and for a space I didn't know where in the devil we were. Then I spotted the Parthenon, and soon after that something urged me to order a left turn. Suddenly things got familiar, or almost so. For no reason except that we had to stop somewhere, I had him turn onto a side street and park in a half-empty lot adjacent to a gas station. Now what?

"What we goan do?" J.T. said.

I sat there in silence for a moment. "We got to stay somewhere. How much money you got?"

J.T. reached in his pocket and took out a handful of bills and some change. He counted it slowly, his lips moving. "Seventy-two dollars and forty-four cents."

"That much, huh. That ought to feed us and get us a room for a little while, maybe. Need to get a job. Both of us." I eyed the gas station, remembering that among the jobs I had held in the past, one was gas station attendant. Besides, I had always been good at getting jobs. And besides that, these clothes of J.T.'s I was wearing made me look fit for the work.

"Hey." J.T.'s face had suddenly lit up. "Bet you Buster Bell's got a house with plenty of rooms in it. All them famous artises like him got big rich houses. I seen pictures. You wouldn't hardly believe them."

He had me there. "That's a thought," I murmured.

"Why don't you go call him up? That gas station got a phone. Here." He handed me the forty-four cents he had been holding. I didn't have any choice.

I was hoping he wouldn't follow me, but he did, right on my heels. Inside, the phone was in a far corner on the wall, the phone book hanging beside it. By this time I had my plan made, and with J.T. watching over my shoulder, I fumbled through the book to the letter B, then to "Bell," and making up a number, dialed it. I had meant it to be nobody's number, but a loud and irritable female voice answered. Lest J.T. overhear it, to muffle the sound I pressed the phone tight to my ear and proceeded to ask for Buster. Of course there would be no Buster at this number, and when I went on anyway to ask when he would be back, the voice came near to injuring my eardrum. Undaunted in spite of the pain, I continued my fruitless inquiries until, with the word 'idiot' shrieked into my ear, there was nothing left but a dial tone barely audible to my benumbed hearing. I talked loudly to nobody for another minute or two, and then hung up.

"Too bad," I said, to a crestfallen J.T. "That was his secretary. Buster's off on a tour, to California. Be gone another week, maybe two. There's such a big demand for him out there. She said try him again in a week or so."

J.T. gave a shrug of resignation. "That sho' was a loud secretary, wasn't' it."

"I guess she gets an awful lot of calls," I said.

There were a lot of old houses along that street, and we soon found one with a room for rent . . . a shabby one that didn't take but half our money for an advance. Right off, I got a job at that same gas station, and the next day J.T. got one five or six blocks away at an otherwise all-black grocery store. I still didn't have a plan any better than the doubtful one I had had all along, so on my second evening at the gas station when there was not much doing, I sat down with the telephone book. Unfortunately my best boyhood buddy (who I hadn't heard from in at least ten years) was named Smith, and there was no Walter Smith to be found anywhere in the practically endless list. So I went at the W. Smiths and, to my great surprise, had luck on my fifth attempt. I didn't recognize his voice, but we soon were on familiar terms. I hadn't expected Walter to know Buster Bell personally, but remembering his liking for country music I had hopes he might have a friend who did. Again I was lucky, beyond expectation. He not only knew somebody, he knew just the person and would put me in touch with him. A little more by way of explanation and expressions of my gratitude, and we ended with some meaningless words about getting together. I hung up the phone with a feeling of elation. It seemed to me a long time since I had had something of real interest to look forward to. Besides, as I was more and more convinced, "Success" was practically my middle name.

It took days of waiting, with J.T. on my back to hurry things up somehow. The time would have passed even more slowly if J.T. hadn't discovered a little place close by called the Angel Song Café, which was a combination bar, snack bar, and hangout for country music lovers and performers. Sometimes there was even a performer of some repute. Flora Bird was one, and the night she was there was the only time that, because of our fast-dwindling funds, we stayed on for more than a few minutes.

There were eight or nine tables and some scattered chairs, all occupied, a bar on one side and, at the far end from the entrance, a small podium with a standing microphone on it. The walls were just about covered solid with pictures of country music stars, and right off, J.T. started looking for Buster Bell's picture. Under the general hubbub he whispered to me, "I don't see him nowhere." His expression was one of downright alarm. But he kept on looking, and after a minute his face brightened. "There he is. Back there in the corner." Then, his brightness fading, "It ain't right, though. Ought be where everybody can see him."

I tried to comfort him by saying, "It's just because this isn't much of a place."

A man brought us stools and took our order. I ordered a beer for J.T. because I didn't know what he might do with a real drink in him.

We were still waiting when an instant of silence prefaced a general swell of enthusiasm. There she was on the podium, a regular sunburst, Miss Flora Bird making everything else in the room invisible. I suppose her name was what inspired her to adorn her hair with a variety of feathers, despite that cranks like me might think it made her look like a chicken from the neck up. The rest of her, though quite impressive, was not only unadorned but also, at first glance, practically uncovered. Her tight hip-to-knee-length pants were the same color as her skin, and except that they made her nether regions invisible it was hard to tell that she had pants on at all. Around her waist was a thick leather belt that supported nothing, and well above this a bra that looked as if it might at any moment give up the hopeless effort to do its job.

After my first uplifting impression of Flora, I had the pedestrian thought that, so attired, she must surely be cold. But this was the briefest possible distraction. There was, as I only now realized, an accompanist with a guitar standing alongside her, one who, as soon as she opened her mouth to start singing, moved a couple of steps away. He had better have. After snatching the microphone from its stand and emitting a shrill soprano note or two, she was precipitated into a series of gyrations that might well have catapulted him off the podium. The song, I gathered, was named "Lowdown Lew" (evidently a favorite with the already enkindled audience), a title repeated with added derision at least twice after every so-called verse. It seemed that Lowdown Lew in the loathsome depths of his betrayal had surpassed all lovers down through the ages, and that no words known to man could adequately describe his depravity. In fact a number of words (some of which I never liked to hear used in public) were given a fair trial, and failed. But Flora got some kind of a point across anyway. The fervid voice, the stomping, grinding, twisting, and whirling around, with pauses timed for belligerent thrusts of her head at the audience, appeared in some illogical way to put the blame on us. Even so, at the end of it, three-fourths of all present came to their feet with thunderous applause. I was glad to remember that I had not been among them, and disappointed that J.T. had been.

Outside, I asked J.T. if he though Buster Bell would have liked that. He lowered his head and rather humbly said, "Naw, I reckon not. That ain't Buster's style."

It had now been several days, and both of us were on edge waiting for a call. The good thing about it was that it gave time for J.T. to get prepared. I had composed a new song that I considered my best, even if it was pretty corny and on the sad side. I called it "Deep Valley," and I had J.T. playing and singing it over and over till he got it down almost to my satisfaction. As it turned out, this happened just in time for the call. The man, evidently a close friend of Buster's, said we would be welcome, because Buster was that kind of a generous fellow that liked to encourage talented young men such as this man had been told J.T was. Of course, since I was supposed to be a friend of Buster's, I told J.T. it was another and higher-up secretary. The news left him jumping up and down and, as it seemed to me, playing and singing "Deep Valley" over again every ten minutes for the next twenty-four hours.

It was on a Friday and at exactly three o'clock in the afternoon when we set out. I had begged off from my boss at the gas station, but I wasn't sure, in spite of what he said, that J.T. had done the same at his grocery. He had that head-in-the-clouds feeling that from now on he wouldn't have to go around like common people with their feet on the ground. It was like that with him until we got almost clear out of town. Then he started to worry. He worried about the car breaking down, and whether I had got our directions right, but most of all he worried about choking up when it came time for him to do "Deep Valley." "You'll do fine," I kept telling him, and pretty soon, after turning off the state highway onto a gravel road and driving on for another mile, I said, "There it is."

There it was, a tall arched gateway bearing, at the summit of its arch, a sign that, along with a few gilded musical notes, read "Bellway Plantation." Beyond the gate was a vast, nearly level field, all green in spite of winter, with the big house, or mansion, at the center. Approaching, we saw on one side of it a large swimming pool with a yellow awning over it, a croquet court where a few people were playing, and a paved lot where half a dozen cars were parked. On the other side of the house, enclosed by a huge stretch of white paling fence, was pasture containing a handsome barn and some grazing horses. There was also a fenced-in ring where a man in a Texas hat was riding around and around on a classy-looking sorrel horse.

But it was the house that grabbed the eye, especially as we drew closer. I couldn't help but stop for a better look before we turned into the parking lot. For a minute or two I sat there imagining an architect who had started out to build a cathedral, but halfway through had changed his mind and decided to make it into a municipal building . . . like, say, an office for the administration of public welfare. A brief flight of steps led up to a small roofed porch and a doorway with pointed arch and massive, inlaid double doors. On each side was a narrow window as tall as the doorway, also arched, with glass of mixed green and crimson colors. Above all this, however, except for a cupola topped with a tiny spire high up on the roof, the cathedral effect was pretty well diluted. From where we were located, it looked like the building had at first been the shape of a perfect rectangle, but that later for whatever reason, and seemingly at random, there had been new rooms added on, projecting out from the original walls. Add to these a couple of unlikely second-story balconies, and you were presented with a confusing picture. The only consistent thing was the color, or colors of the walls. Halfway up, their surface, of pebble-dash, was battleship gray, while the upper half, apparently of cedar board and baton, was red or orange, depending on the light. On the whole, a bewildering mixture.

After our pause I pulled into the parking lot and got out. J.T., guitar in hand, followed suit but then stopped dead in his tracks. "Lord God, look at them cars," J.T. muttered. His astonishment was understandable. There were a big shiny Cadillac, a Mercedes, a fire-red Lincoln convertible, and among the rest several that I had no names for. I looked at J.T.'s car, and he did too.

I finally got him moving, but only as far as the foot of the sidewalk. He had stopped again to watch the man with the Texas hat riding the horse, now at a nifty trot, around the ring.

"Ain't that something pretty, that fancy horse and all." J.T. was again overawed. But it wasn't really so pretty, because just then the rider, instead of posting, was bouncing in the saddle as if he had a rubber butt. I was about to remark on this when, fast rounding the turn, off the rider went, a somersault, and landed on the back of his neck. We just stood there staring, watching the man begin to stir and try to turn over. A black man had appeared in the barn door a little distance beyond the ring. He, too, just stood looking at the fallen rider's struggle, but only for a minute. He turned and went back into the barn. We stayed where we were till the ex-rider finally made it to his feet and went looking for his hat.

We went on and climbed the steps and stood there hesitating. There was a gold knocker shaped like a dragon's head, and I tapped with it a couple of times. I could hear voices, but nothing happened, so on my own I opened the door. Immediately, though there was nobody in sight through the little entranceway ahead, the sound of voices was magnified. The rack with coats on it suggested that we do likewise, and we did. There was also a stand with an opened book on it for people to write their names in, but since the pages were perfectly blank, we passed it by.

A couple of steps more took us into a room the size of a small auditorium . . . two stories high, crystal chandeliers, long, railed balconies on both sides at the second-story level. (As I soon learned, the balcony on my left was a dummy, accessible only by means of a ladder.) I never did get the house plan straight in my mind.

I couldn't tell where the increasingly uplifted voices came from. Off to our right, two men and two woman holding drinks, who didn't look like music people, were in a sort of distracted conversation. But the noise came from the other side, from the second of two adjacent rooms, and it was not the sound of a conversation. In fact, it was much more like the sound of a fight, involving women, and seconds later, when I heard a female screech and a crashing noise, I knew it was a fight.

From where we stood, I couldn't see into the room, but clearly the fight was getting even more violent. The little conversation group had taken strong notice too, and just stood there gaping. Suddenly a black man in a white coat entered from a door in the far rear wall opposite to us. He stopped in his tracks, just as if to witness, or maybe enjoy, the fight. It was a good thing he stopped when he did, because something like a crystal goblet came sailing across just in front of his face, exploding on the parquet floor ten feet from him. Evidently, because I heard his voice, there was at least one man in the room with the contestants, trying, I imagined, to end the battle. Anyway, whether his doing or not, it came to a stop, with closure announced by one or the other woman's shrill last words: "Goddamn bitch!" I think this was the one, probably the loser, who just afterwards came into view on her way toward us and the front door.

She was a sight to see, holding what had been most of her blouse, with trailing bra, against her breast, her long blond hair headed in every direction, and a bleeding scratch down her left cheek. I even noticed that two of her long green-painted fingernails were broken off. She passed us without a glance, hobbling because one of her high heels was missing. My look at her face left me with impression that behind the scowl disfiguring it there was the kind of fleeting prettiness I had often seen in the faces of deep-dyed country girls.

The other woman, as best I could tell, was equally disheveled, but this one, rather than follow the other's lead, left by the door near which the white-coated black man was still standing. A minute later the till-now-invisible male presence, even now in a Texas hat, followed in her path. The little group of innocent observers, after buzzing among themselves for a space, passed us by and went into the room where the brawl had taken place. Approaching just far enough, I was able to see that, despite the wreckage in there, food and drink in plenty were still available.

The black man in a white coat approached us. He was slight of build, had watchful slightly reddened eyes and I could tell by the look in them that he already had us sized up. He said, "What can I do for you genmens?"

"We're here to see Mr. Bell," I said. "I believe he's looking for us."

His eyes settled on J.T. "You'd be J.T. Hogan, then. He said about you." His eyes came back to me.

"I'm his manager," I said, improvising.

"Awright, Mr. Manager. "I'll go see is he woke up yet. Won't be but a few minutes."

"My name's Douglas," I said.

He looked at me once more and, turning away, went and climbed the steps at the far right-hand corner of the room.

In the interlude we stood around half-listening to the little group back there, who seemed already embarked on a festive occasion all their own. Rather, it was I who listened, because J.T. was now practically shaking with anxiety, clinging to his guitar for support. Trying to comfort him, I kept telling him he would do fine, he would do fine, on and on, till something else distracted me. It was the pictures hanging along both walls under the balconies. About half of them were pictures of Buster: Buster smiling, Buster with guitar in hand and singing at full throat, Buster holding up a silver trophy. But the curious thing was that of the others pictured there, I was more or less familiar with every single one. Then I realized that they all were old-timers, most of them dead or nearly forgotten. There were Uncle Dave Macon, Mother Maybelle Carter, Earnest Stoneman, J. E. Mainer, and the like . . . all known to me from my childhood days when my Grandfather Wells used to take me to the Grand Ole Opry. But I was interrupted.

From the far end of the balcony the black man was motioning to us. I don't know why it seemed to me an especially friendly gesture.

At the top of the steps where the balcony ended, we turned and followed him down a hallway past several shut doors to an open door straight ahead. The room, not too well lighted, oversize for a bedroom, was pretty much in a state of disorder. There were papers on the floor, an overturned chair, a large cluttered desk, a stand of guitars leaning haphazardly against a wall. I also noticed the bed, an old-fashioned tester bed with awning. I didn't even see Buster till, from off to my right, he said, "Glad to see you fellows. Set yourselfs down and talk to me."

He was seated, very much at his ease, in a plush chair, with one foot resting on an ottoman and an elbow on a small table beside him where a bottle of whiskey and a nearly empty glass stood. I wouldn't have recognized him from his pictures. I had expected to see a big man but not one with quite that much flesh on him. It was not that he had a real pot or seemed especially fat in any particular part of his body except his face. There was too much jowl and puffed-out, gray-bristled cheeks, and even his eyelids looked painfully swollen. His long black hair was streaked with gray. I glanced at J.T. for any sign of disillusionment, but none showed. In fact he was standing there frozen, still clutching his guitar. Buster was looking at him. He said, "So you the boy I hear got all the talent. Songwriter, too, I hear."

I couldn't tell whether J.T. was trying to answer yes or no or thank you. Obviously Buster was sympathetic, and he turned his gaze to me. "And . . . and you his manager. Named what? I forget."

It was only then I remembered that we were supposed to be old friends, and for J.T.'s benefit, hopefully, I said, "I thought maybe you'd remember me. From a long time ago."

He looked at me for a few seconds, blinked those swollen lids. "Long time ago, huh? I've knowed a awful lot of people." Thankfully, he let it go at this, and so did I. Then I saw that the reason he had dropped the subject was something suddenly had come to his mind. His eyes went to the black man still standing in the doorway. He said, "Ace, what's all that yakking I been hearing from down there?"

"Just some drop-ins. Think they come from up north someplace."

"Yeah. Well what about all that yelling while ago?"

Ace was hesitant. "We best not to talk about it right now, Mister Bus."

"Was Judeen in it?" Judeen, I later learned, was his fourth ex-wife.

Ace reluctantly nodded yes.

"And Betsy Lee?"

"Her, too," Ace mumbled.

Buster drew a long breath. "Next time either one of them shows up around here, you tho' her out."

Ace gave his nod of assent and discreetly withdrew.

Buster settled back in his chair and, after a thoughtful look at his glass of whiskey, picked it up and swallowed the remainder. "Ah," he said, "something for the old nerves." I supposed it was whiskey that gave that fat look to his eyelids.

"Now, boy," he said, "how about a little serenade for old Buster?"

Except that J.T. twice opened and shut his mouth, he couldn't move.

Buster understood. "Try just plucking them strings a couple times. That'll loosen you up."

The Adventures of Douglas Bragg

With tremulous hands J.T. managed a note or two.

"Come on, J.T.," I said, "clear your throat and give him 'Deep Valley.'"

Starting with something like a croak, he managed, bullfrog-sounding, to produce the first few words: "Deep Valley's where my heart. . . ." He choked up, cleared his throat, took courage, and went at it again. He was nearly successful this time and, after the first verse, began, for better or worse, to sound like himself.

> Where a softly cooing dove
> Calls back all the things I love. . . .

He skipped a verse, but it didn't matter.

> Evening sunlight slanting down
> Greens the meadows all around.
> Hear the big red rooster crow
> And Bess the milk cow's gentle low.

By this time J.T. was at his best, but I couldn't help noticing with regret that his best was not as good as it had seemed when he was practicing. However, I was comforted by the expression on Buster's face. At first it hadn't been much more than one of polite attention, but pretty soon it was downright absorption. In fact, before J.T. finished, I could see for sure that Buster had tears in his eyes. I had to think that it couldn't be only because of J.T.'s musical performance.

Anyway, just as J.T. was coming down with the final words, "Old Valley, deep Valley . . . My Home," Buster sank back in the chair with his wet eyes looking up at this shining boy who had just dropped down from heaven. When he could speak, he said, "That was something. Boy, you are sho' something."

J.T.'s grin looked like it was going to keep spreading till it went all the way around to his ears.

"You write that youself?" Buster said.

I jumped right in. "He sure did. Every word."

Buster sat up straight. "I'm goan have a drink. To celebrate this boy." He poured one in his glass, then paused. "You got to have one, too, no matter." He fetched two glasses from under the little table top, poured for all of us, and held the first one out to J.T., who took it without hesitation. He followed with a second one for me, then lifted his own glass on high. "Down the old hatch," he said, and did it. I got mine down smooth enough, but J.T. didn't. He coughed hard two or three times and had to wipe his eyes with the back of his hand. But his smile somehow stayed the same all the way through.

"Now," Buster said. "What we goan do?" He paused. "First thing, though." He sat up straight again and yelled thunderously, "Hey, Ace. Come in here."

As if by magic, Ace appeared in the doorway.

"Take these boys and fix them up a room. Ever which one they likes."

– – –

So for the time being at least, we were adopted, sort of . . . J.T. especially. Every day for a couple of hours Buster would have him in there with him for what amounted to a training session. The door would be shut, but from the hall or even from our room nearby, I could hear them when they were picking and singing. No matter which, picking or singing, it was plenty easy to tell who was doing it. Buster's robust authority in both, I was sorry to note, put poor J.T. way back in the shade. I suppose that partly it was the contrast between them that made J.T. sound a lot more like a bumbler than he had used to sound. But whatever, he sure didn't impress me as a young man destined for stardom, and I kept waiting for the moment when Buster would come to see it my way. Well, what had I expected? After all, I had just got caught up in this business like in a kind of a game, and I surely hadn't looked for any miracle to come of it.

But pretty soon I came to see what should have been obvious right off. It wasn't any talent J.T. had, but J.T. himself that had captured Buster's devoted attention, at the same time deluding himself as to the boy's musical gifts. Also that song of mine J.T. sang for him, that had such as roosters crowing and milk cows mooing, no doubt had a lot to do with it. Here was "Little Buster" revisited, straight from his childhood home in the far-off sticks. Well, there was nothing to do but wait and see what would happen.

My role in this was pretty anomalous. I had decided on being J.T.'s helpful cousin, a city boy who was rather "highly educated" but also interested in country music. Whatever, Buster liked me and turned me over to Ace, who put me to work doing little jobs both inside the house and around the place. I helped with the food, an astonishing lot of it for the still more astonishing lot of "guests" who, as I saw it, had no business to be there. As to the reason why, Ace was curiously evasive, and it took me some time to figure it out. I also helped with cleaning up, including in downstairs rooms I came to know about on my first full day.

At back of the enormous front room, an extended hallway led past the big kitchen, farther on past a bathroom fitted out for one and all, past some other doors, and finally to a door that opened onto a gallery outside. There was a large swing, three or four cane-bottom rocking chairs, and a close-up view of a little walled-in flower garden. Returning, I paused for a look into the three rooms whose doors stood open. One was a well-equipped gymnasium. Another, to my considerable surprise, was (though I had to make inquiries about it) the Meditation Room. And, indeed, it had a meditator, a woman who, I learned, was no part of this household. Wrapped in what looked like a bedsheet and obviously seated on her ankles, she held her arms stiffly straight out sideways and never moved a muscle throughout the whole time I stood there looking at her. The only other things in the room were a small Buddha in a niche on the wall and a hanging quilt with a formidable-looking serpent stitched on it. The third room I looked into was the Overnight Room. There was a king-size bed with a bright orange coverlet, two lamps with orange shades to match, a handsome clothes cabinet, and what appeared to be a Persian rug. Ace responded to my inquiry with a perfectly serious expression. "It's for them as can't make it home from the party. Drunks and all." Despite his expression, I suspected that his "and all" meant what I thought it meant, but I let the matter rest.

I soon got to know the other people on the place. There was a black family that lived in a cottage some distance behind the Big House. Four of the six children, two boys and two girls, were near enough grown, and they along with their father, Cobb, and his wife, Mona, were the regular source of labor around the place. The horses took the biggest part of Cobb's attention, and he was glad to have me around for occasional help . . . like combing them and oiling their hoofs. He despised the "guests" in general, but the ones he really, deeply hated were those that came to go horseback riding. "Damn fools," he said. "Best part of them don't know a horse from a army mule. And me s'posed to look out after them. Don't know why old Bus puts up with it."

The Adventures of Douglas Bragg

He told me that out of the nine horses, he had two that were nothing but nags, and these were the ones that, for the riders' own sakes, he tried to put everybody on. But now and again, along came another kind of jackass (usually dressed up in a cowboy suit or else fancy in jodhpurs and a little red hunting cap) that insisted on riding a real horse. So Cobb had to stand around worrying about them, at the same time half-hoping that the fools would fall off and break their necks. No case of a broken neck had ever happened, but this made me think of the man we had seen fall off some days ago, when J.T. and I first arrived. It also made me think of possible legal consequences.

I soon forgot about the matter, but on the very next day, by what now seemed an odd coincidence, the thought produced itself in the flesh. Cobb and I were currying a horse when I suddenly looked up and knew right off that the little skinny man with darting black eyes who had just now entered the barn was a lawyer. He said, "How are you gentlemen today?"

Cobb, looking hard at him, didn't say anything, and neither did I.

Unaffected by our silence, the lawyer said, "Is this the horse that threw Mister Edward Conway and badly injured him?"

"I don't know nothing 'bout it." Cobb's air of indifference was a comfort to me. I had instantly sensed that this overconfident lawyer was dealing with a pro.

The lawyer turned to me. "And you, sir? It happened just nine days ago. Around four o'clock in the afternoon."

Taking my cue from Cobb, I said, "Beats me."

The lawyer looked at me a bit more narrowly, then back at Cobb. "There were witnesses," he said, as if he had pulled a rabbit out of a hat.

"I ain't seen them," Cobb said, still plying his curry comb.

"Mister Conway said he saw two people watching when he was thrown. Incidentally, Mister Conway is a very prominent man in Nashville."

"Do say," Cobb said, moving to comb the horse's flank. "Anyways it weren't none of us."

The lawyer was showing increased signs of vexation. "I don't suppose the people who come to ride just walk in here and choose their own horses . . . and saddle them, themselves, do they? You couldn't help but remember a man who was thrown just nine days ago . . . and injured."

"Nope," Cobb said. "Far as I know, been two, three weeks since one of them fell off. And he got right back on." Busy now at the horse's rump, he added, "You wasting you time and mine."

The lawyer's face had acquired a definite flush. "Do you know what 'perjury' is?"

Cobb seemed to consider for a moment. "Ain't a disease, is it?"

The flush in the lawyer's face deepened visibly. "It's the crime you'll be charged with for lying in court." He added, "And get sent up to prison for," and abruptly turned and left.

We watched him until he was out of sight, and I said, "That's kind of scary, isn't it? Maybe a big lawsuit. Those things go way, way up in the thousands sometimes."

"Don't worry 'bout it. That guy fell off weren't even hurt. Got back on the horse and kept on riding." Then, "Anyhow, Mister Bus got the best crooked lawyers they is."

It still worried me a little, and it also got me thinking a lot more about why in the world Buster conducted his private business the way he did. I knew he had made millions out of his long music career, but the way he was spending it seemed to me completely out of hand. This place was a perpetual open house, with huge parties once a week, plus regular "drop-ins," and special facilities for every taste. They (it seemed like everybody) were eating him up. It was crazy.

But a little at a time, I was coming to understand why. My first real clue came to me one day when I discovered that he was acting out a ridiculous lie about his current career. It was Ace who accidentally gave him away, by a telephone conversation that I happened to overhear in part. Buster had told us, with every physical evidence of boredom at the thought, that he had to go off for a couple of days because of engagements in and near Atlanta. I had to connect pieces of the conversation before they added up to the fact that it was a lie. Actually he wanted Ace to bring him something he had forgotten, and the place to bring it was a little motel twenty-five miles away, where he had registered as Henry Smith. The fact that he didn't seem to fear being recognized there was further revealing.

There were other related occasions when, because I had now been made wary, I was no less than sure that his claims were fictions. He would talk, in a casual sort of way, about whirlwind tours in places as far off as Wisconsin and California where he had performed before thousands of cheering fans, all as though these were recent events in his life. He would also mention, in an even more offhand way, upcoming tours that later, remembering, he would refer to as having been "postponed."

But maybe the most determinedly misleading of his deceptions involved his fan letters. By this time he and I had come to be good friends, and until now, at casual mention of his place in the music world, he would often indicate, by a nod in that direction, a large file cabinet stuffed with fan letters. That it was "stuffed" I knew because once he had opened a couple of drawers to show me how many. It was only lately that he had in fact (leaning over an open drawer and shuffling among the letters) selected a few for my further enlightenment. Not for me to read, however. From his chair, reared back at his ease, now wearing rimless glasses that looked too small for his swollen face, he read them to me. He read in a sonorous voice, sometimes pausing to give space for words of special praise. At such moments I could see, by the tightening of his rather wide mouth, the look of satisfaction he was suppressing. I never had a chance to read one of the letters, and, especially if it was dated, I wouldn't have done so if I had. The time came when I thought about writing him a few fictitious fan letters, myself, for, as I had observed, the ones he now received were sadly few.

Finally I noticed also that he was reluctant, even when those big outrageous Saturday night parties were under way, to go down among the "guests" and mingle for even a little while. "Too much racket for a old music man," he would say. "Hurts my ears so bad I can't hear my own voice when I sing." But he did go down several times, and I, following along, found it more than unpleasant, in fact humiliating, to observe his pretense of confident participation. Most trying to me were those occasions when, approaching with his hand out, he came very close to being snubbed by some foppishly dressed, or half-undressed, dude of special importance. To my relief, his "participation" never lasted long. Other than these occasions, the extent of his attention to the parties, large or small, consisted in observing them from the balcony, where a post half-hid him from view. I soon figured out the real reason for this. He wanted very much to know when, or if, any of the real celebrities were in the attending crowd.

So, by this time, I felt like I knew the whole story of why Buster kept putting up with this everlasting open house. As I've said, we had come to be on friendly terms pretty soon after we got acquainted, and by this time it amounted to a kind of intimacy. By which I mean, up to a point, because I couldn't just haul off and tell him what I was sure was the truth. The truth was that he couldn't keep himself in the limelight by making this and his whole place a holiday-house for all those whoopee-seeking rascals who didn't care a hoot in hell about him. This, and also that by allowing it, he was inviting them to eat and drink him literally out of house and home. And still more, that it was damn well unworthy of the man he really was to refuse to see it. But since I couldn't tell him these things, especially the last part, all I could do was cast about in search of an answer. I found myself trying to imagine how my father might have handled this.

Buster and I often had long conversations, mostly about him, and I tried to keep them going as long as possible in hopes of finding openings that I could use to my purpose. In doing so, I got just about his whole story, from his babyhood up. He told it with a lot of drama. Time and again he would get up out of his chair (by this, seeming a good deal taller than he was sitting down) to show me what it was like at a plow behind a big mule's ass in rocky ground, rocks big as your hat that could grab a plow point and shoot the handles high enough to hit you in the chin and knock you flat. "Got laid out cold more'n once that-a-way," he said, reenacting with his fist such a blow to his chin.

His daddy had died ("worked hisself to death") when he, Buster, was only twelve, and he had to keep up that little rocky farm as well as look out after his mama and two younger sisters. "They he'ped some with the garden and such, but the heavy stuff all fell on me. Early and late. Planting the corn that never did do much good, and tending our little 'bacco patch. I hated that . . . sticky gum getting all over me. Rain and shine. And me always having to patch the roof on our little old shack. Had a milk cow died on us, and like to never got another'n. Times when things got even tougher, I had to hire out to a man paid me with such as vegetables and old clothes."

He paused, his puffed-up eyelids half-shut, looking back on those scenes. It was the kind of moment I could take advantage of, and I said, "You had to be much of a man even then. Good old-fashioned guts."

Through these last minutes he had been standing, looking tall, one elbow resting on a cabinet top. He seemed now to be thinking about my words, mulling them over. Finally he said, "Didn't have no choice."

The Adventures of Douglas Bragg

– – –

Finally he moved his elbow off the cabinet and held up his hands for both of us to view. "See these-here cotton-pickers? They done more work when I was a boy than most men do they whole sorry life."

They were large hands, powerful, that looked even now like they had the old workman's calluses on them. "I believe you," I said and, hesitantly because I'd said it before, added, "Plain old guts."

As if he hadn't heard me, he said, "They what started me off in music. Picking a guitar. You know where that first guitar come from? That same fellow I hired out to . . . give it to me for my work. A old sorry one but it didn't matter to me. Set up nights learning myself how to play it. Wasn't long before I took the notion this was how I was going get famous . . . like old Uncle Dave Macon." He nodded toward the opposite wall. "There that guitar sets right now. One on the left." It was easy enough to see the difference between it and the other half dozen leaning there.

He said, "Play it for you, sometime." Which he did two days later, head bent down, singing along in his nasal baritone. The song was called "From Jerusalem to Jericho," one I supposed was pretty well forgotten in this generation. This was when he told me he was going to give this old guitar to J.T.

It wasn't long after this that I ventured to approach the real matter in any kind of an open way. I told him I'd been wondering why he kept on letting all these people make free with his property, that it looked to me like it was enough to make anybody go broke. I was afraid he might say it was his business, but he didn't. He paused before he answered that they were music people, his friends, and it pleasured him to have them down there. And that was all, except that he looked thoughtful saying it. I didn't press him.

So, for the time being, I couldn't think of anything to do that I hadn't already been doing, and things went on the same. For a while they did, except for a couple of seemingly minor events that made just short-lived ripples in his show of contentment. One was the fact he was suddenly hit with the threat of a big lawsuit. That skinny sharp-eyed lawyer appeared and was ushered up to Buster's room. The door was shut, but I could hear Buster's voice, getting louder every time he spoke. It wasn't much more than five minutes before I saw that lawyer, looking pale and walking faster than was natural, on the way out. Buster was standing in the door behind him (filling the whole space, it looked like), and his voice had to be resounding all over the house. "Goddamn shyster. Tell your Conway bastard to stick his lawsuit up his ass."

Till he saw me, he stood there red in the face, muttering to himself. He said, "Wants three hundred thousand." Then, "He sho' ain't the first one, neither . . . not by no means. One a few months ago trying for more than that. Said he got rattlesnake-bit walking round the place. Shit! More shit!" I nodded my emphatic agreement.

The other event didn't produce any such display. It was a letter from his accountant, which I saw because I brought it up to him, and it obviously was not good news. At first reading he shook his head in a puzzled kind of way, then sat there brooding over it. At last he simply tossed the letter aside and settled back into his usual comfortable expression. And so, for the time being at least, that appeared to be the end of it, and nothing to speak of was changed.

Or so it seemed. In fact, without Buster's serious notice and not much more from me, things were building up. It had to do with J.T. The two of them were about as close as they could get, doing a lot things together besides holding music sessions. They would walk around the fields, drop in for a look at the horses, and sometimes saddle a couple so they could go riding. But J.T. had branched out. He had not got over being star-struck, and Buster, though still very much his main hero, was no longer the only object of his admiration. He now looked forward especially to those Saturday night parties when, sometimes, there would be a couple of "real" stars among the company. He would try to dress in a way that would make him fit in, wearing jeans and (I don't know where he got it) a sleeveless shirt with silver stars and sickle-moons embossed on the front. He also wore a string tie with a cat's head on it and would have worn a Texas hat in his possession if I hadn't told him it made him look even more like a jackass. He would mill around in the crowd trying to find people, especially important-looking ones, both men and women, to talk to. He would usually be holding a half-filled glass in his hand, but how much booze he actually drank, I couldn't tell. Everybody had come to know who he was, but the fact didn't seem to make it easier for him to get into conversations. Here and there he would nail somebody, usually a woman who appeared to think he was "kind of cute." I'm sure Buster knew about J.T.'s doings down there, but figured that everybody, all his "friends" in the music world, would be hands-off with the boy. It was the drugs that mainly worried him, and he had reason. Otherwise, except in J.T.'s case, he didn't much care about the drugs.

This, with not much change, was how it had been, but on this Saturday night a stunning transformation took place. Along toward twelve o'clock, about the time when things were approaching their noisiest, I was, as now accustomed, in our room, reading. Suddenly, above the conflicting noise, I could hear that somebody was singing. It sounded familiar, and I put down my book and went out onto the balcony.

From there I could see and hear that the singer was a woman, and after a few seconds I could see who it was. There was a crowd close around her (one of two separate crowds, really), but the feathers in her hair, still more feathers this time, told me it was Flora Bird, Flora manhandling a guitar. She was twisting, grinding, whirling around, shooting her head out at one and then another of her swaying admirers. At times her voice achieved a pitch that under different circumstances might have been enough to summon a whole police force. Because of the encircling bodies, I couldn't see what she had on, but I could tell it wasn't much.

I noticed familiar faces in the crowd. Lately I had spent a little time watching country music shows on TV, and sure enough, here were several real stars I recognized. The easiest to spot was Two-man Tyler, so called because one side of his face was perfectly clean-shaven, while the other side sported exactly half a mustache and clipped beard. I remembered, too, because I had heard him perform, that his musical gifts included the capacity to jump from baritone to falsetto and back in the wink of an eye. And then there was Sylvia Rosell, the sleek sex-box with yellow hair obscuring half her face, who had earned her fame by singing "Loving on the Mountain" every chance she got. (It was a title that gave me a mental picture of a very fat naked lady lying on her back with the vocalist stretched out on top of her.) But best of all, there was Eddie (Blitz) Gimbel, a true superstar who I had watched with some astonishment because he never ceased bounding back and forth across the stage like he was playing both sides in a badminton game . . . and this without subtracting anything from the dizzying resonance of his voice. Wearing a cap turned backwards, a gold chain around his neck, and a silver belt buckle you couldn't hide with both your hands, he stood a little back from the crowd with an expression of dissatisfaction at Flora's performance. I was observing him with some interest when a flash of light interrupted. His picture had been taken by a little man with a big camera. It was the first time I had noticed a reporter on the scene. I rightly figured he was from one of the tabloids.

The other, much smaller crowd, probably a competing or hostile one, was across the room engaged in what looked like inebriated conversation. Now and then one or two of them would step out from the rest on a mission into the refreshment room and return with a full glass in hand. A woman among them looked familiar, but there were so many of these blond, tall women that I couldn't be sure of it. I thought it could be Judeen.

Judeen or not, I pretty soon could tell that she was ogling J.T. She had her head bent down close to his (she was a little the taller), and now I could see that she had put a hand on his arm. She might have been whispering to him, but whether she was or not, J.T. looked flustered. Evidently he was trying to step back, and that's when I saw that she had taken his hand, arresting his backward motion. Not only that, she drew him out of the crowd, then paused to say something else close to his ear. This was when, for some reason, I became convinced that the woman surely was Judeen and that she had him almost in her clutches. More than almost, in fact, because now, without any appearance of effort expended, she was leading him away in the direction of the big hall door. A glance showed me the faces watching their progress, and also what I took to be laughter just about to surface.

Judeen had got him as far as the open door, but there was a hitch. It was in the form of Ace, blocking the way. J.T. took a backward step, but not Judeen. She stiffened like a fighter ready for blows, and it was a wonder, no doubt of Ace's making, that the words between them were kept at a level less than clear to their very attentive audience. Before they were finished, J.T. had already melted away . . . to be found later outside in the backyard with the flush still high in his face. Not so, Judeen. The flush in her face, outmatching J.T.'s by far, was one of flat defiance, and she was to be found, minutes after the little fracas had ended, in the refreshment room pouring hundred-proof bourbon down her throat.

As often noted, very small events can produce great changes in the course of things. So it was on this Saturday night. A spirit already lurking suddenly took wing, beginning with an increase of noise, catcalls, and laughter, and reeling of bodies about the room. This was especially true of the refreshment room, which, already well-populated, was now the scene of a writhing mob as desperate for its wares as if they had just swarmed in from a trackless desert. The pop of a cork was followed by cheers, and a bottle with a hand on it rose above the crowd and poured its contents onto a head of blond hair. Elsewhere several guitars appeared, each a summons to lurching music lovers who gathered around the performers in tight and interchanging clusters. At the center of the largest group, largest and now increasing in noise as well as numbers, was Flora Bird, again at full tilt.

I just happened to notice Silvia Rosell standing alone at some distance from Flora and her pulsating fans. Holding her guitar by the neck in one hand, she looked on with an expression as cold as stone. But just for another minute. Suddenly, snatching her guitar into position, she gave one sweep to the strings and, in a soprano that for shrillness rivaled Flora's own, started treating us once again to her "Loving on the Mountain."

Flora was startled. At a dead stop, she searched over the heads of the crowd for her challenger. With a jerk and even greater vehemence, she launched herself again. "I want a man, a man like Jack / Got a wallop, got a wallop, got a wallop in the sack . . ."

The two voices clashed, intermingled, kept right on for another minute or two. Flora suddenly stopped. In a harsh uplifted voice directed at Sylvia, she said, "Try matching this." Whereupon she snatched off her overworked bra and, amid cheers, tossed it into the crowd. Again, most visibly bare-breasted, she returned to Jack and his wallop. The words on Sylvia's lips as he turned away, were, as best I could tell, "Filthy bitch."

Flora, as was, finished her song, but then immediately demanded in a scalding voice that her bra be returned. Not a chance. Already, having been snatched from hand to hand, it was finally in the possession of a waggish young man who was not only wearing it now but was wheeling round and round and crying. "Got a wallop, got a wallop, oh, got a wallop." Flora turned sharply and, leaving a few unladylike words in the air behind her, headed for the back door.

Her departure didn't leave any slack in the crowd's momentum. They wanted music and immediately went for Sylvia Rosell, who gave them not only a refusal but a very angry middle finger in the air. The cry went up for Blitz Gimbel . . . Blitz, of course! . . . but Blitz was nowhere to be seen. Search parties went out through both front and back doors, leaving a kind of sound-vacuum peopled by a diminished crowd headed straight for the booze. The one straggler my gaze fell on was my little buddy J.T. Something paused in my mind.

The reason for this was Buster, whose near presence on the balcony, unnoticed by me before, had clouded the thought already taking shape.

The Adventures of Douglas Bragg

Still there to distract me, he said, "Ain't never been like this before. Like a goddamn circus. Get them out of here."

"How?"

"Get rid the whiskey's one way."

"I think they've about got rid of it already." I added, with emphasis, "Damn bunch of hooligans."

He looked sort of defensive, thinking it over. But he didn't answer back, and I felt like maybe this meant a little bit of disillusionment was setting in. He said, "Try, anyhow. It's done got to be too much."

I could see he was ready to turn away when suddenly, with a jolt, he was smoldering mad. "Ain't that goddamn Judeen I see down there?"

It was. She stood at an angle against the wall like she had been carelessly leaned there and left gazing down at the glass of whiskey she held, apparently baffled by her hand's inability to lift it. "I'm afraid so," I said. "Ace tried to get her out of here. It would have taken two or three men."

Here I took a step to get in front of Buster, because it looked like he was loading up to go down there . . . in his too-tight checked pajamas, needing a shave, his eyes, red enough already from whiskey, now blazing red. "Look," I said. "Don't go down there, in pajamas and all. I'll take care of things. And Judeen too. Ace and I will."

Fortunately he was not too angry to see the sense in this. "Get J.T. out, too." He looked straight at me for a moment, then walked away down the hall and shut his door hard. Instantly my thought, now an actual plan as far as it went, was ready in my scheming brain.

A competing thought restrained me for a moment. Cruel, too cruel. But the moment passed, and as quickly as I could, I went to our room and snatched up J.T.'s guitar. From the stairway I saw that the parties in search of Blitz were returning, and I paused just long enough to make sure they had been unsuccessful. I hurried on down and moved in on J.T., who was standing by himself holding an empty glass. Balmy-looking, I thought with a little stitch of concern. "J.T." I said, "are you all right?"

He looked at me and blinked. "Fine," he said. "Never better. You been hearing all the music? I seen Tux Reed and talked to him. And Billy Randal and . . ."

I thought he sounded just sober enough, and I interrupted, "How's your singing voice?"

"Huh?" he said with a moon-eyed look.

"They all want somebody to sing. How about you?"

"Awww," he said, drawing it way out. "All these famous stars . . ." But a flicker of spirit had come in his eyes.

Somebody, and then others, were calling out the name of Two-Man Tyler, but an answering voice said, "He's too damn drunk."

"You're the very one," I said with all my persuasive power, trusting also in the god of wine. "You're all practiced up. And got your own song. You know what Buster says about you, says you're great."

This made his whole face light up, and I took him by the arm. "Now's your chance. You're going to be a hit. Come on."

"But . . ."

"Come on." I handed him his guitar, took his glass, pulled at his arm. To my great satisfaction he came, moving on his own, following my lead out into the crowd where, at the center point, a heated debate was going forward. Here, among all the noise and bodies. it was my turn to perform. I drew a long breath. Another stitch of conscience didn't restrain me, and I lifted my voice above the clamor. "Listen! I've got a surprise for you. Here's a boy you're going be hearing from . . . and soon."

A tall man in a stocking cap cut in, "Who the hell are you?"

Quick as a wink I thought and said, "I'm Buster's estate manager. This is Buster's boy, J.T. Hogan. Buster's been getting him ready a long time now. And he's ready. Got his own song he wrote, too."

They were all staring at him. Somebody said, "Go ahead, Mister Hog-in."

Thankfully, J.T. didn't get the pun. Instead of looking flustered, he had something like a glow of confidence in his face. I had been right to trust the god of wine. I quickly said, "Go to it, boy."

In a near silence of the crowd, he did. He hoisted his guitar, gave a sweep to the strings. The first sound out of his mouth was a kind of croak, but he quickly swallowed it back and came on in a voice that after the first few words was clear enough.

"Deep Valley's where my heart . . . ," he sang, while my eyes scanned the attentive faces around. Already, without even the thought of how it must sound to other ears, my heart began to misgive me. On he went, still full of confidence, unruffled even by the camera flash in his eyes.

"Where a softly cooing dove / Calls back all the things I love. . . ."

The Adventures of Douglas Bragg

Awful, terrible, I thought: song and singer. And, belatedly as it seemed to me, expressions had begun to change. But it was not until, blissful as ever in his confidence, he came out with the lines, "Hear the big red rooster crow / And Bess the milk cow's gentle low . . ." that the inevitable crack-up hit him in the face. It began with a loud, drawn-out "moo" (from Bess the milk cow) followed by a well-rendered "cock-a-doodle-doo," followed again by laughter and catcalls from every quarter . . . a rising chorus amid which J.T.'s voice concluded with a dying fall. He stood there, his mouth open, even through another camera flash, for all the world as if he had lost consciousness. Poor J.T. It was the most unsuccessful success of my life.

I took his arm and led him, like leading a zombie, to the stairs, followed by blighting remarks about his musical future. Buster's name was among them, with the suggestion that he give his country boy some more and better lessons. And plenty of milk from Bess the milk cow.

I led him up the stairs and to our room and sat him down on the bed. "They're just a bunch of damn drunks," I said. "Don't pay them any mind." And tell Buster? I thought. Was the time ripe? I had touched on this in my mind already, and now was the time for decision. My answer came, unfolding into the sketch of what seemed a quite dependable plan. I said, "And don't tell Buster yet, he might do something crazy." Groggily J.T. appeared to assent. So, once more, there was work to do, and it to be done right now.

I left J.T. sitting on the bed and, halfway down the stairs, paused to search for my object among the crowd. The revelry had suffered no decline. Another singer, a very loud male one in an undershirt, was at it, drawing most of the crowd's attention. A smaller crowd more tightly surrounded a man on his hands and knees who looked nearly naked and who appeared to be in the process of physically portraying some form of life . . . possibly a bullfrog. But these were only a moment's distraction.

I scanned the room, praying "Oh, let the rascal be still here." Almost at once, by a flash of his camera, I spotted him. Preparing myself, limbering up, I tried to give shape to the spiel I had in mind: a mix of details true and not quite true, threaded with my own pure inventions whenever the need appeared. A minute or two and I gave it up, trusting to my gift of nimbleness.

Making my way through the crowd, taking a few smart-ass remarks about my little musical buddy (to which I riposted with the ever-useful upright finger), I caught the guy just as he was heading toward the front door. His looks, even better than what I had expected, gave me heightened confidence. His smallness of stature, black-browed shifty eyes, bird-beak nose, and mouth with a cynical upturn at the corners were features that all together made up an appearance remarkably close to my personal paradigm of a very nasty man. That he was also a reporter for a tabloid called the *Interloper,* along with the fact that our interview ended in his haste to follow my calculated suggestion, had left me quite assured of success.

We were seated up front in the relative quiet of the anteroom, where there was furniture and, to all appearances, a corpse on the sofa. Here, after concluding my summary of real and imagined atrocities, I described in choice detail Judeen with bumpkin lover in tow. I quickly added my description of the glamorous Overnight Room down the hall, where, I slyly remarked, they probably still could be found. This had been a missile well-aimed. It brought him to his feet. If I had counted fast, I might have got to ten before my dutiful reporter, camera in hand and spring in his step, had passed clean out of sight through the crowd in pursuit of this hot little story. I didn't stay for his final departure.

– – –

It was Wednesday evening before the *Interloper,* by my hand, arrived on the scene. Already Buster's state of mind was well expressed by the often repeated, and very audible, gnashing of his teeth. His anger had been on the increase since Sunday morning, when J.T. in person had finally described to him the main details of his humiliation. Because it was late, Buster had gone to see why J.T. had had not yet appeared, and he found him, alone in the room, hunkered up on the bed with his face to the wall. It was not because of a hangover, as Buster had first thought. It took him several minutes to wrestle the outrageous truth out of a blubbering J.T. Immediately following that interlude, Buster's tooth-gnashing had got under way

He sought me out and pressed me hard for more details, which I, with feigned reluctance, related to him. He did the same with Ace, and then, with an air of something like belligerence, did it over again with both of us. What followed at last was like the drawn-out stillness before a storm, issuing finally in a series of old and newly invented expletives fit to blow the top off heads nearby. In this verbal company, "son-of-a-bitch" was high praise, and in his words, there was not one male or female critter in that scumbag mob last night that was good enough to deserve it. At times he would launch himself into scurrilous tirades, working down from that "shit-head crowd" with their bird-brained antics, to individuals who he knew, or imagined to have been present. "Frauds," "thugs," "back-stabbers" all, though "shit-heads" remained his favorite designation. He had it in especially for the famous Blitz Gimbel, who had the singing voice of a constipated jackass. Not far behind came Flora Bird, who was not only a whore but had a sign on her mailbox saying so. Others also came in for it, including ex-wife Judeen, for whom the word "whore" didn't even begin to come close. So it went on until finally, his voice beginning to crack, he came down to the matter of poor J.T. "That good-hearted, talented boy, looking to his future. To see the way he told it to me, it's like they had plumb broke his spirit." There were real tears in Buster's eyes.

So it went till Wednesday evening, when Buster's eyes first encountered the *Interloper*. Up to this moment, in spite of his having declared several times that from now on the gates were shut and that all those blood-sucking shit-heads could go to hell and pay for their big times roasting in the fire down there, I had still remained a little bit uncertain. I think it was because there had been occasions when I detected, or imagined, a softening up in things he said about them, something wistful in the thought that everything was finished. (In which, if my fears were a true herald, I had played a dirty trick on poor J.T. for nothing.) But on this Wednesday evening, my worries were quite stamped out.

The paper's impact, though sufficient in itself as adding to the intensity of Buster's rage, was most noticeable by the fact that it extended enemy territory. He had already, by endless repetitions, about worn out the considerable stock of expletives at his command and, except for explosive interludes, was reduced to intervals of silence (no grinding of teeth) in which his facial expressions did the talking. There were times when I would watch the flush of blood come and go in his puffed-up face, and try to figure which special object of his rage, among the increasing number, had caught his mind's eye now. At these times I made sure to keep my own mouth shut.

It was impossible that the arrival of this tabloid on the scene could make much more of a difference than that it offered new people and things for targets. Buster's vocabulary, near to exhaustion as it was, seemed to have left him without any means for truly adequate response . . . that is, until he at last decided on what he proceeded to do. In a voice made fit for the harshest of epithets, he read, to me and J.T. and Ace, selected bits and pieces from the article in the *Interloper.*

At first, fearing exposure, I hunkered down. But there was no need. Soon enough, though hearing my own words included, I could tell that the writer laid claim to having witnessed the things I had described, fictional as well as real. And besides these, fabrications of his own. Obviously he had been enjoying himself. There were eloquent accounts of Judeen's antics, of J.T.'s inept performance, of staggering drunks and crackheads, of fistfights and sexual encounters, many of which, to my knowledge, never took place. There were several pictures, the featured one, of Buster. Pictures are said not to lie, but this one of him holding a bottle on high and his mouth as wide open as it could get was either doctored or unearthed from God knows where. And of course, though given only second place, there was a striking picture of Flora bare-breasted, with nipples penciled-over for modesty's sake.

But the worst was yet to come, and I couldn't help but flinch when Buster read the first of the references to himself alone: "The old muck-a-muck in person appeared only briefly on the balcony above it all, supporting himself with one hand on the railing and with his other hand supporting a nearly empty bottle. He seemed cheerful enough, apparently enjoying still another of the saturnalian blowouts that have brought him to the edge of bankruptcy."

Buster paused here, clamped his jaw, and muttered to himself. Then he went on, choosing phrases mostly, but off and on, a whole sentence or two. The writer's pretense now was that all items in the article were based on exact quotations from interviews with guests. In any case, they were all more hurtful than clever and, further, were pitched to represent the universal opinion of the crowd. An often repeated question among them, in riddle form, elicited efforts at wit. "Why did Buster keep this up?" A specimen answer was ,"To feed his way back in." Another, more witty than the rest, was, "He can't remember not to."

At last Buster fell silent and, with a violent jerk of his arm, sent the *Interloper* sailing in a flutter across the room.

It was done. The gate was to be finally shut, and all intruders sent on their way with their asses full of buckshot. After opening a fresh bottle of bourbon for him, we left him alone in his room.

The Adventures of Douglas Bragg

No more clamorous Saturday nights with shit-heads making free. This stillness was a terrible anticlimax, and I stood there in the hallway thinking about how easy it had been. Easy for the shit-heads, too, who would suffer nothing more serious than a fleeting disappointment. But already there was something unclear working away in my ever-fertile mind.

It was not yet dark, and I went outside and walked around for a while. A curiously soundless evening, I thought. It began to rain, and I hurried to the barn. Just inside, I stood listening to the rain on the roof and to the crunch of horses eating corn in the stalls. But soon I heard a sound I didn't recognize at first. Plop. Then I knew. It was a horse taking a crap, and suddenly it was more than that to me. The thought I had been mulling took definite shape, and with a burst of laughter, I turned to leave the barn like a man on business. But Ace was there behind me, folding his umbrella. He looked at me curiously. "Look like you done swallowed something ain't quit wiggling yet."

"I did," I said, and quickly told him what was on my mind.

His first response was a chuckle. Then he studied for a second, stroking his cheek. He faintly shook his head. "Have to think about that. Better run it by old Bus." But he was grinning when I left him.

Buster, sitting back in his leaning chair, was pretty drunk and didn't look glad to see me. I had my words ready, but just about the time I got my mouth open, I thought better of it. Something in me said "Go Slow," and I did some quick rethinking. To prepare the ground, I said, "We're letting them off mighty easy, don't you think?"

"Who?" he sleepily mumbled.

"You know who . . . all those shit-heads."

Slowly coming out of his daze he said, "Yeah," then "Yeah" again, more clearly. His eyes were well open now. "What I'd like . . . what I'd like would be take my shotgun to the whole goddamn bunch of them."

"Yeah, but you can't do quite that," I said. "There's other things, though."

He blinked, exposing a glimpse of clarity in his eyes. "What other things?"

Again my advising mind restrained me. "Hold back," it said. I said, "Okay. Have one last big party. An even bigger one . . . a goodbye party. Then, just when it gets going good, you show up with your shotgun. Tell them everything you want them to hear. Then shoot the damn thing off, get them stampeded. Maybe sing them a goodbye song. . . . How's that?"

It was enough to make him sit up in his chair and say, "By God, boy, you done hit on something. Let's do it. Goodbye, Boom."

"Okay," I said, wondering why my sneaky adviser had substituted this more innocent plan. I would trust him, though, and wait till the time was ripe to tell Buster what my real scheme was. Even now my adviser was not finished. I found myself saying, "And one more thing. Why not have the police, or somebody, waiting for them on the way out, to search their cars for drugs?"

"By God, why not!" he blurted, and seizing the half-glass of whiskey beside him, slugged it right down. "By God, we'll get them! You in charge of setting it all up."

Of course what I went about setting up was my own idea for revenge. Already chuckling to myself, I took the car Buster had assigned to me (and money from the kitchen stash) and drove into town. But it had got too late in the day, and I had to go back the next morning to finish with my purchases. What I wanted wasn't all that plentiful, and besides that, I had to press the several druggists I consulted about quantities and proportions needed. Of course they all wanted to know why, and I, with a casual air, had to explain that it was for pigs, as recommended by my veterinarian. In fact I did all this with a certain gusto, giving nourishment to my scheming appetite. By now I had rejected my idea about involving the police, in favor of an idea not so problematic. Ace finally went along with this one and would be prepared when the time came.

I did something else on that trip town, mostly to help fill up the slow train of hours remaining till Judgment Day (as I now privately referred to it). I drove around the city for a while, comparing its features with my twelve-year-old memories. As it seemed to me, even so short a space of time had made a real difference: much more traffic, new and larger buildings and renovated old ones, crowded sidewalks, and a sense of an almost ferocious bustle that I had no memory of. Nostalgia, I reckoned. I drove out West End and turned off into a district of modest houses and stopped in front of the small yellow-brick house that had been my home back then. This, except that it now had a spruced-up look, was much as always. I had no trouble imagining my father, who for long-considered reasons I had never even tried to contact, standing on the front steps. Still in my nostalgic mood, I drove back downtown and then farther down to the old Ryman Auditorium.

Though also spruced-up, it looked much the same, a big old hulk of a red-brick building that now appeared out of place. I understood that its interior had been renovated, but in my mind it was the same poorly lighted, huge and lofty space, with rows of seats slanted upward from a stage which the seats half-encircled . . . a place dusty and soundless in the absence of musicians. Anything but soundless, though, when the music started up, because in that whole interior there was not one seat in any nook or cranny where even the least resonant of notes fell short. The best in the world for music, it was said. But that was the old music, even if, as my grandfather sometimes remarked with disgust, it, like everything else in the world, was already beginning to change. Anyway, I had got an early taste for the music my grandfather loved, and so was inclined to watch with a critical eye as it "evolved" to its current and still-growing pitch of vulgarity.

Saturday finally came. It was a day of excitement for all of us, including Buster, who still didn't know what the real plan was. When I visited him that morning in his room, he was, besides drinking, cleaning his shotgun. He looked up at me with red eyes and a grin on his mouth. "This here's Old Faithful," he said. "Had it all my life." It was a big old double-barrel twelve-gauge with a little rust around the muzzle. "Shoot it off inside the house, it'll be like a war done broke out."

I thought that might be all right, too, a good addition to the festivities. Not that I thought he would put a stop to my plan if he knew about it, but why take a chance? I went down to the kitchen.

They were waiting for me, Mona and her two girls and Ace (even Cobb, who came in later), because they wanted my supervision. I was the one to say, though with Mona's educated advice, how many bottles of untreated whiskey were to be served up first, just to get the party going good. After that came the mixing, exactly so much in every bottle, with me hoping that what I had learned from the baffled druggists who sold it to me would turn out to be right. For pigs, I had told them, because I figured that was the animal closest to what our "guests" were like . . . especially when they were already half-drunk.

It was a tedious process, but one enjoyed by all. After the drudgery, not to mention the disgust, of having to furnish for all that long series of Saturday night parties, here at last was one of their own, a revenge party. There were guffaws and jokes a-plenty, some of which were pretty stomach-turning. I didn't mind, I fell right in with it.

"Ain't seen no castor oil in a long time," Ace said. "How come it don't taste like it?"

"They do something to it now," I said. "Still works, though."

Both of us had tasted of our product and agreed that even if it was a little bit oily, it wouldn't matter . . . the more so when he told me it tasted a lot like moonshine. It would suit them to think it was . . . something exotic.

We decided not to tell Buster. I was more and more sure he would like the idea, but this way the surprise would add to his satisfaction. I was careful to remind J.T., again, to keep his mouth shut.

Just one thing was left hanging: that idea about the police and drugs and all. We kicked this one around for a while and finally decided it would be too much. In the wake of it, though, I came up with a simpler idea. I told Ace to be ready when the time came.

It started raining. In the afternoon it rained hard, and I became seriously worried about the effect on the party. But around five o'clock the rain stopped, and the keenest of my worries passed off. I paced around, watching the clock, helping them set up in the refreshment room. As to the food, olives and nuts and anchovies and so forth, it seemed to me too much, because full bellies cut down on the drinking. So I had some of it taken back to the kitchen, along with a few of the bottles of untreated whiskey, for fear our guests might overdo it before the real stuff came on.

That only a few people had drifted in before ten o'clock didn't much concern me because Buster himself, by telephone, had put the word around. This was to be his goodbye party, the biggest blowout yet, and all true music lovers were welcome to come and see the last of him. He didn't even mind if his announcement, on top of the rumors, suggested that he was bankrupt (which he was), guessing that such would likely add a titillating factor. As it turned out, my confidence was justified.

After ten, they began to arrive in considerable numbers, and by eleven the crowd was bigger than I had ever seen it. At an early point there was some pretense that they had all come to pay their respects to Old Buster. A good many called out for him and even paused (or most of them did) to toast him with drinks on high. I told them he would be down among them in a little while, which led to some isolated, and soon forgotten, expressions of anticipation. Already the party was promising to be a humdinger.

Not only was Blitz Gimbel present again, there was an equally shining superstar, Boman (Bubba) Lunsford. He was readily distinguishable by his long muscular arms, bare and tattooed from the shoulders down, but most of all by his plentiful silver-white hair. He couldn't have been over thirty, and I knew the color had to be "boughten." That he was a great magnet for the girls was evident as soon as came through the door (a little late, of course) and immediately without trying gathered a train of female worshipers. Another thing evident was that he and Blitz were not friends. In no time each one had a part of the crowd around him, Bubba's being the larger, and you could already feel an unpromising (or maybe promising) friction at work. Later on, when the party got really hot, it seemed that an actual physical confrontation might break out at any time. This was especially true when the moment came for individual musical performances. The two, including their groupies, were menacingly head-to-head on the question of which one should go first. For now, at least, the dispute was resolved when Bubba, with an air of majesty, turned his back and, at a few steps' distance, hugged up his guitar and launched his famous bass voice into a rendition of "Better Not Cheat on Me." Not to be outdone (and like a replay of last Saturday's event), Blitz did the same. So, "Unfriendly Woman" and "Better Not Cheat on Me" were rending the air at the same time, each to its own swooning audience.

There was at least one interlude when hostilities were suspended. Sometime earlier Judeen, in a low-cut, fire-engine-red dress and a clutter of bracelets on her arms, had arrived on the scene. She was already drunk, but she headed straight for the refreshment room and half an hour later was almost too drunk to see. Finally realizing this, to her credit she decided to go for a shower. After two or three tries, including one when she bumped into the wall, she located the door to the hall and disappeared. Evidently it was a brief shower, because in just a few minutes she reappeared and, to make a grand entry, paused in the doorway. Seconds later her presence was acknowledged by a dying away of noise throughout the crowd, soon followed by hoots and loud guffaws. Obviously puzzled, she looked around for a second or two, then finally down at herself. Except for the bracelets on her arms, she was buck naked, as well as dripping wet. As best I could tell, she didn't even blush. All she did was look with defiance at the crowd, take a few uncertain steps forward, then turn and head straight into the refreshment room for more of the dog that had bit her. The last time I saw her that night, she was seated in a corner, looking sulky, wrapped around with a tablecloth that some modest person had furnished for her.

Except for some menacing and one serious threat of a fight between Blitz and Bubba, nothing very spectacular happened for the next half hour. It was about here that Ace and I, conferring on the sidelines, decided the time had come. We did it without attracting notice, removing the untreated bottles and replacing them with at least a dozen bottles of the real thing. Then, a little uneasily, we watched. And sure enough, a couple of people did notice the difference. A man with a drooping mustache and a newly tasted drink in his hand remarked to the man beside him that it was moonshine. The other one obligingly agreed and in a slurred voice added that this was just another sign of how near broke Buster was. Clearly, though, it was good enough, and Ace and I were reassured. We withdrew and, after working our way through the crowd, took up posts of observation on the balcony.

In the interlude while we waited for results, the hubbub all around took an upward turn. Again there were two centers of special interest. Somebody had dragged a table out of the refreshment room, and an alternately cheering and groaning crowd had assembled around it. From our posts we could plainly see the two contestants with hands locked in an arm-wrestling match. Not surprisingly, the two, both with faces burning red, were Blitz and Bubba, and so far it looked like a permanent standoff. Bets were going around, voices overtopping one another. But there was a competing event, one that especially got to Ace.

Additional shouts and cheers were coming from the area around the front door. There, resisting the efforts of some drunk fool to climb aboard, was one of Buster's saddle horses, a handsome roan with a blaze face. The man was about midway of his third or fourth effort to mount the skittering horse, when I saw Ace come onto the scene. There wasn't the least indication of apology in the way Ace grabbed the man by his shirt-front and sent him staggering against the wall. In one quick movement he seized the halter and led the horse out, leaving behind him what I imagine was a stream of very black English.

After a few moments of intense gratification, my attention shifted back to the arm-wrestling match. In fact the match was over, and so was what I quickly understood to have been an ensuing match of fists. In fact, in an atmosphere of relative silence now, the loser, silver-haired Bubba with a very bloody nose, was being helped up off the floor.

Through an interval in which nothing else spectacular happened, Ace and I stood there on the balcony exchanging what had now become rather discouraging thoughts. Would it work at all? Would it come too late? Till suddenly Buster, shotgun in hand, followed by a gaping J.T., was there beside us. "'Bout time for me, ain't it? To give them a little shaking up." Pointing with his gun, he said, "Like how 'bout them things there for starters . . . all them pieces of glass raining down on them." He meant the chandeliers hung at intervals along the high ceiling.

I put a restraining hand on the gun. "Don't, Buster, not yet. We got a little surprise coming." I didn't add "I hope."

And I needn't have. What I rightly took to be a first indication of "movement" was taking place. A young woman in jeans was something more than just threading her way through the crowd, heading toward the rear hall. She reached it and, barely in front of a tall and very determined man, passed out of sight through the door. To Ace I said, "This is it, I think."

"Look like it."

"Better go fix the gate," I said, and Ace was gone in an instant.

"What's going on?" Buster said. "Do what to the gate?"

"Just hold on. You'll see in a minute." But an interval followed with nothing to show, and my nerves tightened again. "Just wait," I murmured.

"What the hell," Buster said. "I aim to let go."

"Don't," I said, and then, "Look!"

"At what?"

There were two more en route, and then a third, a big man clearing his way with his elbows through the crowd. "See that guy? The one bulling his way through? He's on the way to the bathroom."

Buster looked puzzled. "Well, better'n him doing it out here."

"He's full of castor oil."

"Which?" Buster looked even more puzzled, his lower lip hanging slightly. "Castor oil? he said. "Like what my mama used to gimme?"

"Same thing. We put it in the whiskey."

Buster's mouth shut tight for a moment, then spread into a grin of the kind usually described as "ear to ear." "By God!" His chuckle quickly expanded into a heehaw that all but prevailed over the clamor below us. "By God, boy, you something." Then, "Look, there go another'n. See him moving with them little short steps." He let out another still-louder heehaw.

A lull followed, and continued on. Though growing uneasy again, I said, "There'll be more in a minute."

"Got to be," Buster said. "Castor oil don't never fail."

He was right, though it took a while. In the meantime, as if to contradict Buster's assurance, a man standing on a table near the front of the room, wearing a Texas hat and accompanied by the whine of an electric guitar, started singing a song of his own composition called "Love My Sweetie Halfway Up." But he hadn't even got to the second verse when, suddenly, with a funny expression on his face, he stopped. He handed his guitar to somebody in the audience and gingerly, like an uncertain mountain climber, got down off the table. It was clear enough where he was headed, but his audience just stood there looking tentative until he passed out of sight in the crowd.

That was a defining moment. The man holding the late-singer's guitar handed it to the woman at his side and in considerable haste set out as if to overtake its owner. Another and then another followed suite, and it wasn't long after that before a small migration was under way.

But they got going too late because, as I now saw, there was a traffic jam building up around the back hall door. That wasn't all. A curious stillness had settled on the crowd, and even those apparently unafflicted were reduced to mumbled questions among themselves. In fact it was so quiet that Buster's spasms, which had him doubled over at times, were bound to be audible down there. That they were being heard was soon demonstrated by the faces looking curiously up at us.

In the crowd stacked around the hall door, there came a surge. Two of its more resourceful members, bursting out, made headlong for the front entrance. A swarm followed them, shouldering each other, tripping here and there, a maelstrom of desperate bodies. But something else happened. One poor woman, with an oath on her lips, stumbled to her knees. Righting herself, she left on the floor a specimen of her trouble. The laughter died in my throat.

It was anything but a moment of high glee for either of us. Buster's laughter, too, had stopped, his wide mouth fallen shut. But for him, this one moment that we shared alike was a mere hitch or question interrupting his merriment. Not so for me. It was as if each renewed surge of his laughter served only to deepen the feeling of regret, even shame, that had taken hold of me. A mindless dirty trick of a kind to set a schoolboy roaring. And all of my own doing. What remedy, then? Since there wasn't any such in sight, all I could do was bear it.

Suddenly Ace was there beside me. "All done," he said. "Chain and all."

"What?"

"That'll hold them a long time."

The gate, I thought, murkily.

It took a minute for Buster, with spirits renewed, managed to get things straight. "Boy, you a genius," he said, and fell back to laughing.

It seemed that all at once the house was empty, at least empty of guests. A few minutes later, amid whiffs of lingering odor, we descended the stairs and made for the open front door. The drizzling dark out there was already shredded with beams from the headlights of cars, some in motion now, joining the stream of traffic moving out toward the distant front gate. Beams from cars still in the process of moving into position swept across the landscape, here and there exposing as in the blink of an eye figures in awkward and embarrassing postures. Occasionally we ourselves, observing from the porch, were also caught in moments of display. And once, right in the wake of such a moment, a voice hoarse with rage screamed out of the dark, "You dirty goddamn son-of-a-bitch."

Whether directed at him or not, Buster assumed it was. He took it with a chuckle and seconds later called back in a loud voice, "How 'bout coming in for a drink, Shit-head."

No answer. The turmoil kept on as before, but I sensed that Ace, standing beside me, shared my uneasiness. Not so with Buster. He even repeated his challenge, raising his shotgun into view. When we noticed that now the parade of cars clear out to the gate was stalled in a hopeless jam, he let go with a huge burst of laughter. I said to him, "Better soft-pedal it. They could get too mad." I was thinking, maybe . . . To Ace I murmured, "Maybe we ought to go out there and open it."

"No way," Ace quietly answered. They'd lynch me right off. You too, likely." In a louder voice he said, "We best get back inside."

Buster quit laughing, but he didn't do anything. As we watched, some cars in the long line, in the flush of headlights, were beginning to turn off into the fields on either side in search of an exit elsewhere. It was a bad move. We could tell that one by one, at only a little distance from the driveway, they were all miring down . . . wheels spinning, motors whining. People on foot, some of those who evidently had exited from the back of the house, kept appearing. I said, "Come on, Buster, let's go back in."

He stalled for a minute. Then, after making another pointless display of the shotgun in his hands, he turned and, accompanied by J.T., followed us in. But even there with the door shut and locked, Buster stood for a while, still grinning, peering out through one of the narrow windows in the entryway.

There was nothing to do but wait and see. We went into the anteroom and sat down in chairs we turned to face the front windows. We could still hear, though faintly, the futile whine of motors and sometimes upraised voices. Buster had not lost his good humor, and every time he got up for a good long look out a window, he came back grinning. "Be a field full of high-priced mud-mucked cars in the morning." And once he said, with a show of sniffing the air, "This place going to have to have a real good washing." He laughed, and J.T. echoed him.

Too late, I was thinking. And anyway, they had it coming.

"Bring a fire hose in here," Buster went on. "And scrub buckets." He laughed again, followed again by J.T.'s echo. "Way I reckon, it likely won't be nothing to me what they do with this place."

I hesitated, decided to be direct. "You mean, you think you're going to lose it?"

"Look mighty like it. What they tell me."

"Everything?"

"What they say."

"And leave you with nothing?"

"Pretty near that, maybe."

Buster got up for another look out the window, and I could hear him chuckling again. From appearances he was not at all disturbed about his prospects. When he got back to his chair, I said, "What would you do?"

He didn't even pause to say, "Go home."

I let it go at that, and after a minute he said, "Just one thing, though." He looked at Ace. "Ace, you be all right?"

"Be fine," Mister Bus."

As if reassured, Buster looked away and then came up with, "Cobb, too . . . with all that big family." Which made me conscious that but for us the house was all empty now.

The Adventures of Douglas Bragg

— — —

120

After a moment's ruminating, Buster looked at J.T. "I'm hoping this boy'll want to go along with me."

J.T. didn't hesitate even for a second. "I sho' will, Buster. Anywheres you want me to."

Buster nodded. "That's good," he said, and we all fell silent, listening again to the still undiminished ruckus of cars and voices down the drive.

There was another sound. It came from somewhere close by, a kind of bustling noise. The front porch. Before we could get squarely on our feet, the clang of the big brass door-knocker, repeated two, three, four times, resounded through the house. Then raucous voices, punctuated by heavy blows on the door.

"By God!" As if by a single impossible leap Buster was there with his shotgun at the ready. Standing three or four steps back from the door, he lifted his voice about as high as it would go. "Get your asses off my porch, and quick."

There was a moment's pause, then again the banging and the voices.

"Last chance, Shit-heads!" Buster yelled. There was no pause this time . . . or not till Buster pulled the trigger. Boom! What followed was a screeching noise and curses and a hole in the door about the size of a pancake. When the voices took up again, a furious litany of threats and blasphemies, they were uttered at a safe distance from the house. It was a thick door, and I figured that the worst any of them suffered was a few number-six shot lodged under their hides.

Buster opened the wounded door and loudly issued some memorable advice to the departed ones out there in the dark. He shut it and returned and, with an expression of rapt satisfaction, sat down in his chair. We sat there with little to say, listening.

It might have been a whole hour before we noticed that a change had taken place. Ace got up and went to the window. After a moment he said, "Look like one of them had sense enough to figure how. They moving out." We all went for a look, and after that, though we kept to our chairs for a while yet, we were breathing pretty easy. Buster too, but not because of any real change in his frame of mind. I think he had been hoping all along that they would make another try at the door.

It must have been about four o'clock, after Ace and I had taken a quick tour around the house outside, when we all finally went to our rooms. J.T. was already fast asleep when I got there. Too exhausted to

The Adventures of Douglas Bragg

take my clothes off, I lay down and tried for sleep. I didn't have much luck. A series of heavy dozes was what it amounted to. At one wakeful point I heard a stirring somewhere, which, before I lapsed back again, I figured to be Buster having the same trouble I was having. But I don't think I ever came completely awake until, all of a sudden, I had good reason to. It was smoke in the room, and more than that, smoke enough to set me really coughing.

I yelled at J.T. and got to Buster's room at just about the same time Ace did. The light was on, and there was smoke in there, too, but Buster looked like he wasn't paying it much attention. He was reared back in his easy chair with a glass of whiskey in his hand. With real urgency Ace said, "Get up from there, Mister Bus, 'fore that fire get to us."

Buster put his whiskey down. "Just having a last little goodbye drink," he said, and got up. He went straight to his lineup of guitars against the wall and picked out his best one and also that old one. With Ace urging us on from behind, we went out and down the steps in smoke that had got almost too thick for breathing. Then out the front door to where, from a little distance, we stopped and turned around. Just in time, it seemed. Already, through the open doorway, we could see how the pall of smoke was assuming a deadly crimson glow. Ace said, "Tried to call the firemen. Phone wouldn't work."

We stood and stood without speaking, at intervals backing farther away as the heat in our faces required. Soon enough the flame in tongues appeared in a burst through the roof, renewed themselves, gathered at last to form one towering, swirling yellow cone. Just loud enough to be heard above the crackle and roar. Buster said, "It was them shit-heads." And a little later on, "Goodbye, house." These were the last words I could remember hearing Buster say.

That morning, which it was by then, with a couple of fire trucks and firemen and spectators and owners of expensive mired-down automobiles all over the place, things seemed to go every which way. And on top of all this, my physical exhaustion. Somehow I made it to a not too distant truck stop and got a bed and died for ten or twelve hours. When I woke up, it was night again, and so I had to wait till next morning to go back.

The gate was locked, and I had to climb over the fence. There was nobody in sight, but with the big house out of the way, I could see Cobb's little one in the near distance. I headed for it, pausing only to view the spread of heaped-up and still-smoking coals and ashes. Cobb didn't know much, only that Buster and J.T., and later on, Ace, had been gone since yesterday. He, Cobb, had been told to stay on in order to take care of the horses and such. He didn't know for how long.

So I didn't know, and didn't know to how to find out, what the outcome was for Buster. In spite of his saying it was the shit-heads that did it, I think it was Buster himself. I think he did it just to wipe the slate clean, be rid of it all. Knowing what I knew, this made sense. I would have bet he had headed straight for *home*. I couldn't stop wondering whether he had gone on his way flat broke or with a lot of money in his pockets.

IT WAS ABOUT NOON OF THAT DAY, after brooding for a long time over the ashes, before I got clear enough in my head to start thinking about myself. What now? The gas station, maybe, if the guy would take me back. I reached in my pocket to see how much money I had left, and I was surprised. There were half a dozen twenties and two or three tens, all from that moment when I had hurriedly grabbed a handful out of the kitchen trove to go and buy castor oil with. A piece of luck, but it wouldn't get me back to town. I couldn't remember two pieces of luck in a row ever happening to me before, but now, for once, it did happen. Beyond the heaps of ashes, the parking lot was partly visible, and a few steps sideways showed me a single car: J.T.'s little pile of junk. I hurried around and, holding my breath, opened the door and reached in under the seat. Thank God the key was there.

It took me probably twenty minutes, and three or four vigorous applications of heaves into the gas tank pipe, to get the thing started. My next problem was that of the locked front gate. But I soon remembered a gate at the back of the place, and driving across the field, always at peril of miring down, I made it there and found it not locked. Home free, I thought, bouncing along the little log-road toward the highway. My exultation was momentary. That gas station fixed in my sights was a sorry destination. But where else?

It happened that the boss, Mr. Cook, had recently lost the employee who had taken my place, and after a lengthy show of reluctance, he hired me again. A place to stay came next, and since I reckoned my former one was out of the question, I searched a little and found another just like it (old and shabby, that is) two blocks up the street. So, feeling dismal, I settled in.

Those first few days didn't do anything for my state of mind. It was as if those weeks at Buster's and their grand finale had sapped any yearning I still had for the road. The only thing really on my mind was the matter of Buster and J.T. I kept imagining the two of them, down there in "Deep Valley" hard at work restoring that little shack where young Buster had lived fifty-something years ago. Where was it, exactly? Near a small town named, as I remembered it, Rocky Creek. The state road map didn't confirm my memory, but it did show a Boulder Creek around seventy-five miles east of Nashville that I figured could be it. So what?

On the day that had followed the big event, the *Nashville Times* had carried a considerable story about it, but the bare facts in the case were all it gave. When, a couple of days later, there was still no follow-up, I had about concluded that this was the end of the matter and that I had better turn my mind back to my own circumstances. Doing so didn't produce anything, but at least there was one occurrence in these days that momentarily diverted me. I guess I could call it a domestic event.

My room was on a back corner of an old two-story frame house in need of paint and a good deal of carpentry. Among my blessings was the fact that an inside door of my room opened on the kitchen, where I had minimal privileges. My landlady, Mrs. Grimes, a small, middle-aged snappish woman, was very precise about my privileges. I was to take nothing from the refrigerator that I had not put in, and what I put in must be confined to a single shelf, the bottom one. I gathered that a violation of this rule would amount to automatic termination of my occupancy, maybe without reimbursement of my advance. Thus, my scrupulousness.

There had been times when I had heard, just barely, sounds from overhead, but I had supposed they were made by Mrs. Grimes herself. I was wrong and, in the circumstances, startled. Bent down at the opened refrigerator, I was reaching for some of my personal items when suddenly a low, strangled-sounding voice grabbed my attention. I thought that partly it was the way I jumped, hitting my head on the refrigerator door, that put the look of terror in the old woman's face. Anyway it was this look that for a space scotched my intention to say something. She was the one who spoke first, or, rather, second, repeating the words, "I am calling the police."

Standing upright now, I pulled my self together. I said, "Please don't, ma'am. I'm the new boarder." When this seemed to make no difference, I added, "Ask Mrs. Grimes. I've been living here three days."

This made impression enough to change the old woman's look of terror to one of mere suspicion. I now supposed, when she finally answered, that the quaver in her voice was natural to her. "My daughter is not at home."

Apparently she still didn't believe me. I didn't know what to say. I said, "I always use the back way in. That's why you haven't seen me before this."

Still the look of suspicion. Now she just stood there silent in the doorway, walking cane in hand, her faded blue eyes fastened on me. If 'fastened' is the word, because her eyes looked so bleary that it was a wonder she could see anything. My gathering impression of her was that not only was she old, ancient in fact, but the shrunken relic of herself was wrapped from neck to foot in some kind of a faded robe that might very well serve as a shroud. Or such was my impression to start with. Her voice, with more energy now, surprised me. "Thieves always use the back door."

"But I'm not a thief," I protested . . . to no response.

She seemed to draw a breath. "Then why are you stealing from my icebox?"

"But I'm not. It's part of the deal, with Mrs. Grimes. Ask her."

"My daughter is not at home."

I had a thought: the key to my room. But when I suddenly reached in my pocket to get it, the old woman gave a little cry and, except that she had lifted the walking cane in apparent self-defense, seemed about to faint away against the doorjamb. Alarmed, I quickly held up the key. In a matter of seconds she was herself again, but the look of suspicion in her face had hardly diminished at all.

"It's the key to my room," I said, holding it on display with my fingertips. "That your daughter gave me."

The Adventures of Douglas Bragg

Whether the old woman could see clearly or not, she looked hard at it. She said, "All keys look about the same."

After standing there in her gaze for a space, I said, "I can show you. You can watch me lock the door with it." Getting no response I could think of nothing to do but give a shrug and start to turn away. I was interrupted.

"Wait! What is your name, young man?"

"Douglas Bragg, ma'am."

"Bragg," she said reflectively, a little as if it was an unwholesome word.

"Yes, Bragg," I said with emphasis, all of a sudden vexed.

"Bragg. I have heard that name." She was regarding me with a new intensity. "Where could I have heard it?" Then, "Yes. But I would hate to think that . . ." She didn't finish, just stared with a growing expression of alarm.

To hell with her, I thought, and really angry now, I said, "That I'm a wanted criminal who robs people's refrigerators. That's me."

She was looking at me aghast. I stood there waiting to see what she would say or do next, and when nothing more came of it, I turned and, just to spite her, took my time selecting a couple of my own items from the open refrigerator. I had just straightened up and shut the door when I heard a noise behind me. "Thump." No, more like "kerplunk." I turned around.

She was stretched out face-up on the doorway, eyes shut, mouth barely open, hands crossed on her belly the way undertakers fix them. Dead? Down on my knees beside her, I said, "Can you hear me?" I said it again, but no answer, no response of any kind. I put a hand on her chest, leaned closer. I couldn't tell whether she was breathing or not, but I thought I could feel, ever so slightly, a heartbeat. For some moments all I could think to do was keep repeating the words "Are you all right?" Do what? I thought of the telephone, but what was that number to call? It came to me, and I quickly found where the telephone was. The address? I remembered and shouted it into the receiver. "And quick!" I yelled and left the receiver hanging there.

Back beside her, I felt again for a heartbeat. But the pulse I felt was as likely my own, throbbing in my hand. A wet cloth? In haste I snatched a dishcloth hanging over the sink and wet it and laid it across her forehead. Just the same, nothing doing. A corpse, I thought . . . I was looking at a corpse. I stood up.

The Adventures of Douglas Bragg

I don't know how long I stood there in the perfect silence of that old house. My fault? What would they say? . . . Mrs. Grimes, and maybe the Law. A mess in any case. The insistent thought of simply absconding came and went in my mind, a stupid thought finally squelched by the sound of heavy footsteps.

I met them at the front door, two serious-looking young men in white jackets, and motioned them toward the body. The man with a stethoscope bent down and held it on her chest for a few seconds. "She's alive," he said, and proceeded to lift one of her eyelids with his thumb. I didn't see the exposed eye move, but I was sure it was looking straight at me.

"What happened?" the man said.

My throat felt too clogged for speech, but in a croaking voice I managed, "She just fell over. She was standing right there in the door and she just fell over."

"That's all?"

"Just fell over," I repeated.

"Hmn," the man said. "Well, we better take her in. Billy, go get the stretcher."

Billy obliged, but just at the front door he stopped, confronted by somebody coming in. It was Mrs. Grimes. "What's going on?" I heard her say.

"The old lady," the man answered.

Mrs. Grimes, with a certain knowing movement of her head, passed him by and approached us with what seemed to me something less than full speed. We stepped back to make way for her. For a moment she stood there looking down at her mother lying stretched out on the floor. The man with the stethoscope said, "A stroke, probably."

"Yes," Mrs. Grimes said, with a peculiar intonation. "Another 'stroke.'" Then she looked at me, and I went cold. "Was she fussing at you?"

I managed to nod and tried to say something.

Mrs. Grimes breathed a sigh, then said, "Oh well," and, stooping down over her mother, said with that same intonation, "Wake up, dear."

No response, not a stir.

"Wake up, dear," she repeated, louder this time. Still getting no response, and to my astonishment, using the tips of her fingers, she gave the old woman a smart little slap on first one cheek and then the other. The faded old eyes came open, then blinked.

The Adventures of Douglas Bragg

"She will be fine," Mrs. Grimes said. "It happens all the time."

The bleary old eyes were in motion now, searching from face to face. They stopped on mine, her mouth came open. "Thief," she quavered. "He's a thief."

"Come now, Mother."

"He was robbing our icebox,"

Mrs. Grimes, ignoring her now, said to the two men, "Help her up, will you? She'll be fine. And thanks for coming."

As quick as I could, I faded away, and after that, following Mrs. Grimes's needless advice, I was more than careful to keep my ears well-tuned for the old girl's footsteps.

It was two days later when a second "Buster story" appeared in the newspaper. This time it was much more than just a relation of bare facts. The story was right up there on the first page, headlined "FORMER MUSIC STAR SOUGHT ON CHARGES." It proceeded to state that efforts to locate Buster had failed so far and that investigators were searching for anyone who might have relevant information. In spite of the paper's use of the plural, there was only one actual charge: Assault With A Deadly Weapon. It boggled my mind for a moment . . . until I remembered Buster's shotgun blast through the front door and the yelps that issued therefrom. Those creeps! But there it was, portrayed as serious business. The rest of the article focused on accounts of what he was "wanted" for, and by whom wanted. That the insurance people would be after him might have been expected, but the other matter, in which he was sought for questioning, was pretty chilling. It appeared that a man named Bruce Clark, though no remains had yet been found, might have died in the fire. Credible witnesses swore to his presence on the scene and that he was one of those most determined to get revenge on Buster. More telling was the fact that after five days his whereabouts were still unknown. The chill was still on me while, for the second time, I scanned the two and a half columns in search of my name. It was not there.

Pumping gas, washing windshields, and goadings by old man Cook to "git on with it" were not enough to distract my thoughts through the rest of that afternoon. Bad news, that, I was thinking, wishing I had a whole lot more than a skimpy knowledge of law. I got off at six o'clock, and still thinking about it, walked along the half-lighted street to my room at the back of the house.

The Adventures of Douglas Bragg

There was a big surprise waiting for me. I had just got inside and turned on my light when somebody knocked on the door behind me. A stealthy knock, ominous-sounding, that came again before I turned the knob. The dim light that fell on him didn't illuminate anything but a small figure in a long fog-colored overcoat and a hat with the brim turned down in front. A newspaper comic came to mind: Fearless Fosdick.

"Finally found you," the man said in a voice I seemed to remember. He already had a foot on the sill, and now the other one followed. He took off his hat. "Know me now?" he said.

Unfortunately I did, in a shock of recognition. I wouldn't have remembered his name from that interview at Buster's, but his byline in the *Interloper* article had fixed it in my memory. Loman Snipes. In a flicker I thought how often it was that names fitted their owners, and his was a perfect case. A small man with darting eyes and tangled black brows to shade them, a keen obtrusive nose, and not much more in the way of lips than any fish has got. I said, "Yes, I know you."

"My article suit you?" A fast-paced nasal voice.

"Only in a way," I quietly said.

He eyed me for a moment. "Doesn't matter." Then, "We need to talk."

"Why," I said.

He was studying me, head to foot. "You read the *Times* today?"

"Yeah." He was already beginning to give me the creeps. I wondered how he had found me.

"Let's talk about it. I figure you probably know where he went. Being close to him and all."

"You're wrong," I said firmly. "I was just a flunky. He never let me in on his private business."

He was studying me harder now. He said, "What about that black man. Ace, they called him."

"I don't know where he is, either."

The only thing about Snipes that seemed to move was his eyes. Now they too stopped moving, and blinked. "You don't know much, do you?" Then, "It would be something in it for you. Maybe something nice. Looks to me like you could use it."

"I'm fine."

"Okay. They'll be coming for you, you know. Police. Insurance dudes. Lawyers. Keeping an eye on you. They can find you easy as I did."

The Adventures of Douglas Bragg

"Let them," I said. "I've got nothing to tell them."

His mouth widened a little. Then, "Okay. And I've got eyes, too. Good ones. Think about it."

"Get out of here," I said, sharply enough to sound threatening.

"Okay." He turned and took a step toward the door, then all in one motion wheeled around with a tiny camera held up in both his hands. He flashed it in my face.

"You sonofabitch!" My forward lurch was too late. Before I could even reach the open door, he was gone in the dark without so much as footfalls sounding behind him.

I guess you could say my daily boredom had been a little diminished by that visit. Not in a pleasant way, however, because it had left me with an uneasiness I hadn't felt before. That was his intention, I figured. He had let me know he was on my case, that he would be watching if I should decide to bolt. Anyway he gave me the creeps, and all the more so when, after dark the next day, I got a glimpse of a shadowy figure standing on the other side of the street.

My "creeps" of course were foolishness, and anyway, since he couldn't keep watch all the time, I could easily arrange to abscond without his knowledge. Not that I intended to . . . at least not yet, not with the pressure to locate Buster clearly on the rise.

That it was on the rise was made plain soon enough. I was visited, successively, by insurance people, by reporters from two newspapers, and by the cops. It was only the cops who gave me much of a hard time. The others were merely insistent and left after clearly expressing their belief that I was lying to them. By the time the last of them left, I was a good deal more than vexed, and already playing with the idea of getting back at them somehow. And after the cops, to make things worse, two detectives showed up and began to verbally pummel me. It was this preparation that determined me to do the thing I do so well: invent.

That one of them was fat and the other thin somehow led me to wonder if it was going to be a case of that old TV "bad cop, good cop" cliché. In fact it was a little like that. The fat detective with the small mouth and insidious tenor voice not only did most of the talking but also was the more menacing of the two. He didn't start off that way; his first questions were put in a perfectly civil tone. But as soon as he concluded that I was going to continue denying any knowledge of Buster's whereabouts, things changed. He had been seated on my only chair, face-to-face with me where I sat on my unmade bed. Now, heavy as he was, so as to bring the full weight of his authority down on me, he got to his feet. "All right," he said from above. "It's time we had some straight talk. You understand me?"

I nodded yes, assuming an expression I hoped was one of budding intimidation. Not so easy, considering the anticipation I felt.

"I hope you can see we got serious business here. There's the charge of assault with a deadly weapon."

Baloney, I thought.

"What's worse, we think a man died in that fire, probably . . . and that Buster Bell set the fire, himself."

Maybe not all baloney, this one, but where was the proof of it?

"And the doctored whiskey," the thin detective added with a tone of satisfaction "You might say 'poisoned.' Several of those poor people were hospitalized."

Pure baloney this time, but now I was trying to look stunned.

"Exactly," the fat one said in a voice gone perfectly flat. "Now understand me." He lifted a hand and made a fist out of it. "To shield a man under criminal charges is a felony . . . with prison time behind it. You might ask yourself if that's what you want. Because that's what you'll get for lying to us."

He paused to let this sink in. I slumped a little.

The fat one went on, "To be plain about it, we think you know where this guy is . . . or at the least where he might be. So let's have it."

To enrich my performance, I fumbled for a second, letting my mouth fall open in a vain attempt to swallow. "I . . . I don't know . . . not for sure."

"All right. Where do you *think?*"

His eyes made me think of a pet owl I once saw, distracting me just briefly. With my best shame-faced expression, I faintly said, "I heard him, two or three times, talk about going back someday to a little town . . . called . . ." I really did have to pause here because it had to be a real place, and also one remote from Boulder Creek, which just might be close to Buster's old home. After a blank moment, for some reason I came up with "Reel Foot."

"That's a lake," the thin detective said. "Over near Memphis."

"That's it, though," I said, congratulating myself on a choice that would make extra trouble for them.

The Adventures of Douglas Bragg

For a space in which the only sounds came faintly from the kitchen beyond my wall, the fat detective kept me tight in his gaze. "That all?" he said.

Humbly, anxious to oblige, I said, "That's all." But another thought popped to the surface. Why not, since memory all of a sudden had befriended me, double their trouble? I thought of a little place I had visited once, for some reason. "Wait," I brightly said. "I remember something else. He mentioned it a couple of times. A little town named Shalon or Sharon or something like that. Where he had kinfolks he was fond of."

"You know where it's at?"

"No. But a road map ought to have it."

"All right," he said, pondered for a second, and then got heavily onto his feet. With a little hint of grudge he said, "We're obliged to you." He had turned and taken two or three steps toward the door when he evidently decided he had been too civil. He turned back and lifted his voice. "Understand me. Shielding a man under criminal charges makes *you* a criminal. With prison time to follow." The two of them turned and went out.

I shut the door behind them and, thinking about food, started for the kitchen. But I hadn't much more than started turning the doorknob when I heard a noise alarmingly familiar. Kerplunk. And sure enough, there she was, just beyond the open door, stretched out flat of her back with that dead look on her face. Evidently 'criminal' had been the operative word. After a moment of doing nothing at all, I murmured, to no avail, "Are you all right? I stepped over the body and went out and across the hall to Mrs. Grimes's bedroom door. I softly knocked.

"Yes?"

"I'm afraid Mother has had another stroke."

After a short pause, "Very well. Thank you." Nothing more.

I went out the front door and headed for the Toddle House.

— ⸺ —

Every morning upon waking up, I would tell myself that today would be the last one before I left here. Up in the day, however, remembering the glimpses I had had of Snipes or somebody else equally interested in me, I would change my mind again. But aside from these glimpses, real or imagined, I couldn't help but be conscious of the growing interest in the matter of Buster, as shown by the newspapers. In fact it might be that I, in a small way, was responsible, having shot off my mouth not only to the detectives but to others as well. Even though in one way it was self-defeating, I couldn't resist the temptation to spread idle rumors likely to be repeated on and on, as to his whereabouts. The Toddle House, where I often ate, was a good place for this. I would initiate friendly conversations and proceed to work them around to Buster: who he was and once had been, what had happened out there, and where I had heard he might be now. My contributions couldn't possibly have played a major part, but I did notice that one of them appeared, anonymously, in a column in the *Nashville Times*. Anyway, Buster had become a "topic," and I congratulated myself for having participated in his resurrection . . . if you could call it that.

This of course greatly pleased me, but as I have remarked, there was this other side to it, and this displeased me. There were times when I gave myself a good verbal drubbing. It was not only that this "resurrection" would, since I was a "person of interest," stand in the way of my departure from this damn place; it must also, surely, spur the cops' determination to find Buster. I never was able to leave well enough alone.

So it went on for another week, with nothing to divert me but work at the gas station and occasional walks in nearby Centennial Park. In the park, at least, I could enjoy viewing, with a kind of surly satisfaction, that massive structure believed by its graceless and deservedly dead architect to replicate the original Parthenon. I also enjoyed, with a satisfaction not much different, observing the late afternoon traffic on the avenue in front of the park. It was always, always the same: a nightmare tangle of automobiles and trucks as far as the eye could see in both directions, all dead stopped between interludes of creeping forward motion, fierce honking of horns, scraping of fenders, drivers with murder in their hearts. Alas for triumphant industrial man!

But I couldn't wait around forever, and I made my decision regardless. Almost immediately, however, there was a hitch in my plan. J.T.'s car would not start. I spent most of an hour, to the point of exhaustion, blowing into the gas tank pipe, and in desperation ended by having it hauled to a shop. There, the next day, the much-vexed mechanic expressed his firm opinion that this was the only car of its kind ever manufactured. He did get it running, though. He also offered a piece of mechanical advice. After raising the hood, which was hinged at the front end instead of the back, he put his finger on a little rod in the motor. " When it stops, give this a good jiggle or two and it'll start . . . you hope." I paid him, a considerable whack out of my trove, and went back to my plan.

Late that night, having given notice where it was due, I picked up my skimpy belongings and put them in the car. Then, after hesitating, I walked around to the front of the house and stood there searching shadows up and down the street. All clear, it seemed. I left on my table the amount of money I thought I owed and went back to the car. Happily, it started without a hitch, and minutes later, with frequent glances into my rearview mirror, I was headed east toward Boulder Creek.

— — —

It was a long drive and a slow one in this car. I found the turnoff onto Highway 29 all right, but shortly afterwards the car stalled, and I had to get out and, with blessed success, jiggle the little rod in the motor. After a couple of hours, I started dozing, so I turned off onto the road shoulder to take a little nap. It didn't turn out to be little. When I opened my eyes it was daylight . . . which I was glad to see.

After a couple of hours, driving on a road more up and down than before and with hardly any traffic, I passed a sign that told me Boulder Creek was just ten more miles. After that, as I rounded a curve, I saw a man in the road some distance ahead of me. I could see he was staggering, and before I got that far, I saw him fall down. Naturally I stopped and, after a second, got out.

He was sitting up, propped on his arms behind him, his legs stretched out. It was dry weather, but he looked like he had been rolling in mud. The filth was all over his ratty overalls and tattered cotton shirt and also on his face, along with bristles. Still more, he had one bare foot, and the shoe on the other foot had no laces. His melted brown eyes looked up at me with a rapt expression, as if he knew and loved me. After a moment, with effort he said, "Glad to see you, Jesus."

Hurt? Sick? Drunk? I was sure it was the last one when I noticed a broken bottle on the pavement beside him. What to do with him? "You better get out of the road," I said. "I'll help you."

To my extended hand he said, "Jes' touch me, Jesus."

"Well, I'm not Jesus, but I can help you out of the road. Give me your hand."

Still with that rapt look in his eyes, he said, "You got a drink? Mine done broke."

"Jesus doesn't drink. Come on."

"Comf'able here. Goan die here. Take me, Jesus."

"All right." I said. I got behind him with my arms under his, but I couldn't lift him. God, how he stunk! He made no resistance when I tried to drag him, but I didn't get far. I couldn't just go off and leave him here, in a place with not a house or a soul in sight. I got an idea. "Wait," I said, as though anything else was possible. I went quickly to the car and drove it around to where the passenger door was right beside him. Taking hold of his arm I said, "Okay, here's the Sweet Chariot . . . swung low for you." To my surprise this enlivened him some, and with a little help on his part, I managed to get him up onto the seat. My next problem was keeping him from falling back out while I reached to shut the door. I managed it, and he turned his head and looked at me with a glow of adoration. Just audibly, he said, "Carry me home."

After a cranking or two, I got the car under way, but now I had another problem. To keep him from falling over against me, I had to drive with only one hand and hold him back with the other. Thank God it was only ten miles, I thought, and then I started thinking about what I was going to do with the drunkest man in the world when I got there. The police station, of course . . . or the sheriff's office or whatever they had in that town. I was also wondering how in the devil he had got way out here by himself.

After a few miles passed in silence, he suddenly stopped leaning against my hand and pitched forward, his head now resting on the dashboard. When he stayed that way, I assumed he was asleep, and for a while I quit paying much attention to him. But little by little I got to thinking something wasn't right. Leaning for a glance at his face, I saw that his eyes were open. A second glance and then a third showed me no change at all, and I let the car drift to a halt. "You asleep?" I pointlessly murmured. Nothing. I reached with both hands and turned his head to face me. I was looking into the open eyes of a dead man.

The chill running under my skin passed off in a minute or two, and thinking "Just my luck," I put the car in motion. At a top speed of about forty, it was surely the longest five or six miles in my life. But finally there were scattered houses and, shortly after that, stores and a traffic light. The light was red, but I saw it too late and stopped with the light now behind me. No cops, however, but only a man who had had to jump out of my way. I hailed him, to no effect, and went on to the next light, where an old man with a cane was crossing. This time I had luck. He approached and answered my question by pointing at a rusty-looking brick building just to my right. He added, "It's on around back of that." Then his gaze stiffened. He was looking at my passenger, who, as I now saw, lay arranged in a sort of heap against the car door. The old man kept looking at him. "Is he dead?"

I managed to say, "I picked him up out on the road."

"By golly," the old man said, "that's Harmless James."

There was a honking behind us. "Got to go," I said, and took the corner and turned in behind the building where it said "Sheriff's Department" on a sign by the door. No patrol cars, I vaguely noticed, and got out.

I stood face-to-face with an old fat officer (if, considering how he was dressed, he was an officer) seated at a long cluttered table. No badge, wearing a sloppy-looking gray cotton shirt. He put aside the little box puzzle he had been working and said, "Okay, what?"

"Look," I said, trying to clear my throat. "Got a dead man out there in my car. Picked him up on the road ten miles out. And he fell over dead."

"Well," the man said. And finally, "Let's have a look." He stood up with some effort and waddled around the desk and out through the door, with me behind him. He reached in through the car window with both hands and turned the dead man's head for a full view of his face.

I said, "Called Harmless James, a man told me."

"Sho' is. Pfeuw. Even smells like hisself. Mostly whiskey. I reckon he been in this jail twenty times. . . . And now he done bought it."

After a silence I said, " Well, what?"

The officer looked around at me with a vaguely puzzled expression. "I don't know. Sheriff and them all gone. Drug doings or something over at Ludlow. Got me filling in. Policeman, myself, but it been a while." He drew a breath. "Don't know when they be back. Might be a long time."

"Can't I just leave him here?"

He mulled this for a few seconds. Then, "I reckon not. Can't have no dead body lying around the station. 'Specially one stinks like he do."

"Then what?" I said. "Can't you reach him someway? On the radio?"

The Adventures of Douglas Bragg

"Nope. Not likely." He thought again, laboriously. Finally, "It's __ something 'bout calling a coroner. He's down there at Bentonville."

It was my turn to draw a breath. "How far is that?"

"Oh, 'bout thirty mile."

God! I had another thought. "Hasn't the poor stiff got any family?'

This called for further weighty consideration. "Some kinfolks, seems like. A old aunt, it might be."

"Where?"

"Seem to me it might be out north on Timber Road." He actually lifted his arm and pointed. "Keep on this same street out of town till you come on a fork where's a little grocery store. They likely to know where she's at." With this he turned away and was back in the building before I could get in the car.

It was a long three or four miles out of town, with me looking straight ahead and hoping nobody could tell what it was I had in here beside me. A couple of times on right-hand curves I had to push him hard back against the door. I passed an incoming patrol car, but I wasn't going to turn back now. Every few minutes an impassioned stream of cusswords came ripping out of my throat.

But the man in the little grocery did know where she lived, and then I was on a dirt road billowing dust behind me and looking sharp for a cabin-size frame house back off from the road among cedar trees. Pretty soon I spotted it, one of only three or four houses and a little church along this road so far. I turned and bumped across a ditch and stopped in back of an old rusty car a little way from the house. She was standing in the door, a small hump-shouldered woman with gray hair tied back, wearing a loose faded-blue dress almost down to her ankles. The straw-colored head of a child was peeping out from behind her. I got out and had taken just a step or two when she said, not friendly, "Who you looking for, stranger?"

I stopped and said, "Are you Harmless James's aunt?"

"Who wants to know?"

"My name's Douglas Bragg. If you are his aunt, I'm afraid I've got bad news for you."

"What kind of bad news?" She had a rather high-pitched nasal voice and a missing upper tooth. But before I could answer, I noticed that her gaze had come to focus on what could be seen of my passenger. I said, "That's him there."

The Adventures of Douglas Bragg

— — —

"Drunk, huh? How come you brung him? Comes out here drunk by hisself all the time. Eat a whole loaf of bread and go back looking for whiskey again."

"No, ma'am, not this time. He's dead."

She stiffened and stayed that way for a moment, then stepped down and walked deliberately to the car. Reaching in through the window, she put a hand on his head.

"I found him falling-down drunk out on the highway. I tried to help him and finally got him in the car. He just hauled off and died on the way into town. They told me to bring him to you."

Finally she withdrew her hand and said, "Well, it's a wonder he lasted this long, poor fellow. Ain't never been nothing but drunk since he first could lift a bottle full of whiskey." She turned and walked back and sat down on the doorstep. She just sat there for a space, the little girl seated beside her now. A spotted hound dog came up and licked the girl's cheek.

All of a sudden the woman looked up at me. "I'm obliged to you," she said and looked away again, deep in her thoughts. A little later in a quiet voice, "Wasn't never one good thing ever did happen to Jimmy. No mama or daddy neither one, since he was a sprout of a boy. Th'owed out on the world. I wish I could of took him in. Couldn't do it."

I decided that now was the time to say, "I'd like to help you any way I can . . . with burying him and all."

She didn't answer, but seconds later she looked up at me with a different, almost lively expression. Her voice, a good pitch higher, said, "Naw. It ain't me goan bury him . . . not by my hands. Jimmy goan have a *real* fun'ral." Her voice pitched a little higher still, almost excited, she said, "He's goan get embomed. And have one them fancy boxes to rest in. And whatever else they got goes with it . . . to give him something nice 'fore he goes in the ground." Her expression now was downright triumphant.

I let the moment draw out. I hated to, but finally in the gentlest voice I could manage, I said, "You know, don't you, those things cost an awful lot of money?" I wanted to say "a thousand," but I didn't have the heart.

"I got money. I got a fruit jar pretty near full."

I hoped it was a big fruit jar. I would let the matter drop for now. But she didn't allow it. She stood up suddenly and went in the house and after a minute or two came out with that fruit jar. Standing there by the door, she made a show of reaching in and coming up with bills in her hand and stuffing them into the big pocket on the side of her dress. I would have bet they were one-dollar bills (though some of them were not) and also that they were all she had in the world. She said, "I want you to take us in to that fun'al house."

"Right now?" I pointlessly asked.

She didn't answer. To the little girl she said, "You go down there and play with Sim. I'll be back tirectly. Now, git going," and headed straight for my car.

Well, I thought, maybe the funeral man took charity cases.

But she didn't get in. Instead, as soon as she opened the door and leaned forward, she abruptly stepped back. "Pfeuw," she said. "Sho' does stink, don't he?"

"He was already doing that before he got dead," I remarked.

"Well, can't take him in there this-a-way. Goan have to give him a washing."

"A washing?"

"Drive him on around back," she said, and set off ahead of me.

Oh My God! I thought, and stood there considering whether or not to pull him out of the car and drive away. But I couldn't do that. I got in with stinking Harmless and drove around to where she was waiting beside a huge iron pot just beyond an open gate. As soon as I stopped, she came back through, saying "I'll git some soap," and while I sat there cursing myself for a damn fool hauling all over the country a dead drunk bum better left out on the highway, she went in the house and quickly returned with a big cake of brown soap. "Let's git him out," she said.

We did, with me holding him under his arms (and no free hand to hold my nose) and she by his forked legs, one on each side of her. We carried him through the gate and laid him down beside the pot. It was nearly full of water. It was for the two cows I saw in the field a little way off, and which, evidently attracted by the spectacle, were approaching for a look. So, I noticed, were some chickens. She said, "Git them sorry clothes off him."

We proceeded, I zombie-like. It wasn't much of a job. There were only the shirt and overalls, no underwear, one shoe, and no sock on either foot. "Awright now, let's dunk him." We lifted him up and let him down in the water without splashing. There was not quite enough to float him. "Hold his top end up," she said, and I did, and watched her set to soaping him good . . . hair and face and all of him down to his middle. Then the other end, every inch of it, grunting a little as she worked. At one point I felt, barely flinching, the hot breath of a cow on the back of my neck. "Now roll him over," she said, which we did and kept rolling till all the soap was gone and nothing was to be seen but flesh about the color of a fish's belly. She stood up and looked down at his clothes lying in a heap. "They ain't fitting for nothing." She studied for a second. "May be I still got some clothes my poor dead husband left." An instant and she was gone, leaving me alone among chickens and cows to swap gazes with Harmless's , or Jimmy's, wet blank eyes. I took time out to kick a red chicken clear over the fence, and to nearly throw my leg out of joint by kicking at another one.

She came back with clothes, and we lifted him out. I held him partly upright while she dried him off good with a grain bag. The clothes didn't fit, but it didn't matter. "Long as they's clean," she said. Which put me in mind of my own appearance, so that once we got him back in the car, I got a clean shirt out of my bag and put it on. She didn't seem to mind about her own dress being wet.

We drove in silence, with Jimmy bent and balanced against the door, and she in the little back seat, where, though but dimly reflected in my rearview mirror, I could see how her face was set with determination. The only time she spoke, a couple of minutes after we had passed the town limit where now small houses lined the street, was to give me instructions.

We turned off into a street with only scattered houses, though the one she directed me to was isolated more by its tall enclosing hedges than by its distance from neighboring ones. There was no hedge in front, however, and the large sign reading *Mortuary of Eternal Rest: L. J. Hibbs, Director* was clear to see. The well-groomed front yard was small, but the building, surely a converted residence, was of considerable size. There were two stories and, halfway up the front, supported by twin wooden columns, a roof that in the past must have sheltered a now-missing porch. The flawless paint job, a soft pearl gray, did a lot to conceal (as I soon learned) what the sides and back of the house clearly revealed: that it was an old, old building.

I turned in the driveway, and noticing the narrow space like a tunnel between house and hedge, I moved on to take advantage of the concealment offered. After all, how many people showed up at a funeral home with the corpse in hand. Helping the lady squeeze out of the car, I had another thought: I didn't even know her name. She answered my question in a faint, shaky voice. "It's Bell Loomis." Then, looking at me with her bleary eyes wide open, she said, "We goan carry Jimmy in?"

"Naw. They'll come get him." I didn't add "I hope so," or that I hoped to God some kind of a charitable arrangement could be negotiated. Or, again, considering her now obvious state of mind, that maybe we ought to just call it off and bury Jimmy in some good old country way. The money, I thought. I said, "Look. You can tell from here it's going to cost an awful lot of money. Hundreds of dollars, maybe more."

For my purpose this was the wrong thing. She straightened up and gave me a look that meant she didn't know nor care nothing about no hundreds of dollars. She said, "I got money. I got this-here whole pocket full, like I showed you."

"All right," I said, and falling back on the only hope I had, I took her arm and guided her around to the front door.

The button I pushed instantly produced the sound of a bell tinkling. A brief delay, while Mrs. Loomis stared at the well-polished door as if she expected it to do something peculiar, and we stood in the very sympathetic presence of Director L. J. Hibbs. Or so it appeared, even before his soothing voice offered conclusive evidence of his sympathy. "Welcome," he said, reminding me of Bela Lugosi in his role as Dracula. "I suppose you are here about a Loved One."

A glance at the lady told me she wasn't sure what he meant. I murmured yes, and he stepped back. "Please come in."

He didn't look anything like Lugosi. He was a tall man, but he appeared less so by the fact that he stood with his head thrust forward in an attitude of humble interest in our bereavement. His unusually wide mouth was vaguely upturned at the corners, suggesting a gentle smile that never quite materialized. He had on a black bow tie with an immaculate white shirt, of which the sleeves, a little too short, exposed his wrists and pale, long-fingered hands that he held serenely folded just above his gold belt buckle.

But once we both had got inside and stood facing him in the little entryway, his demeanor underwent a change. It was most evident in the way his hands had come unfolded and now hung rather stiffly at his sides. I guessed the reason. Before this, he had not got a good straight-on look at Mrs. Loomis. But now he had done so, and as a result had lapsed into this uncomfortable silence. It lasted only seconds, till his gaze, gone a little frosty, came back to me. In a strictly business voice he repeated, "You are here about a Loved one, I suppose?"

"Yes," I said, a little stumped as to what should come next. As for Mrs. Loomis, I noticed that already her attention was not with us. Just on our right was a wide doorway to a spacious room where gentle indirect light fell on radiant white walls and holy pictures and plush purple carpet and a golden stand with candles (unlit) . . . and, commandingly at the center of it all, a coffin that looked to be made of copper or bronze or something. The coffin was inhabited. Part of a face in profile, mainly the big hooked nose, and a crest of up-swelling torso farther down, were clearly visible. Somehow visible because, judging by the depth of the coffin, the Loved One should have been entirely out of sight. Jacked up somehow? It was curious.

Anyway, Mrs. Loomis was obviously smitten by the sight. Even as I noticed, she was under way and didn't stop until she was standing by the coffin with her hands on the rim, staring at the dead man as at a miracle. "Lor . . ." she said.

Director Hibbs's perturbation was obvious, and when he saw her reach out and touch the Loved One's nose, he was at her in a flash. "Madame," he blurted, "please don't!"

"Feel just like a sho-nough live nose."

Hibbs took her arm, not politely, and moved her back out of reach of the coffin. "Don't touch anything, please."

"Sho' is red in the face, ain't he? Bet he drunk a lot of whiskey. My poor Jimmy used to look that-a-way."

An obviously disgusted Director Hibbs said, "Madame, that is Mr. Edward Hamilton. Among the most distinguished gentlemen in this community."

"All the same," she said, and shifted gears. "Anyhow, that's just how I want my Jimmy to look. All embomed. In a gold box like this'n, too."

Hibbs drew an obviously deep breath. "May I ask, not meaning to offend, whether you are able to pay a very high price?"

"Don't worry, I got a-plenty."

Losing patience, Hibbs said, "How much money have you got?"

Put that way, the question did offend her. "All right, Mr. Smart." With a small show of hauteur, she said, "I got seventy-three dollars. Right here in my pocket." She touched the pocket. "I'll let you count it."

The Adventures of Douglas Bragg

Hibbs looked up at the softly lighted ceiling. "And how much insurance do you have?"

"How much *what?*"

Hibbs didn't bother to explain. "Madame," he said to the ceiling, "this *box*, as you call it, quite alone, not to mention other necessary services, sells for twelve hundred and seventy-six dollars. The sum you have would barely pay for the handles on it."

The poor woman looked as if it was only his high-flying language that had her stumped.

Hibbs, in the same voice but more slowly, repeated the figure.

It was different with her this time, reflected in the turn of her head so that, with her mouth slightly open, she was looking sideways up at his face. A moment passed. She said, "It ain't no such a thing. You ain't telling me a true thing."

"I assure you, Madame, that I am telling you a true thing."

I was standing only a few steps away, and she turned to me seeking assurance. I could only nod and gently say, "I'm afraid it's true. I told you."

Her gaze fell away. She looked down, looked back at the coffin, and at last let her eyes go slowly wandering all around the room. Like nothing that could exist in the world, was what I imagined her thinking. I quietly said to her, "Why don't you go outside a few minutes and let me talk to Mr. Hibbs." She looked at me and did so and closed the front door behind her.

I looked at Hibbs, but he spoke first. "Is that ignorant woman kin of yours or something?"

"No," I said and, giving just enough facts to make do, added, "I felt sorry for her. I was hoping you took charity cases sometimes and maybe gave them some kind of a little funeral for not much money."

He drew a weary breath. "What I could get for her case would not nearly pay for my least expensive casket . . . not to mention necessary services. I have to make a living. It's not easy in this little town. Especially," he added with a show of disdain, "because many send their loved ones up to Bentonville." He drew another long breath. "Moreover I am shorthanded at the moment. I dismissed two helpers, my whole team but one, only day before yesterday . . . for lack of seriousness." I noticed the little flare of his nostrils.

He paused, and I could tell that something had clicked in his mind. He was looking me up and down. He said, "What do you do, Mr. . . . ?"

"Bragg," I said. "At the moment, not anything."

After another pause, "Are you, by chance, an educated man?"

I was pleased to say, modestly, "I graduated from college."

"And you are just out wandering, I take it. Looking for something. Anything that might suit you. Right?"

"About right."

He cupped his chin and stroked it for a space. "Possibly we could make a deal. You work for me in exchange for this woman's funeral. A very modest funeral, of course. Naturally you would have nothing to do with the basic work, I have a professional for that. You would be free to leave, assuming you wished to, as soon as your work has paid the full cost of the funeral. At which time you would receive a certain bonus. . . . What do you think?"

At first I thought "Hell no," envisioning a stretch of days in this lugubrious atmosphere, with dead bodies lying around and unimaginable business going on somewhere close by in this building. But I thought again. I thought about poor old Mrs. Loomis, and also about how it's said that sacrifice is good for the soul. In any case, as things stood, I was practically out of money. But just as I was about to start bargaining with him, he interrupted with another condition, a seeming afterthought, that took me aback. He said, "Of course there must be a small down payment. For security."

"Yeah?" I finally said.

"I think a hundred dollars might be enough."

"She hasn't got a hundred dollars."

"I know," he said. "But since you are so anxious to help her, I thought you might be willing to chip in. Do you have that much?"

Cheapskate. But I sensed that something more was going on, something I wouldn't figure out till later. It was aimed at discovering whether I had money enough in hand to walk out on him before I had paid my dues in full. If anything but foolproof, it was still a sort of trap, the best he could manage offhand. At the time, though, I assumed that his motive was only greed of the regular kind that can't resist a moment of opportunity, and not necessarily the kind to really look out for. Anyway, there was poor, poverty-wrapped Mrs. Loomis and, on my part, the certainty that I could take care of myself. So, to his question I said, with a measure of defiance, "No, but I can pay some of it."

The Adventures of Douglas Bragg

This was enough. "Agreed, then. And, who knows? You might just find here what you are looking for . . . a profession." There was a small though curious narrowing of his eyes as he said this, but I was otherwise engaged and didn't think much about it. After dickering for a minute or two, I accepted a salary (suspended of course for the interlude) that was reasonable enough considering that a private room upstairs was included.

I had anticipated, and was amused to see, the expression of astonishment on Hibbs's face when I told him we had her Loved One out there in my car. In fact there probably was disappointment, too, in that he was accustomed (as I soon learned) to an added charge for fetching bodies. But he quickly recovered and, in a quiet but still commanding voice, told me to drive around to the rear of the building, where Mr. Fischer would tend to the matter.

I did so and, in the hedge-enclosed back yard, stopped between the house door and a shed where there was a pile of lumber and a few tools scattered around, and parked in back of that, a large cream-colored hearse. A couple of minutes later, Mr. Fischer, a rather pallid and completely bald man in late middle age, appeared with a rolling stretcher. He never said one word, unless you could count his muttering as he hoisted Jimmy, who had stiffened somewhat by now, out of the back seat. Mrs. Loomis, still wearing a look of satisfaction, tried to help, but he, without seeming to notice, elbowed her aside. He had his burden loaded and through the doorway before we could even think to ask a question. Half an hour after that, I left a gratified Mrs. Loomis at her own doorway, loudly anticipating the burial day to come.

— — —

So here I was, employed not by a grocery store or gas station manager, but by an undertaker who was not even an undertaker but, by protocol, a 'mortician' or 'director.' It was that way here with every funeral term in common usage. Dead was 'departed' or 'deceased'; a body was a 'loved one' or 'Mister' or 'Mrs.'; a hearse was a 'coach'; flowers were 'floral tributes,' and on and on. And right away, in the process of being instructed in this matter, I got off to what seemed a bad start with Hibbs. We were standing in the Slumber Room near the coffin of Mr. Edward Hamilton when I demonstrated my insensitivity by a wisecrack at the expense of poor dead Jimmy, referring to him as "the drunk one."

The Adventures of Douglas Bragg

— — —

Hibbs fixed me with a look of what at least appeared to be real indignation. "We don't joke about the 'departed' here. Even when no visitors are present." The look in his sharp greenish eyes continued for a space, a reevaluating look. My nod of humble contrition, however, didn't stop me from imagining just such an expression on the beaked face of Mr. Edward Hamilton. Anyway, after that I kept my tongue in check.

His composure restored, Director Hibbs returned us to the business at hand. It was necessary that I be made aware, and appreciative, of all the refinements contributing to the 'feel' of this Slumber Room. The immaculate white walls, the floor-length rose-colored drapes, the deep-piled purple carpet, the rich gold candle stand. And there was the soft ethereal music (reserved for visitation hours). And most of all, perhaps, the lighting, the gentle twilight glow that wakens memory. 'Otherworldly' was the word. I thought how contented Mr. Hamilton must be, lying there in his comfortable coffin.

At rear of the Slumber Room was a little chapel, the doorway crowned with a Gothic arch. "Chapel of Peace," the small sign read. The large window at one end was of rose-tinted glass, and under it, facing half a dozen rows of folding chairs, a stand with an open Bible on it. Pictures again, holy ones.

We passed back through the Slumber Room and across to a parlor nicely fitted out with a sofa, three or four plush chairs, and a small bookcase containing books with titles like *Peace of Soul*. Then on through a door in the rear wall that opened into the Selection Room. We were just at the point of entering when the tinkling sound announced a presence at the front door.

By coincidence, as by something scripted, the presence was a bereaved couple, a Mr. and Mrs. Dozier, uncomfortably here for the express purpose of choosing a coffin. Or 'casket' as Hibbs insisted. So, as he covertly let me understand, here was a lucky chance to advance my education.

It did that, all right. By the time he had got to the end of his extended sales pitch, I was much more than a little impressed. I had come to see, for instance, that the arrangement of the coffins, a dozen of them set distinctly apart in groups of three (and not according to cost) was itself a part of his strategy. The whole was clearly a work of art, perfected no doubt by years of dubious refinement. The very tone of his voice, his air of consideration as he guided the bereaved from coffin to coffin, all but compelled confidence. Resting a hand on one especially rich in surface texture he said, as no doubt he always said, "This splendid one, of everlasting copper, at a bit over twenty-three hundred and fifty dollars, is absolute top of the line. Needless to say, only a few families are prepared to go this high. It is for you, of course, to decide whether you are one of these.

In answer, both Doziers nodded as if in sympathy for those not prepared to go this high.

Moving on to another group, Hibbs, his fingers just grazing the coffin designated, announced with a hint of boredom that this one, at less than $1,150, was at the bottom of the line. Then on to another group, where the coffin indicated was, at $769 more than the previous one, in the popular range. But still another in the same group, almost identical except for silver instead of gold handles, was only $670 more, a saving of $99. So it went on. At the end, when humbly asked for a little clarification, Hibbs proceeded without impatience to more or less retrace his steps through the thicket. No help to the Doziers, who finally, by devious suggestion, were reminded that the casket's worth was not only a reflection of how deeply the family valued the Loved One, but also of their standing in society.

I don't know exactly how much the Doziers ended up spending for their coffin, but I would bet it was a good deal more than they had counted on. Nevertheless, they left there looking satisfied, if maybe a little uncertainly so, just as I expect most of Hibbs's customers did. I had witnessed a masterfully slick piece of work. It was hard not to admire it.

Besides this, later that same afternoon I was also privileged to observe the perfection of his technique with the families and friends of the 'departed.' There were official visiting hours from five till seven o'clock for Mr. Hamilton, and Hibbs had firmly advised me to follow him around and listen. I didn't have any good clothes, but he did, in plenty (maybe from the families of corpses), and he had me dressed up almost like a true gentleman host. I surmised that he was already hoping to keep me on as a regular . . . mainly, I thought, because I was a college man and should be quick to learn. In any case, I stayed in his tracks and listened for pretty much the whole two hours.

In the entryway he welcomed the visitors with a humble stoop of his head and a perfectly convincing expression of heartfelt sympathy. "So glad you were able to come. Mr. Hamilton has so many dear friends and admirers." If Hibbs didn't know the visitors' names, which was usually the case, he would say, managing to appear as if the name was right on the tip of his tongue, "And you are Mr. and Mrs. . . . ?" To their reply he would nod and murmur, "Of course," and proceed to usher them into the Slumber Room.

Most of the visitors stood gathered in little groups about the room, with frequent migrations from group to group as conversation attracted them. But practically always, as I noticed in the following days, there would be at least a few standing around the coffin to gaze upon the deceased lying there in eternal repose. These, with me in tow, Hibbs would approach and stand among them, secretly reveling in compliments paid to his handiwork. (In fact the handiwork was Fischer's.) Some such as "He looks like he's not dead at all," a viewer would remark. "Like he might wake up any minute." Which would inspire Hibbs to modestly say, "That's the effect we strive to produce. Except that 'produce' is not the word. We try to call up the man himself, just as he appeared in life, in all his dignity." Swelling a little now, he would go on to say, "You can imagine the benefits for his dear ones. It is grief-therapy. Seeing him like this, they form a picture-memory that will stay with them all their days." But sometimes there would be a callous rascal in the group who would respond with something like, "Good job, anyhow," rather shattering the established mood. Hibbs would give the man a huffy look and shortly thereafter abruptly turn away.

Each day, after further murmured instructions, I would be introduced around as a *young associate* (it seemed that things were moving awfully fast) and set to mingle. Talk about Mr. Hamilton or whoever, with praise for his or her life and works, was a popular topic, and I was expected to pitch in. Other than what I had so far heard said about the deceased, there wasn't much I could do but put on a little show of having heard these same wonderful things in other places. Being a pretty good actor, I was, as it seemed to me, quite convincing enough to make an impression. In fact I would even get a little emotional and just barely stop myself before I went too far. In any case I was a success with Hibbs, who on several occasions discreetly sent me definite nods of approval. He may have been thinking that I could become just like him. No danger, surely, I thought.

But the Deceased was not everywhere and always the topic of conversation. Especially as the number of mourners increased, there would come to be, at least among some groups, conversation of a definitely profane sort. I heard at least one group, exclusively male, discussing baseball, and several, though with voices a little hushed, telling jokes. That they were indeed telling jokes was made pretty clear by unacceptable outbursts of laughter. Immediately I would look about for Hibbs and the obligatory expression of outrage on his face. He would be halfway there before the jolly group saw him coming and hurriedly scattered away.

It was on one of these occasions, and I think my third day on the job, that something happened inside my head. I don't really know why, but all of a sudden I was seeing Hibbs's demeanor in a different light. Now it seemed like something, a behavior, not truly belonging to him, but instead a mere role that I described to myself as 'essence of undertaker,' leaving him with practically nothing of his former self . . . a caricature, in fact. Which amounted, then, didn't it, to what the word 'phony' well described? But thinking again, more generously this time, the cause could just as well be ambition, the simple determination to be perfect in his job and the inborn skill of an actor to achieve it. After all, as the saying went, "Practice makes perfect." So it was only fair to assume that this was the case with Hibbs, and that I was in the hands of a flawless model for the true mortician. If the ethos of his world occasionally clashed with that of other worlds, so it was all around. I might have settled for this view completely if it had not been that the word 'phony' (and sometimes a word still harsher) had got stuck in the back of my mind.

— — —

I was kept fairly busy through those days, but not busy enough to counter my growing impatience . . . an impatience that surely was no match for that of Jimmy's aunt. As for the deceased himself, he was, as Hibbs assured me, resting comfortably in the cooler downstairs, waiting his turn. I had not yet gone down there; just the thought gave me the creeps. Once, in an off-hour, I drove out to reassure Mrs. Loomis. At other times I took little walks around town or went for a meal at a little restaurant two blocks away, where I usually got the once-over from other customers.

But the hour finally came. It was that of my descent into the lower regions, the 'Preparation Room,' where, as Hibbs a little deferentially suggested, I probably was needed by now. It was for Mr. James, he told me, and indicated the door at the rear of the Selection Room. The rather sweeping gesture of his hand instantly called back that fleeting moment when my first glimpse of him had put me in mind of Dracula. And more, the nugget of wisdom he now proceeded to bestow on my reluctant self seemed quite to fit in with that pattern: "It is all a part of life."

Even if it was, I didn't have any desire to experience it. I had seen plenty of animals gutted, with the blood and everything, but those were animals, and for all I knew they did the same thing with people. Standing there on the next to top basement step, I was amazed to think I had gone all these hours without giving this matter more than glancing thoughts. Even in much later days my memory of these moments still took hold of me sometimes. But now I drew a couple of shaky breaths and finally descended.

The light at the bottom of the steps came from the open door of a room where it seemed almost blinding. At the door was where I stopped, with my gaze riveted on a body (clothed, thank God) stretched out on a table, and a bald-headed man, Fischer, leaning over it. Around it all were shelves and shelves of bottles and jars and tins of something awful, and wickedly glittering metal instruments and, worst of all, bucket-sized containers that seemed to have no tops on them. And another thing: a sort of little pump, I thought. The voice, that sounded as if it had never been used much, came with a jolt inside my skull. "We are pretty near through, now," he had said.

We! And what was left to do?

"Come look at him," Fischer spectrally said, still without turning to look at me.

Half a dozen reluctant steps and, stopped beside him, I was looking down at Jimmy. Or was it Jimmy? I had seen him both alive and dead, and this 'departed one' didn't resemble either of my recollections. In fact he didn't resemble anybody I had ever seen. I thought he could have passed as a dressmaker's dummy with too much makeup on, and a smiling dummy at that. And a frayed red necktie, besides. A sudden gust of what I might call lugubrious merriment came on me and pretty well cleared my head.

Fischer's voice again. "I was hurried. Not my best work, I'm afraid."

I said, "Maybe if you could take that smile off him . . ."

After a pause, "Let's see," he said, and, reaching with thumb and first finger outspread, he slowly drew down the corners of the mouth.

The Adventures of Douglas Bragg

"Too much," I said. "He looks sour now."

Fischer made the adjustment, and we both stood there considering the result. Then a strange thing began to happen. With slow and eerie progress, the corners of Jimmy's mouth made their way up and finally into the smile again. Oh, well, I thought, maybe Mrs. Loomis would like to see him smiling. And the red tie, too.

"I can fix that," Fischer said. "But we'll go ahead and casket him." He also had the jargon.

It was out in the dark near the back door, on rollers. We pushed it in and lined it up next to Jimmy. Stiff as he was, it was trouble getting him in because, though the lid stood open, the aperture was only half the length of the coffin. And speaking of the coffin, it was nothing anybody could brag about: a plain old homemade wooden box, varnished, all right, and with a few strips of shiny metal tacked along the sides and over the top, but which didn't succeed in making it look like anything more than just what it was. We finally got him settled in, supine on what looked like a blanket trying to imitate a soft velvet cloth, and a plush pillow under his head. I left him lying comfortably there, still smiling, and climbed the steps giving thanks that this had been the extent of my initiation down here.

For some unaccountable reason I went straight to the little restaurant and quite without thinking ordered bacon and eggs which, after all, I had no taste for. I ate most of it anyway, mainly, I think, because the only customer besides me was a policeman drinking coffee, and who, to my discomfort, kept eyeing me from time to time. Why? No doubt it was just that I was a stranger in town.

My room upstairs was all right, with two chairs, a table, a small closet and a bed comfortable enough. But this night I couldn't go to sleep for a long time, and I lay there thinking about the funeral tomorrow, about my situation and how long I would be able to put up with it. Off and on, since I hadn't heard any sounds, I wondered if Hibbs was in one of the other rooms asleep. To amuse myself I imagined him in one of his coffins downstairs, no doubt the most expensive one. Or else wandering about in the night, routine for his kind.

My sleep was fitful, and twice I had to get up and go to the bathroom. It was at the back of the house, and the open window looked out on the dim, hedged-in backyard. On my second trip I heard voices down there and after that a car start up, but I couldn't see anything. Probably a

Loved One brought in, one that couldn't wait. I shook my head to expel an image of some poor mangled corpse.

Then it was burial day for Jimmy. Considering my part in the matter, I had expected to go along for the funeral. It was not to be. Hibbs was firm against my arguments. "There is cleaning to do. And new caskets to be polished. I need you here." So it was, though I couldn't see any real need for it. The only things I did that were at all necessary were to help to get a fat new Loved One into a coffin and, early in the afternoon, Jimmy into the hearse. Or 'coach,' as Hibbs insisted. I participated with a good measure of anger, thinking also that this delivery was a service I would be paying for . . . and probably overcharged.

Starting a couple of hours later, what happened, or began to happen, was a series of events I am not likely to ever forget. I was still in the basement polishing away on one of those damn coffins, when the hearse returned and stopped out back. The little driver, Eddy, a young red-haired guy whose face, in contrast to my recollection of it, was curiously pallid, got out and came in looking for Hibbs. His shaky voice also told me that something was wrong. The instant I pointed to the steps, he was on them and up in a hurry. Since Fischer wasn't present at the time, I quickly followed suit and stopped at the door he had left open. I could hear voices, but not many words, only here and there a phrase. "You did what?" And then another, the young guy's voice: "I had to. He . . ." I missed most of the rest of it, but there was something aside from what they were saying that puzzled me for a moment. I could tell which voice belonged to the young guy, but the other voice, which had to be Hibbs's, didn't sound like Hibbs at all. I supposed it was just because he was angry about whatever had happened. Anyway, I soon retreated back downstairs no wiser than before. Actually it was a matter made perfectly clear to me not much later on.

The whole story was this: there was something in that coffin besides Jimmy. It was drugs, down where his feet were, and it was scheduled to be delivered to a receiver at a specified point on the way to the graveyard. But Eddy, driving the hearse, got spooked and made a big mistake. The place of intended delivery was a short dead-end dirt road that at some little distance past the grocery store turned off the road leading to the graveyard. But it happened that a patrol car with a cop in it was parked beside the grocery. The driver of the hearse saw him and immediately panicked because it seemed to him that the turnoff place was within the cop's range of vision. He was afraid it would look funny if he turned around and drove back past the cop again, so, stupidly, he went on and delivered the coffin to Mrs. Loomis and company at the graveyard. After all, how likely were they to go poking around down in there where the body's feet were?

But Hibbs was a long way from satisfied. I didn't lay eyes on him for nearly an hour after the little driver left, and when I finally found myself in his presence again, he seemed to have quite cooled off. In his usual voice (with maybe a little slip or two) he had a convincing explanation for the boy's excitement. "A small accident," he said. "No damage to the coach, but some to the car it struck. The young man is very excitable. And too inexperienced, really, to be driving such a large vehicle. I should have known." Then he added, with a casualness that caught my attention, "He also mentioned that it didn't look as though they were ready for a funeral out there."

He was quiet for a little space, in which, as I could just discern, he was giving me a new kind of once-over. "There is something we need to do. I'm afraid Fischer did too hurried a job on the . . . the deceased. It simply won't do to keep him out of the ground any longer." A faint grimace, and he added, "I would not want to be responsible for the probable consequences."

I accepted this, though a little uncertainly.

"What I want you to do is go out there and be sure she understands. Let her know how ugly it would be to have on hand a Loved One who," he grimaced again, "both looks and smells bad. Think of the picture-memory she would be left with. . . . Do you understand?"

I did, sort of, and nodded. He stood waiting for my departure, and I set out.

J.T.'s car required some jiggling of the wires in the motor, but it soon started, and twenty minutes later, some few hundred yards this side of the Loomis estate, I arrived at the Ebenezer Bible Baptist Church. It was one of those small, frame church buildings, with a treeless graveyard out beside it, that you can see all over the rural South. There was a big yellow backhoe standing idle in the graveyard close by a ridge of red clay scooped out to make the grave. A few men were standing in front of the church, but I couldn't see a coffin anywhere. Inside the building, then. A bad sign, I thought, but maybe not. I got out of the car, under scrutiny from the men, all in clean long-sleeved cotton shirts and suspenders, standing around. Right off, though, their scrutiny gave way to cordial nods and murmurs of welcome. It seemed that I had already become, so to speak, famous. They directed me into the church where Mrs. Loomis was to be found . . . and of course, Jimmy in his coffin.

As soon as her eyes fell on me she came out with something like a shriek of delight. "Lor," she said, "I'm so glad you come." She rushed up to me and took my arm and turned me around two or three times for the ladies present to see, saying, "Looky-here. The one done it all and give Jimmy this fine fun'al, besides. The lord bless him." She called off the names of the half-dozen smiling ladies, now up from their folding chairs, the Bakers and Smiths and Millers in their Sunday-best dresses from the Sears catalogue, and made every one of them step up and shake my hand. When the uproar died down, I said, sort of like taking a risk, "When's the funeral going to start?" I had not seen anybody who looked like a preacher.

"Lor," she said, "I done put it off to tomorrow. Want everybody have chance to come see Jimmy one last time, looking so nice. Even looking kind of happy. And my sister and her husband coming all the way from Paris."

Paris? Then I remembered: Paris, Tennessee.

"You come look at him." Taking me by the arm again, she squired me the few steps up to where the open coffin stood crossways in front of the pulpit. I looked. There was Jimmy, still smiling.

"And that purty necktie they put on him. Don't he look nice?"

I thought that probably once upon a time he had looked nice. I quietly said, almost at a whisper, "I got to tell you something. The funeral man told me to. He said you've got to bury right away . . . because he probably won't keep till tomorrow."

She just looked at me.

"That's what he said. That his man hadn't done much of a job embalming him, so it wouldn't last but a little while. You know . . . what would happen. That you wouldn't want people to see." Suddenly I really felt like a liar.

She looked down at Jimmy, then back up at me. She reached into the coffin and with thumb and first finger lightly pinched Jimmy's nose. She looked at me again. "It's no such a thing. He don't feel no-ways different from that old hook-nosed man in the coffin the other day. Just look at him." She stood waiting for my response.

I finally and quietly said, with unexpected relief, "You're probably right."

She smiled, showing the gap in her upper teeth, and my mission at least in name was now completed. I would try, I told her, to come back for the funeral tomorrow, and amid kindly expressions of farewell, I went out and, hurriedly now, got in the car. But there was more to come.

I had just got turned around to drive away when I saw one of the smiling ladies come out of the church door and head for me with something, a box, in her hands. No, it was three boxes stacked on top of each other, which she held up to my open window, saying, still sweetly smiling, "Bell forgot all about these. She reckons they's something from the fun'ral home got in the coffin by accident. She just happened to go poking around down in there to see if Jimmy had shoes on."

"Did he?" I vacantly said.

"Sho' didn't. He was barefoot as the day he was borned."

I don't know what my face must have looked like. By now, recalling again what I had heard about drug doings in these parts, I was practically sure what it was in those boxes, and I felt like my face, eyes nose and mouth all screwed up together, was about to give me away. I braved it. I just succeeded in muttering an ungracious "Thank you," took in the boxes, and drove off.

For God's sake, what would I do now? But after a minute some thoughts broke through. One thing I certainly would not do was return the stuff to Hibbs . . . and so be complicit in his nasty and dangerous business. So, what? An idea came. I slowed the car, watching for a turnoff place in the woods to either side. I saw a path, a log road. With a glance to make sure all was clear behind me, I made the turn and drove a few hundred feet to where dense thicket concealed me. Now, to be double sure. The boxes were wrapped around with paper tape, and it took me several minutes to free and lift one corner of a box. Sure enough, little plastic bags, soft as if it were dust inside. No matter that it would take a while to scatter it bag by bag in the thicket and so be done with it all. But another, better thought crept up on me and put a smile on my face. The back seat of the car would lift up, I discovered, and that's where I put the boxes. I had, I hoped, all the details clear in my head before I got under way again.

The sun was just setting when I turned in the driveway and parked behind the hearse in back. Hibbs must have been intently watching for me out front, because he had managed to be there in the back doorway when I got out of the car. Sunset, I thought, and he just fresh from his coffin. He waited till I got inside and the door shut behind me. In the basement gloom, I thought again, and girded up my loins. Fixing me with eyes a little narrowed, he waited in silence for my report. Yes or no . . . did it matter? I decided to split the difference. "She wouldn't really say. She just said Maybe. I couldn't hardly push her."

A flicker of anger appeared in his face. "Why didn't you stay to find out?"

He had caught me a little off balance, but I bravely said, "I didn't see any use in it. I had told her just what you said."

Deliberately he looked away and stood there as if he were hearing something. When he looked back it was with a different expression, a long, reading look. I didn't believe I would like what he was thinking. At the same time I was half-conscious of no longer being in the presence of anything resembling a model mortician. .

But a sudden change came about. "Well," he said in a voice approaching the friendly. "She will do what she will do. I suppose you did your best." Then, "Let's go upstairs."

I couldn't tell what was in store. As it was, there seemed to be nothing in particular, because he went upstairs to his room and didn't come down in the interval while I waited, expecting something. But this did give me occasion to enter the Slumber Room for a glance at the presiding Loved One. He was there, of course, big belly and all, comfortably resting. My heart gave an extra beat or two.

When, after a few more minutes, Hibbs still hadn't come down, I decided it would not be unexpected if he found me gone out for supper. At the little restaurant I saw my cop again. He was on the way out, but he gave me another look in passing, and this started me thinking about what I would do for a grand finale. But first things first.

Luck was on my side, maybe. Approaching the house I saw that Hibbs's car, which had been parked out front, was gone. Where? If my guess was right, troubled as he clearly was, he had gone out there to the church to see for himself. There would be, as old country custom required, watchers in the church all night, but it needn't matter. Secretly parked somewhere at a little distance, he could approach in the dark and get close enough to see if the grave was still open. So now that he was away, rather than up in the night, this was surely the time to do it. A risk, however, of getting caught red-handed in the act. I went inside and, pacing about waited for a while. I decided to risk it.

Out in the dark I took the boxes from under the car seat and hurried back in and up to the Slumber Room. After another listening pause, I proceeded. It turned out to be a good bit of a procedure. This Loved One's great belly all but filled the cavity at midpoint, and working the boxes through and down was at considerable expense to his repose. I had to rearrange him afterwards, being careful to get his head almost straight on the pillow and his clothes back in order.

But it was sometime yet, a trying time, before a flash of light across the front windows signaled a car turning in. For a moment I stood there undecided. Then I headed for the stairs and up to my room and left the door wide open. What should my posture be? I switched on the light and sat down on the bed and waited. Then I heard him, his feet uncommonly heavy on the steps.

He was standing in my doorway, no friendly gaze fixed on me. In a level voice he said, "Where are they?"

A blank expression was all I could manage.

"The boxes. She gave them to you."

I have been in other situations where I was compelled to do some fast thinking, but never one to match this. Clearly this man whose narrow glare held me, as it were, pinned to the wall, was so far out of his assumed role as to make it nearly impossible to believe. That he had on an unlikely, well-fitted sport coat would have been no great matter if it hadn't been that his face had that expression of practically murderous intensity. Even his right hand, that he held in a tight fist, was positioned as if readied to deliver a blow.

But this, as I now discerned, was not all: he was not alone. There was somebody standing behind him, a man much bigger than himself, who chose this moment to step into the light. He was somebody I would not want to encounter on a deserted street at night. That he didn't say anything I attributed to the likelihood that he was unable to master human speech. It was Hibbs who finally said, "Where are the boxes ?"

All of a sudden it was like I was participating in one those blood-curdling TV dramas, or a Mickey Spillane novel where the bad guys would as soon as not either shoot you or beat you to death. In that same moment I just missed saying, "In the coffin down there," but something, a thought, held me back. What would it get me if I did? No expression of gratitude, I am sure. After all, I was a mere wandering waif, and this was actual gangster stuff. Imagining what Mike Hammer would have done, and imagining possibilities in the thought, I haltingly said, "I hid them out in the woods." I will always admire my readiness here. Maybe in the deep woods in the dark I could make a break for it.

"Where in the woods?"

Faintly, "Out not far from the church. Up a log road."

"Still intact . . . in the boxes?"

I nodded yes."

Hibbs paused for a second. Still glaring at me, he said, "If you are lying . . . Mr. Nails here can be a very unpleasant companion."

I nodded again, in agreement.

"Get up. You are going to take us there."

I stood up, slowly.

Because of the way my mind was racing, it seemed that mere seconds had passed before I found myself standing there in the dark beside Hibbs's car, with a heavy hand on my arm. "Who you want to drive?" Nails said in a voice like a growl.

Hibbs, speaking to me, said, "How far along this log road, where you hid it?"

My mind was suddenly clearer. I jumped at the chance. "Pretty far. I wanted to get where the woods were thick."

"Still a road, though?"

"Yeah. Like a road."

Hibbs paused for a second. "All right, you drive. And don't you even think about trying anything smart. Because Mr. Nails is not always a gentleman and he's going to be sitting there right tight up against you. Now let's go."

Nails went around and got in the passenger seat, and Hibbs firmly ushered me in under the steering wheel, uncomfortably close to the hulk beside me. Hibbs got in the back seat, and I, on orders, cranked the car.

Starting here, with desperation already gathering around me, my memory of the following events is not so much cloudy as simply disjointed. I turned onto the main street and headed out with a single static thought in my mind, the thought that I must do "something." Hadn't I had some thought before this, one that escaped me now? Throw myself out of the moving car? That the bastard's heavy arm rested where it did, across behind my neck, signaled that this was impossible. Once the voice behind me said, "A little faster," and after that, or maybe before, in a threatening tone, "Stay in the lane!" Hopeless. Somebody, come to my aid! The scattered houses along the road gave place to empty fields.

Suddenly, Hibbs's voice again, "Slow down. Pass him slowly."

The reason was clear. It came at me like something flung directly into my eyes: a patrol car with red lights blinking, parked behind a pick-up truck with a cop standing at the cab window. Cry out? This, thank God, was not what I did. As I have often allowed myself to imagine, the decision that came to save my neck was not so much my own as that of some intervention from outside. Anyway, it was my hands on the steering wheel that swerved the car and sent it with a grinding noise smack across the front corner of the patrol car. Stopped dead on the road shoulder, I again had reason to give thanks, because the cop arrived maybe just in time to literally save my neck . . . from Nails, who already had both hands on it.

The cop yanked my door open. "Get the hell out!"

Again, this time to make double sure of my salvation, I was inspired to say, "Fuck you."

His hand with his long arm squarely behind it glanced off my chin and grabbing my shirt front yanked me violently out of the car. "We'll see who gets fucked." Holding me upright with both hands, he said, "You drunk, boy?"

There was a moment, before the gust of rage came on me, when I almost could have congratulated Hibbs for his footwork. What he had said was, "The boy must be on drugs. I hired him to . . ."

"Drugs, hell," I raged. "He's the one, the drug dealer . . . him and his goon, there. He's trying to . . ."

"Shut up," the cop said, and gave me a hard shake or two.

It didn't stop me. "There's drugs in that coffin right now, the one on display. You can . . ." The stab of pain from his fist just under my rib cage stopped my voice but not the sudden realization that I had made a mistake, a big one, maybe.

A brief pause, and Hibbs went on, "I didn't suspect. I hired him to drive us to Bentonville, because I don't drive at night. And my friend has no license. I am L. J. Hibbs, director of the mortuary."

Cool, by God, was not enough of a word for it. But I hadn't got my mouth open good before the cop slammed me against the side of the car. "One more word out of you, you little fart . . ." He put cuffs on me

The Adventures of Douglas Bragg

in a way that hurt and walked me around for a look at the other side of Hibbs's car. Then, "Okay, Mr. Hibbs. You got a front wheel locked up tight. You all wait here. I'll send somebody to take you home. Come down to the station in the morning."

It was a mistake, a hell of a one.

Without another word the cop turned me sharply around toward his car and opened the back door and gave me a hefty push inside. His car didn't have but one headlight now and made a scraping sound as we drove off, but it wasn't put out of commission like Hibbs's was. I thought maybe I had reason to be glad of this, at least.

— — —

Under threat of getting my teeth knocked out, I kept my mouth shut all the way to the station. I wasn't able to make any impression on the cop who processed me and locked me up in a cell. Later, grinding my teeth all the while, I vainly tried again with the cop who replaced that one.

It wasn't till morning, after my grueling night on that hard little cot, that the sheriff himself appeared, and I tried once more. At first he didn't seem to be listening. He just sat there rustling through papers at his table across the room from where I stood gripping the cell bars. But finally something I said made him look at me. It was a beginning. "Look," I said. "If you find him still there or anywhere in this town, I'll eat one of these bars for you. If your guys had listened to me last night they'd have found the stuff right where I told them it was . . . in that coffin. It'll be gone now, though, along with Hibbs and his gorilla." I regretfully added, "Because I shot my mouth off."

I had rung a bell somewhere. The sheriff, his long, weather-beaten face turned squarely on me now, was listening with real interest. I added on, brought in Mrs. Loomis and Harmless James and Fischer and the young guy Eddy who had driven the hearse out there to the church. I still hadn't finished when the sheriff put his hands on his chair arms and stood up. "Booker," he said, and right away another officer appeared in the doorway to an adjacent room. "We need to go check on something. And bring this here boy along."

The result was just as I had predicted. There was no answer at the front door, and the other officer had to pick the lock. The clearest single evidence of flight hit us squarely in the face as soon as we stepped into the Slumber Room. It was the fat Loved One, sitting half upright in his coffin, his head at an awkward angle that, if his eyes had been open, would have put us directly in his line of vision. It was because of his belly, I supposed, that they had found it too difficult to get him back into his proper position, and so, in their haste, had decided to leave well enough alone. No repose for him, poor fellow.

There were other signs of flight, such as disarray in Hibbs's room upstairs, but clearest of all was the absence of the hearse. Without his car (mine being unthinkable), Hibbs had had no other choice. The hearse was later found some fifty miles down the road, but there was no sign of the desperate duo.

To the very considerable vexation of my arresting officer, I was soon released, with the sheriff's not unfriendly suggestion that I get on my way out. I nodded my thanks to him.

I **DIDN'T WASTE MUCH TIME** getting out of Boulder Creek. It was a place I didn't expect ever to see again, and I was even entertaining the thought that I might just as well go on back home. For sure the likelihood that I could see the inside of the Boulder Creek jail again was the farthest thing from my mind. Yet, in late afternoon of the next day, there I was, looking out through those same bars just as if nothing in the last day and a half had happened.

What had happened was that at a point about twenty miles out of town, my trusty little car had once again betrayed me. This time my trick to start the motor refused to work. So my only recourse was, with a goodbye kick on a front fender, to start walking. Throughout the rest of the afternoon my upraised thumb got me nowhere, and I spent a cold and miserable night, amid arms-full of moldy hay I gathered around me, in an old half-collapsed barn. It was up in the afternoon next day before I got a ride, a compulsory one in a patrol car sent especially to hunt me down.

I was soon to find out why, and this from inside the same cage they had had me in before. They had searched my room at the mortuary, carefully this time, and found some of the stuff neatly tucked away inside the mattress of my bed upstairs. I was told that it was young Eddy, the hearse driver, who had squealed on me and would swear in court that he had overheard me talking with Hibbs about the plan they had in mind. This and other lies, including that he had actually seen me in the act of pocketing several of those little bags that I had got from Hibbs. Of course I wanted to know why poor Eddy wasn't here in the cage with me, but this was soon made clear. For one thing, he was out on bail, paid for by a responsible family member of this town. For another, he was very young, only seventeen, with a clean record, and, once he had discovered he was working for dangerous criminals, he was too afraid to speak out, poor kid. Which was surely baloney, but apparently swallowed by the local cops.

Anyway, here I was, duly charged, not young enough not to know better, and with nobody to bail me out. But as to a record, there was nothing they could find out about me, and when questioned about a home and family, I thought it just as well for now to represent myself as a homeless orphan. Besides, as I stoutly believed at first, I did have a real ace in the hole. Why, I asked them, if I had been one of the gang, myself, would I have acted as I did by deliberately bashing the patrol car? But this stumped them for only a little while. In part by wavering confirmation from poor little Eddy, they seemed to conclude that it was the old double-cross, inspired by gang rivalry. 'Seemed' is the right word, because when the time came for a decision about my fate, this was the very matter that caused them to stumble. The result would be good luck for me . . . if you could call it that.

After a couple of hours I was moved to Bentonville, the county seat and a larger town, where I spent the night in a cage identical with the former one. Here, in the morning, I endured some more questioning and then, for a nervous interlude, was left alone. But relief, if qualified, finally came. I was to learn that in cases of uncertainty, there was a legal alternative to a court trial. 'Pretrial Diversion' I think it was called. Anyway, somewhat later, I found myself seated, in a posture of humility, across a desk from a solemn old judge appropriately named Cooper. Here I received, in the course of an extended lecture on honor and morality in general, my sentence. "Six months," he said, his fingers caressing the wattles under his chin. "But that don't mean the jailhouse. . . . 'Long as you behave yourself. I'm putting you under Ezra Carnes. He's a preacher and upright a man as walks on God's earth. Just don't be a fool and buck up against him. Jailhouse be waiting for you."

Wearing my best sincere expression, I promised.

The Adventures of Douglas Bragg

It was quick work. In the evening I was transported a short way out of town to the home of Reverend Carnes. It was a fairly small frame house, fresh-painted white, that sat next to a thicket on one side and three or four acres of pasture behind and on the opposite side. A little farm, with a milk cow and a couple of hogs out there, and a chicken house and yard in back of the dwelling house. The hogs especially made me uneasy. And so did Reverend Carnes, on first meeting.

I don't know exactly what I had expected, but the Reverend was not it. I had not imagined 'upright' to mean 'in body,' but it did, physically as well as morally. He was a large man, not fat, with square shoulders and a neck that rose as stiffly straight-up as if it had been stretched. He also had a disturbingly loud high-pitched voice (from much preaching I guessed) that put me a little off-balance. It expressed geniality, though, saying, "Son, I'm glad to see you. You welcome here in Christ Jesus."

I had had just enough religion in my life to know pretty well who Christ Jesus was, but the way he put it, like the title of something, made it sound like this place was more than just a little farmhouse. I even glanced at it for reassurance before I murmured, "Thank you," and followed him up the steps and in.

He sat me down in the small living room, where there were more pictures of Jesus and other holy-looking people on the walls than there were places to sit . . . and the places to sit were all, except for one cane rocker, stiff-back chairs that looked hugely uncomfortable. The cane rocker looked so out of place, so trifling, that I wondered what it was doing there. For the likes of me, maybe? So, when he told me to have a seat, I chose one of the other chairs. I don't think I just imagined an expression of approval in his rather dour face.

This settled, he moved to summon his wife. Or rather, though I shouldn't quite say "yelled," did so far lift his voice that it made me jump. Evidently it made her jump, too, because in a matter of seconds she was standing there in the doorway, small compared to him, with graying hair and a sweetness of expression that was not without a hint of harassment. I was quickly on my feet. "Yes, dear," she meekly said.

"Here's my beautiful wife and comforter, Miss Maggie," the Reverend said. "She used to be Margaret, but I got her calling herself Maggie. See can't you figure why." He gave me time to answer, watching my face.

I finally said "Why?," but only with my lips.

With a look that said I ought to know, he answered, "Puts you in mind of Magdalene, don't it? Mary Magdalene. The woman Jesus loved so much."

The blasphemous words "How much?" crossed my mind, but I squelched them with an understanding nod.

The Reverend at least appeared to be satisfied, and after a mention of supper in the offing, they left me alone in the room.

That even now, all by myself, I chose again one of the stiff-back chairs to sit in (or "on," rather) was a measure of the need for wariness I felt. The way I already had the Reverend figured, it was sure to be tough going here . . . and that for six months. Six months! Better than the jailhouse, though, where I would at least be allowed act like myself? But maybe even longer than six months, and unknown miseries besides. Better to stick it out with the Reverend and Maggie Magdalene, I thought, and set about trying to comb up any religious items I might find buried back in my memory. There couldn't be many. I could remember going to church a few times and my grandfather occasionally quoting verses from the Bible. My mother rarely had anything to say about religion, and to my father the subject was nothing more than occasion for the exercise of his ready wit. I knew there was Matthew, Mark, Luke, and John, but I wasn't sure what they did. So I had a role to play, that of eager learner, and I had better be careful to stick to it. In fact I was soon put to the test.

At the small supper table, with good things like smoked ham spread out in front of me, my sudden burst of appetite almost caused me to forget about being wary. My hand was poised, if only tentatively, to reach out for the nearest dish, when I felt his gaze focused on me. It was not an approving gaze. "Son," he said, in a voice surely too loud for the occasion, "when the good Lord puts food on our table, it's the least a man can do to thank Him before he partakes." He made sure my hand was back in my lap before he shut his eyes and bowed his head. But even then, I thought, he sneaked a glance my way before he got started.

I well remembered the prayer that Roland's mother had afflicted me with, and I hoped to God that this one wouldn't turn out to be a match for it. For expansiveness it was not, but I didn't much like the way he kept referring to me as a boy who had sinned and needed redemption, especially since he couldn't have known anything of the kind about me. He did admit that all of us were sinners, but it sounded like I was a special case and needed more forgiveness and grace than other people did. Another part I especially didn't like was where he called on Jesus to guide his hand in bringing this boy to Salvation, like it was going to be a particularly hard job. This was when I covertly glanced at his folded hands and noticed how big they were. Over all, compared to the attention bestowed on me, the Lord got mighty little thanks for the food he had put here on the table for us. Nor, I noticed, did poor little Miss Maggie get even a mention, though she sat there through it all with humbly bowed head and an expression like piety itself.

But there was one thing that rankled me more than any other. Right after the prayer, loud Amens and all, the Reverend reached out with his fork and speared a rather small slice of ham and put it on Miss Maggie's plate. The slice he put on mine was larger, but on his own plate he put two slices. To his credit, I suppose, he at least felt it necessary to explain. A man his size required more, and so on according to scale. For a man to eat more than he needs was waste, he said, and cited the fact of hunger so widespread in this selfish world. "And it's gluttony, too. Which is sin in the eyes of the Lord." Whereupon he proceeded to dish out corn pudding and green beans in proper proportions. I reckoned that later he was going to pack up the leftovers and send them off to Haiti or someplace. There were just such other things I noticed later on, but this was the one that first called the word 'hypocrite' to mind.

All the way through supper I was uncomfortably wondering where in this little house they would put me and what it would be like to live in close quarters with them. So, afterwards, I was more than just relieved when he led me out the back door and, in light from a bulb fastened to the house wall, past the chicken yard and a little way on in near-darkness to a small, board structure. It was a single room, maybe twelve by twelve feet, with one high window and a door he had to duck his head to pass through. From the dark inside he said, "Light quit working, but you'll do fine with this till I get it fixed." What he meant was a kerosene lamp, suddenly visible when he struck a match. In seconds he had the lamp burning, its pallid light just defining a cot and a chair, a large box serving as a table, and a very small potbellied stove. "Lamplight's fine," he said. "Growed up with it. Turn the wick up a little, you can read the Bible by it." And sure enough, there was one lying there on the box.

I didn't need to ask any questions. Over there by the fence, he told me, was a privy that didn't get much use anymore. And there was fire wood just outside in case I got cold. I was already cold, and I kept wishing he would get going and leave me alone. He didn't. The important matters were yet to come; he even sat down on the cot in preparation.

"Now, son," he gravely said, "I'm going to be looking for a little he'p from you about the place. Feed the chickens and such. But that ain't the main thing. The main thing is what ever' man ought to be about. It's Salvation. It comes by prayer and instruction and by reading of God's word. And there it lays, right there on that box. I look for you to read some of it ever'day and then tell me about it." His change of voice with these last words clearly told me he meant business.

It was no wonder he had first greeted me with every sign of satisfaction. At no cost to him, he had got hold of both a farmhand and a helpless victim to instruct about Salvation. And from the ready look of this little hut, I concluded that I was not the first one. I would have bet that he had an ongoing arrangement with the judge who had sentenced me. That I was right about not being the first one pretty soon proved to be the case.

On the whole my farm chores were not too onerous. I fed the chickens, one of which, a huge red rooster, took an immediate dislike to me and, with feathers all puffed out, would come charging at me with a ferocity that had me backing off in alarm. But I soon solved this one. One day, with nobody around to see me, I let the rooster have it with a barrel stave and knocked him flapping and squawking. I fed the two sows, which I hated, and endured the Reverend's look of vexation when I failed at milking the cow. I finally learned and got pretty good at it, mainly because of Miss Maggie's help. For three days running, she came out to the barn and showed me, kept showing me, just how to take hold of the cow's tit so as to squeeze first with my index finger.

It was on one of these occasions that I first noticed on her cheekbone a purple bruise just half-disguised by face powder. I didn't ask, but she saw me take notice and explained that it happened in the dark when she bumped into a door frame. At the time I accepted this, even though I had already had enough experience enough with Reverend to know how quick to anger he was. After all, it was hard to imagine such behavior in a man whose every other word had to do with righteousness.

My farm chores were a small matter compared with my (pretended) labors to achieve Salvation. The Reverend's church, a fair-sized white-painted structure a mile down the road, was the location of some of my more trying hours. There I sat like a stone, in a crowded pew, through Sunday morning and evening worship and prayer meetings through the week, determined to maintain a posture that would indicate my fixed and awed attention to the Voice. The Voice more than filled the church and at least had the effect of keeping me awake, if not entirely conscious. Those intervals when my gaze was really focused on the Reverend up there at the pulpit were the most trying of all: his hands in passionate motion, the stiff neck and the face uplifted in invocation of that Power able and wanting to rain down Salvation on this congregation of desperate sinners. And apparently, judging by the scattered and momentary outcries I kept hearing around me, a good many of them really were desperate. Anyway, when the end came and the noisy exit was under way, it was pretty clear that even the most afflicted had quite recovered. Slinking away, as I always tried to do, didn't spare me from being the object of many curious eyes.

If going to church had been the whole of my religious trials, it wouldn't have been so bad. But the almost daily private sessions with the Reverend were, if anything, worse. Seated on the cot, facing him across the box where the Bible lay open, I struggled through my renditions, often interrupted by him, of what I had read that day.

I had learned right off that there were two testaments, New and Old. With the Reverend's approval (he ranked the new one higher), I started by choosing it not only because it was newer but because it seemed less complicated. But less so or not, it gave me trouble, resulting mainly from my carefully hidden conviction that half of what I read could never have happened. Still, I was genuinely curious about how he would explain some of these things, and keeping to my role of eager learner, I innocently inquired about them. For example, there was that pool at Bethesda where an angel came down every evening and stirred up the water so that the first sick man in after her got cured. I said, "I keep wondering why an angel would need to take a bath."

"The Book don't tell us,' he said, without reflection. It's one of them things we don't need to understand."

This was his usual kind of answer to such questions. But he wasn't exactly a fool, at least about some things, and the next time I took a risk, though still more careful of my demeanor, I went too far. It was about the demon-possessed man and the Gadarene swine, and how Jesus, when he drove the demons out of the man, put them in the herd of swine, which then jumped off the bluff and drowned in the water below. I said it didn't seem fair of Jesus when you thought about the poor man that owned the swine.

A stunned look was the Reverend's instant response. He had rather intense blue eyes that could go hot with anger, as in this case. "Boy," he said, in a voice that sounded like he was under pressure from On-High, "You better git to thinking about your soul before you talk like that about the Lord Jesus. That's His book that He wrote by man's hand laying there and it don't say nothing but what's true and good. Get down on your knees, boy."

I did it with angry reluctance. It still seemed to me a better choice than the risk of going to the jailhouse.

I decided that instead of the New Testament that wasn't about anything but Jesus, I had best switch back to the Old Testament for my readings. I did and was glad. It was ever so much more fun. Of course, like everybody else, I had already heard about Adam and Eve and the serpent, and such as David and Goliath, and the walls of Jericho falling down. About the whole big picture, though, I didn't know anything. I needn't have worried. Here was more than a plenty of new stuff that grabbed my interest, what with Philistines and Malachites and Midianites, not to mention Israelites, smiting each other, and Jehovah coming down on them whenever they were starting to have a good time. And those crazy dietary laws. And, to boot, no lack of scandalous stuff, a good deal of which didn't seem to bother Jehovah. He was a big surprise to me, not a bit like Jesus, hurling curses every which way and not caring how many wives and girl friends they had. It also gave me some ideas. Since I didn't have to be quite as careful in talking about he Old Testament, I figured I could have a little fun with him on a good many counts.

So, just a couple of days after my discovery, sitting across the box from him with the lamp turned up high, I set to it. I had noticed that he always came down especially hard on adultery and fornication and such (like these were the unforgivable sins of them all), and I had chosen an instance in point. Adopting my best demeanor of anxious humility, I mentioned a few names, Zilpah and Bilhah for instance, who were among the maid servants that Jacob had "come in unto." For a clincher I also brought in how many wives all those patriarchs had had, something Jesus wouldn't have put up with. The result was, No Dice. Not only did the Reverend know who Zilpah and Bilhah were, he also pointed out (what I evidently had missed) that for the occasion of Jacob's "coming in unto," they had got married to him. As for all the wives, that was God's special dispensation in order to build up the power of Israel . . . which, if it didn't satisfy me, seemed to suit him well enough. But "seemed to" was maybe right, because for a second there I thought I saw a glimmer of something in his lamp-lit eyes.

Anyway I was silenced, and as the silence ran on and on, so that I began to hear first spring crickets out there in the dark, I finally took it that he was seriously considering what my fate should be. But it didn't turn out as I had feared. After first muttering something about my soul being in danger, he went on to say, "Reckon from now on you better stick with the New Testament and Jesus. Which is where the whole and only Truth is at." Though I didn't have any really good reason to think so, I still felt like I had scored some kind of a small victory.

There were still other though lesser trials sometimes required of me, evidently to round out my education. (I often wondered if he really thought of me as a promising candidate for preacherhood.) I learned that among Jesus' admonitions were the obligations for Christians to visit the sick and bury the dead. Right at first I thought 'bury the dead' meant we Christians would have to show up at the graveyard with picks and shovels. But to my relief it only meant that we should be there standing around while my Reverend or some other one, without consideration for the standers-by, carried on and on with prayer and example about the virtues of the deceased.

Visiting the sick, a thing he once in a while required my company for, was the least burdensome of things pressed on me. There wasn't anything like a real hospital in Bentonville, and the sick, if they hadn't been removed to distant hospitals, resided in their own or their relatives' bare and half-darkened rooms. I didn't have much of a role in these visits, except to sit there, in reverent silence mostly, a few feet from a bed where, usually, an old man or woman lay. The Reverend would be seated near enough to hold a feeble hand in his, speaking, in a voice astonishingly subdued, of the Lord's tender mercies (no matter the subject's degree of pain) and of the glorious Hereafter waiting up there in the sky. His words were always appreciated, as most often attested by a plaintive voices interrupting with "Blessed be Jesus" and the like. I was not even those days a complete cynic, and at times I couldn't help but be moved by these little scenes. In fact there were moments when it crossed my mind that the Reverend was not in every case the creature of self-willed and boneheaded platitudes I was accustomed to.

But there were also moments that set me chuckling to myself. One white-haired old lady with a pointed and tremulous chin apparently had found in reading her Bible a phrase that stayed with her, and just when she saw the Reverend moving to stand up, she stopped him with her hand on his arm. She quavered, "The Bible says about the Kiss of Peace. I'd be right proud you'd gimme one." With her head lifted just a bit, she was holding her dry old lips puckered with readiness. The Reverend stopped in a way that put me in mind of Goliath when David's stone hit him between the eyes. A few seconds and he leaned a little toward her, and stopped again. He lifted her hand to his mouth, then turned away and got out of there as quick as he could. Outside, "Not very gallant," I almost said to him.

Once every Friday evening I was allowed a short interval of recess. It was a space just long enough for me to walk (my car was held impounded) the mile into town and see a picture show . . . one approved by Him, of course. It was the third Friday night of my sentence when, seeing the kind of movie it was, I turned away and crossed the street to a drugstore for a leisurely chocolate soda. There were tables, but none in use except one where a guy about my age, with long, very black hair sat holding an empty glass. His gaze was very intent on me, and when I started to leave, he gave me a friendly nod that invited me over. Why not? I accepted and sat down across the table from him. The welcoming grin, though not so expansive now, was still on his face when he said, "You're Bragg, ain't you?"

"How did you know?" I said.

"I've seen you before. Asked around. I hear he's got hold of you, this time."

"I thought as much . . . that I wasn't the first one. Who was?" I said.

"I don't know, but I was one of them. He's got him a good thing going out there."

"I reckon he does," I said. "They ought to get him for involuntary servitude . . . except that damn judge is behind it." I mulled for a second or two. "I don't know if I can stick it out."

"I didn't," he said, the faint grin still on his face. It was a long thin face, with flesh stretched across his cheek bones and pale eyes he kept blinking as if the light didn't suit him.

The Adventures of Douglas Bragg

— — —

"What happened?"

"I told him where he could stick his Bible. That and other such."

I hesitated to ask what kind of other such, but he seemed to read my mind. He said, "I never was 'pure in heart.'"

"How did you get away with it? . . . or not get away with it?"

"Like you're doing right now. I never went to one of them goddamn picture shows. He finally gave me a test, wanted me to tell him what happened in one of them. I flunked." His persistent ghost of a grin widened a little. "You better go over there and check on that one 'fore you go back to your cell . . . if that's what you want."

"'Cell' is right," I said. Or 'Sunday school room.' I've had more scripture stuffed down my throat than I knew was in the world."

"Think I don't know?" he said. "God, I hated that. The old hypocrite bastard." His small grin was absent for a second. "And by the way, is 'Miss Maggie' still alive?"

"Sure," I said, slow to catch what he might mean. "Why wouldn't she be?"

"Poor woman. You wait a while, you'll see why."

"I haven't seen anything. I know he's pretty tough on her, that's all."

"Okay." For a space he was silent. Then he said, "Believe it or not, jail's got its good points."

"They sent you up," I said.

"Went to court. Got a year. Wasn't long enough to make me forget the parson, though." He stood up. "Got something on. Good chance I'll be seeing you."

"I don't know your name," I said.

"Smit," he said as if that was all of it, and left me sitting there.

I puttered around town for a while, then finally went to the picture show and sat through the last mushy half of it. I got back to my cell at just about the right time.

Except that I spent most of the next day repairing the fence around the pasture where the cow was getting out, everything appeared to be fine. Everything, that is, except the little stewing in my mind that Smit had put there. It was true that I had never seen anything . . . or at least nothing of more consequence than his bullying manner with poor little Miss Maggie. Most probably it was only Smit's bitterness that was speaking to me, and well before suppertime I had stopped thinking about it.

The Adventures of Douglas Bragg

— — —

It happened to be one of our less pleasant supper hours because, as seemed clear to me, something was troubling the Reverend. But since nothing was said and the cause of my notion was nothing more than a few sideways glances cast my way, I finally supposed it was just my imagination. It turned out I was right in the first place. When, back in my cell after supper, I heard him coming as usual, I still didn't look for anything different. I quickly sat down and opened the Bible and turned the lamp up in readiness. But as soon as he sat down with the lamplight in his face, I knew something was coming. I didn't even have time to wonder what, before he said, "I come out here to warn you about that Smith . . . if that's even what his name is. How come you to know him?"

So, I thought, the Reverend had spies. I swallowed my surge of anger and said, "I don't know him. I just talked to him a minute in the drugstore. I never saw him before."

The Reverend's voice wasn't even loud, for a change; it was just hot with anger. "That young rascal's a liar born. Had me fooled for a while. He's bound to told you a bunch of lies."

Feeling justified in telling a few lies, myself, I quietly said, "I don't know. He just told me you-all didn't get along. That's all."

"Even that's a lie. He stood right there where you're sitting and blasphemed the Lord Jesus right in my face. Throwed the Bible I gave him out on the ground. He even made a big thing out of fornicating with harlots." His heavy jaw had set itself in a way new to me.

"I'm sorry to hear that," I said, trying for a hint of outrage in my voice.

"Smith," the Reverend said, like an oath. "I ain't even sure that's his name. It's some Smiths in these parts, but I never heard of any of them connected up to him." He pondered for a moment, relaxed a bit. "You see him again, turn your back on him." Then, "You're a good boy at heart, and I been seeing signs of you turning toward Jesus. Which means to keep away from such as him."

This called for a brief blessing, in which Jesus was asked to defend my soul from evil powers. Then he said Amen and left me alone.

Nothing more was said on the matter, and after a couple of days I had all but quit thinking about it. Then something happened that finally led me into a mess I couldn't even have imagined.

About ten o'clock at night, half an hour after the Reverend's invariable bedtime, I had just got through putting out my lamp and lying down when I heard a noise at the door. Then a voice, "Okay if I come in?"

Because it couldn't have been anybody else, I knew right off it was Smit . . . that rascal Smith as the Reverend would have said. He had the door half open before I said, "Sure," and sat up. Then his silhouette in the doorway and, ducking the low lentil, he came in. I said, "I guess you came through the thicket back there."

"Only safe way. Old bastard's got ears like a fox. Used it all the time when I was here." Then, just as I was starting to, "Don't light that lamp."

He didn't have to feel for the chair, and once he had sat down he said, "Hope you're glad I came. Wanted somebody to talk to. That town ain't exactly friendly to me."

"Well, the good Reverend's not so friendly to you, either. He said . . ."

"Oh, I see," Smit interrupted. "Had his spies on you."

"He sure did. And gave you hell . . . where he wishes you were."

Smit chuckled, a small cold sound. "The feeling is mutual. Ever since I got out, I've been trying to think of a way to puncture that old windbag. Maybe send him down where he's always talking about. Along with me, he'd say."

"I know how you feel," I said. "No danger to him, though, not with Jesus his best friend."

Smit chuckled again. The sound of it somehow appealed to me, and right then I started thinking that maybe we could get to be friends. It wasn't only the chuckles. He had a dry way of putting things and, as I soon learned, a readiness to talk about himself and his experiences even when his narrations didn't exactly cast the best light on him. He was very interested in girls, and evidently he had had plenty of them, of all kinds. He even touched on minor criminal acts of his: peccadilloes, as he saw them, like one I had never known anybody to actually do: yell "Fire" in a crowded theater. And when I asked why he had been arrested, he described, dramatically and with obvious pleasure, just how it felt to punch a cop in the nose. I didn't know how much truth there was in the things he told me, but as he told them, they made good stories.

It was just before he got up to leave that he said, "You didn't believe me about Miss Maggie, did you?"

"I reckon not. I figure you for a good yarn spinner. No offense."

The Adventures of Douglas Bragg

"Okay," he pleasantly said. "But not all the time. Try this one. I bet you don't know the old parson put her in the hospital a couple of months ago. Over at Brenton. Oh, he kept it quiet. So did she. Told lies about how she fell down the steps. It got whispered around, though."

"That's likely just gossip," I firmly said.

"Not when it came from the doctor that took care of her."

"You mean he told you?"

"Nope. But I got it from somebody I know mighty well: his grandson." He waited for my response, a shake of my head, then went on, "Anyhow, it didn't surprise me. I look close at things. And listen, too. It wasn't just seeing how she jumps when he wants something, scared of him. Times when I was close by the house I'd hear him raging at her . . . for some little nothing she had or hadn't done." He paused. "I reckon he's trying to be on his good behavior with you around. But like you told me, yourself, he's damn tough on her."

I finally said, quietly, "I still haven't seen anything . . . out of the way, I mean." But pictured there in my mind was that purple bruise on Miss Maggie's cheekbone.

"Okay," Smit said. "But I aim to get him."

"How?" I said. He didn't answer. After a time of silence he got up and left.

That Smit from pure hatred had made it all up, seemed to me not unlikely, and I then believed that if it had not been for that bruise fixed in my memory, I could have remained content with this view. But I soon discovered that Smit's account of what went on had made a difference; it had made me watchful. It had always been plain enough that the old boy's way with Miss Maggie was that of an obvious bully, and hard to ignore. But here was new light on it. I found myself counting the times when he raised his voice or put her down with a sometimes punishing remark. What else might he do, or have done?

This was a state of mind that couldn't last long, however, and after those first few days in which nothing different happened, it had mostly passed off. Then, one morning at breakfast, it was suddenly back again. That Miss Maggie failed to appear was not especially curious. "She's feeling under the weather," the Reverend said, and tended to his bacon and eggs. But that the table was set just so and the food perfectly prepared did catch my attention. And when it happened the same way at both lunch and supper, my suspicion was fully aroused. I didn't ask my question till the meal was nearly over. Innocently I said, "Are you doing all this cooking?"

With the loaded fork halfway to his mouth, he paused. "A little help from Miss Maggie. She feels like getting up just a few minutes at a time." He went on eating.

Feeling brave, I said, "Are you going to have to call a doctor?"

"Don't need one. She'll be fine."

The bastard, I thought, indifferent if she was really sick, and lying if she wasn't. I felt bold enough to ask, "Do you think she'd like for me to drop in?"

Unruffled, he said, "Naw. She's sleeping now."

It was the same next morning, but late in the day I saw her out hanging clothes on the line. When I asked her how she was feeling I was close enough for a look. "I'm fine now, thank you," she said in voice that maybe sounded a little too chipper, and turned away from me. Was that a swollen lip I had glimpsed? Or just imagined? At supper, though I managed glimpses from over my food, I was still unsure.

So that was how it stood with me that night and most of the next day . . . until I finally settled, or almost did, on the conclusion that the old guy was in fact that kind of a son-of-a-bitch. I hadn't wanted to agree with Smit, but here I was, brooding on it, casting about for a scheme of my own that would maybe somehow give him a punishing little jolt. If, a big *if*, it wasn't a scheme likely to get me in trouble. Even so, I was glad when Smit didn't show up that night. In fact it was three more nights before he came.

He sat in his usual place. There was a chirping of crickets and, from the window, moonlight enough to nearly reveal the details of his face. He wasn't long in getting to it. "You want to hear what I got in mind?"

A plan, of course. I said, "I'll listen."

"Okay. I got it all worked out." He launched right in and had just got to the heart of it when, all of a sudden, my thoughts took a turn of their own. More than just appropriate, I thought, recalling the scenes of the last two nights between the old coot and me. I have often wondered whether, if this had not happened as it did, I would have agreed to Smit's plan.

On the Friday night just past I had brought a couple of magazines back from town with me. Not that they were to my mind especially girlie, but such as they were was too much. I had been careless in hiding them under my covers, and our Bible study had not even got started when the Rev spotted one. I saw his jaw set itself. He said, "Mind if I have a look at that?" and held his hand out. Unfortunately, just as if by instinct, he turned right to a large-scale photograph of a nearly naked woman posed as if ready to offer herself up. His gaze lingered just long enough to take it in, then fastened on me. "This here the kind of thing you study in place of God's Word?" I tried to tell him this was something that just happened to be in there, and that I hadn't even noticed it before. I don't think he so much as heard me. "Boy, lust has likely put more souls in hell than any sin I can name you. More of the same followed, with emphasis on Satan's involvement, and he ended by turning his back on me and leaving without a word. No Bible study this time. The omission was fully redressed, however, by the scourging he laid on me the next evening. I was surprised at the number of Jesus' pronouncements on such as fornication and adultery, in which, so to speak, the Reverend rubbed my nose.

The effect was to leave my hackles raised, a condition still prevailing when Smit finally arrived. All to the good, he said (though he had to convince me of this) because the old fool had showed something about himself that fit him just right for the plan. "Ain't you ever noticed?" he said. "When a man bad wants something he's dead set against, he'll more than likely make a big lot of noise about it. Just fits. Sets him up. Don't it, now?" I couldn't see his face plainly but I knew the little grin was there.

"I don't know," I said. "It probably doesn't fit everybody."

"Trust me. Get him lathered up pretty good and I bet you my soul, if I got one, you'd be surprised." He chuckled. "Think about the old boy up there humping away."

I thought about it, seeing it with Smit's eyes now: Our God-fearing Reverend stripped to his knees and hot as a boy in the saddle. A good thing for him, too, I thought, like a lesson on being human. I said, "Okay, but what about it? How are you going to bring all this off?"

"Here it is," he quickly said. "There's those two whores I mentioned, live out on the Clayton Road. In a old house nowhere close to anybody. They do a good business; I ought to know. Sisters. Named La Grand, for God's sake. They bound to made it up. Fanny and Lola La Grand. Fanny's ugly, but Lola ain't. A little threadbare but good-looking, nice ass. A little sickly-looking, but that's good for us. Poor thing lying there, needing spiritual comfort. She's our gal."

"Well," I said, more and more interested now. "But what's to make it work? What's in it for those sisters, for instance?"

"It'll tickle them. I know it. Old Reverend Upright cut down to size. I'm sure they've heard about him. 'Course I do figure they might be wanting a little something to grease their palms with, too. We can take care of that, though."

I wasn't sure I knew what he meant by this last, but I put it aside. I felt a grin coming on my own face.

"Like I told you, she'll write a letter. Fanny, I reckon. Way the Rev is, he'll take the bait. I got it all worked out."

"All right. But what's the rest of it?" I said, still dubious.

But Smit had an answer for everything, and now he got down to a matter I had been waiting for: my part in it. "When that letter gets here saying where to come to, for comfort to poor sick Lola, you got to come along with him. Like you done other times."

I started to raise the obvious objection, but he cut me off. "That's the second thing, though. First thing is, you got to go out there by your-self and get them ready, because I ain't really put it all to them yet."

"You sounded like you had."

"No way. I just give them a little outline . . . to tease them with. They'll take to you better than they do me."

I didn't ask why.

"Just explain it all to them. Tell them about him . . . all the shit he's rubbing your face in. They'll go for it." Then, "How about tomorrow night? Give you time enough to think on what you're going to say to them."

I was still feeling doubtful on more than one point, but then I thought about Miss Maggie. "Okay," I said.

– – –

Around ten o'clock I found Smit in his car waiting for me on the far side of the thicket. He said ten was late enough, because the Reverend, a heavy sleeper, went to bed at exactly nine-thirty. As with everything else, he seemed to have carefully studied the old coot's habits, a fact that gave me a little more assurance that he knew what we were doing in this case. He was full of advice about what I needed to say to them, and he didn't hush till we had almost reached our destination.

It was a lonely road, with a few darkened houses at first and then a little store, after which I didn't see anything till he started slowing

The Adventures of Douglas Bragg

– – –

down. There were a couple of lighted windows, and when we turned off onto the dirt driveway, I could see two parked cars and also details of a fairly small, frame country house no different from many another one along these roads. With his door already half-open, he said, "Okay, let's go." After a pause I got out.

There was one difference about this house: a gallery with a couple of chairs that 1could see as we approached the steps. That was when I also noticed that now it was not "we" but "me" all by myself. I looked back. He was getting in the car. "Aren't you going with me?" I said.

"Told you I wasn't. Better this way. I'll be here when you get through."

So I went on, stopped, and stood there in the clamor of crickets, then climbed the steps and paused at the door with my hand raised to knock. The door opened. The woman looking at me, as I saw right off, was Fanny, the ugly one, wearing a plain gray dress that came clear down to her ankles.

"You the boy?"

"Yes'm," I mumbled.

"Come on in."

I did, but before any other words could pass between us, we were interrupted. It was an old man, shaky-looking, who obviously was on the way out but seemed to find the path hopelessly blocked by us. It looked like a desperate moment for him. "Please lemme through," he quavered, lifting a hand as if in his own defense. We stepped aside. He passed at a sort of rocking gait, followed by astute advice from Fanny, saying, "Careful on them steps, Mr. Bandy. Anyhow you ought to think about giving it up, at your age." To me she said, "He'p him down."

I did and left him tottering away toward his car.

Shutting the door behind me, she said, "I try to get him not to come, but he comes anyhow. A heap more than makes any sense. A thing we don't need is a dead old man around here." Then, "You can set down if you want to."

The place for sure didn't fit what I had expected of a whorehouse. There were several comfortable-looking chairs around the room, but the walls were bare except for a faded picture of a much bewhiskered aged man on the wall opposite me. She saw me looking at it and said, with a hint of pride, "That's my old daddy. He was a good man, part of the time." I nodded appreciatively. I wondered what he would have thought about being pictured here. Another glance around the room showed a rough stone fireplace and a small table with a vase of obviously fake flowers. There was a door in the rear wall and a hall leading into darkness. Back there would be where the action took place.

She said, "Go on and set down," and waited for me take the nearest chair. Then, "What that Smit told me, you ain't here for our regular services."

"That's right," I mumbled, trying to think how to start, glad that the light wasn't any brighter.

"Something about a 'trick,' which he didn't exactly mean what some folks means."

I cleared my throat and was about to commence when a figure in a housecoat appeared in the hall doorway. This would be Lola. Wondering whether it would be the right thing to stand up for a lady in a whorehouse, I just sat there looking at her. Smit was right; she wasn't bad, with blond hair (dyed no doubt) and sexy lips and evidence of curves in the best places. He was right, too, about that slightly frayed look that he had called "sickly." Still, it was a wonder if she didn't take all the trade away from her sister, who had a nose that must have been broken long ago by some impassioned client. Add to this a palpable excess of flesh where it didn't sit too well, and you weren't left with a very sexy impression.

Lola came on and, with what had to be a breath of relief, sat down in a chair close by. She followed with a sound like "wheeoh" and said, "Fanny, you got to keep that old goat away from here. Wheezing and blowing like a old suction pump. I can't stand no more of him."

"All right," Fanny said dismissively, and sat down in a chair next to mine. "How about what your name is, to start with?" she said.

"Doug," I said, which loosened my tongue, and I went on, "Maybe Smit told you. Do you know of a preacher named Ezra Carnes? Has a church near town. Calls it Mount Hope."

She thought for a second or two. "Just from your buddy naming him. I might, though." Then, "Maybe I do, heard about him a little. Another one of them hard-shells. Like I know them all. Had a hard time with them when I was a gal. Caught me once when I laid down with a boy. Shamed me, right in front of the whole church watching me."

This was just right, I thought, but it got even better. She went on, "Last thing was, I showed them in the Bible how them old Israelites all had conkebeens, which wasn't nothing but just girlfriends. Took a awful hiding for it. That's when I lit out for good. Later on, Lola come after me."

Lola gave a smile of self-approval.

"Sounds kind of like my case," I said. "Having that bonehead preacher on my back all the time, rubbing my face in it. I guess Smit told you. The old rascal can send me to jail if he wants to." Then, "Just seeing all that holy hot air shot out of him would be one big payback for me. Smit, too, he went through it. And he got a whole year in jail."

"And you want us to screw him?"

"One of you, anyway," I said.

"I'll fuck his brains out," Lola said, her smile now become a grin.

"Liable not be that easy," Fanny said. "Hard-shell like him. Might end up bad for us. Like it is, we got enough trouble keeping the Law off. We couldn't even do that if it wasn't for having a couple of them for good customers. We give them a cut rate."

"He won't squeal when I get through with him," Lola proudly said.

"What if he holds off, though?" Fanny said.

"He won't," Lola said.

"Look," I said to her. "Here's what. Mostly you just lie there feeling bad, down in the dumps. Just do little things, like by accident, like give him a little glimpse of flesh where it counts. Tease him. Maybe take his hand and put it on you where you hurt. You know what I mean."

"You can bet your ass on it," she said, with a little curl of her lips.

"That way, if it turns out he doesn't go for you, he'll probably leave here all lathered up, anyway. Just thinking about it'll make him want to come back, likely. Then, after a few days, send him another letter. Say how much he helped you last time. All real spiritual. That ought to get him."

"Just watch me," Lola said, with a full grin, this time.

"Either way, make it on a Wednesday," Fanny said. "Everybody knows we're closed on Wednesday." So she had come around.

"Today's Monday," I said. "If you sent it tomorrow, it would get there early Wednesday." I took the letter out of my pocket. "I've got it all written out. You can copy it. Better in your handwriting."

She took it and started reading, chuckling to herself. Starting to leave, I stood up with a gallant bow to the ladies. Fanny stopped me. "You want some cookies." I wasn't sure what she meant, and I just said, "Cookies?"

"For free, I mean. I makes them to sell. With chocolate in them."

A good idea for a cover, I thought, and accepted her offer. Holding a little bag of cookies, in an atmosphere of something like merriment, I bade the ladies goodbye for now.

But there was an interruption. Somebody was trying the front door and, failing that, began to bang on it. Even before Fanny got there I had put myself out of sight. Fanny opened the door. It was Mr. Bandy again. They left him up to me. I got him down the steps, all right, but once down in the yard our progress toward his car was a kind of a reeling struggle. Smit finally came to help me, and we got him in his car. He kept saying, "Lola . . . Tell Lola . . . ," but finally, after some threatening words from us, he shut up and went to sleep. There was nothing for it but just to leave him there.

– – –

The next day and night were waiting times, made especially tough in the hour when the Reverend had me in hand for Bible study. My lapses, caused by visions of his big old stripped-down carcass hard at work, were a special worry. Once, in the middle of what he called the Beatitudes, he did reprove me for my wandering attention, but just the same I made it through all right. Smit never did show up, and I spent most of my wakeful hours mulling my little problem.

It had been only a little problem, but here alone in the night I couldn't stop thinking about it. The question, when the letter came, was what I should do about accompanying the Reverend on his mission. If he required it . . . or did not, for that matter. Wouldn't my presence on the scene be enough to chill the whole project? Or was there some credible way I could manage to be absent for the event? I mulled and mulled.

At breakfast time and still with no answer, I hid my excitement by downing eggs and bacon with a look of satisfaction. The mail always came early, and when the Reverend pushed back his empty plate, I figured the time had come. Not pausing because of the rain, he went out to the mailbox and came back with three letters and sat down to open them. He chose the right one first, then pondered it for a space. He said, "I don't know this woman. Named La Grand. Her sister needs help, wants a minister." He paused. "Sounds kind of urgent. I'll have to go."

"Yes, dear," Miss Maggie said.

The Adventures of Douglas Bragg

– – –

"Out Clayton Road. I don't know anything about out that way . . . but I'll find it."

"Of course you will, dear," Miss Maggie said.

This was my moment, the one I had been trying to prepare myself for. Still unsure as to what I was going to say, I had my mouth open . . . until, thankfully, I was interrupted. After all, there was no need. It was because of the rain; the Reverend didn't like to drive in the rain. "So Douglas won't mind driving me," he said, and went for his Bible and raincoat. From the doorway, with me already out there in the wet, he stopped to say to Miss Maggie, "Rain or no rain, it's the Lord's work."

"Of course it is, dear," I heard her answer, and then went on to the car.

The rain had let up by the time we reached the Clayton turnoff, but I still drove with the kind of care a man takes when he doesn't know where he's going. Now and then the silence between us gave way to pious remarks from the Reverend, along with observations about the fewness of houses and farms out this way . . . to which I responded in tones that somehow called Miss Maggie to mind. My one spontaneous observation came as we passed the little store a mile from our destination, a remark aimed only at pointing it out for possible use as a strategy.

"Slow down," the Reverend said. "Frame house with a gallery. This got to be it."

I turned in and stopped beside an old Ford car much in need of paint. I hesitated. Here was the real problem I had been thinking about. Half out of the car, the Reverend said, "You coming along?"

I had thought to say no, but how would it seem, when I had never done so before? I almost refused and then decided, and reluctantly got out. I thought of the little store. But what for a reason to go there? I trudged along behind him and up to the front door.

I was soon to learn that Fanny was a woman as sly as a fox. Wearing the same gray ankle-length dress, her hair drawn modestly back into a bun, she greeted us quietly. In fact almost in a whisper when she said, "Sister's been waiting for you. She's so depressed. Thank you so much for coming." Then, "Here, I'll take your raincoat."

In a voice as soft as her own, the Reverend said, "I'm glad to come. The Lord be with her," and submitted to help in removing his coat.

This was when I became aware that Fanny's gaze was taking me in, that the something shaping itself in her brain must have to do with me.

The Adventures of Douglas Bragg
– – –

I was right. Folding the Reverend's coat across her arm, she suddenly looked at me again and said, "Oh" and then, "This boy?"

"My young friend Douglas. He likes to come long with me sometimes. A learning experience for him." I nodded.

"I see," she said, then hesitated. Something was on the way. Finally, as if a little fearful to say it, she said, fumbling, "Would it be too much . . . too much to ask if I could borrow him for a little while?" Then, reading the Reverend's expression, "To help me with something?" She went on, "It's to help my dead brother's wife move some furniture in. It's hard for just us two. It's just down the road a ways and we wouldn't be long. And with you here, I wouldn't have to worry about Sister."

This last, delivered with a perfectly straight face, required that I duck my head and hold my mouth tight shut. I still had not looked up when the Reverend said, "Of course. I'm sure Douglas will be glad to help." He didn't even say "Won't you, Douglas?" Which, under the circumstances, exactly suited me. A little more, and I just might have given the show away.

So we left, but not before I was granted an illuminating glimpse. Not into the shadowy hallway but into a room in the rear wall that I had not noticed before, to which the door was now open. A very small room where a bed seemed to occupy nearly all of the space, and very clean-looking. No doubt for VIPs, I thought. As for the occupant of that bed, I could see only the swell her feet made in what looked like the brightest pink bedsheets in the world. Starting to choke up, I got outside as quick as I could.

Driving away, Fanny said, "'Course there ain't any dead brother's wife. We'll go down to Stedman's place, buy a few beers. Not to drink, though, he'd sniff it right off." A little later, "I figure this'll take just about the right amount of time . . . if anything comes off. It depends on the man, but you take a average one he'll get good done in twenty to thirty minutes. Though I've knowed some to take a whole hour at it." Still later, passing between scattered houses, she had begun to look a little concerned. "I reckon he won't catch on," she said. "He won't if Lola does like I told her. Risky, though. Might not ought to of done it."

I murmured something meant to be reassuring, and added, "We can tell for sure when we get back, though."

"I reckon," she said. She seemed to have something more on her mind, but I didn't ask.

Fanny's business in the store took her a while, and on the way back she drove a little faster. When, approaching the house, I could see the Reverend's car, I said, "One thing's for sure. He's still in there."

Turning into the drive, she said, "You best stay here," and stopped and got out. I did too, but it was only to watch her walk, not fast, to the steps and hesitate there. Then she started up, and stopped again. The Reverend had appeared. I heard her voice and saw her climb to the top and stand there facing him in apparent conversation. That no sound of a voice reached me seemed at first to mean something good. But maybe not. I strained to hear. The Reverend was in motion, coming down the steps. Getting into his car, I hastened to form an innocent question for him.

He rounded the back of the car and opened the door. Did I only imagine a certain heaviness in the way he entered and leaned back in the seat? Cranking the car, I said, "Did it seem to help her, you talking to her?"

He was slow to answer. "I believe so. In a way," he said without much force. It was the "In a way," however, that caught my real attention.

But suddenly I was distracted. Just as I was about to put the car in motion, another car with a mangled fender pulled up and stopped beside us. It was on my side, and in the moment before I started backing out, I got a look at the driver's face, a face with a grin on it. It was Mr. Bandy, here on a Wednesday, even, breaking the rule. I hurried, backing out onto the highway, observing the lack of any sign that the Reverend had noticed him. This small event was not a good thing, I thought, though I took comfort in the reflection that Mr. Bandy's grinning gaze had seemed directed at nothing else but me. Soon, though, as we drove along, the Reverend's silence quite replaced my thoughts of Mr. Bandy. "In a way" came back to mind. I considered for a moment and said, "Is she very seriously sick?"

"What?" It was like he had come out of a trance.

"Is she very sick?"

"Oh . . . not too." A long pause followed. "I'd say . . . depression, mainly." He seemed to be considering whether he had used the right word. "They are awful poor. And way out here by themselves. She's just wanting something to . . ." Another pause.

A wandering mind was not a thing I had noticed in him before. I chipped in, cunningly I thought, "Something to kind of uplift her. Spiritual, I mean."

He gave me a sideways look, and for a second I thought it was a look of suspicion. But whether it was or not, he took up on the word and, for the next two or three minutes, in a key surprisingly minor for him, was off on a spiel about God's love and mercy for all, especially for the poor, and even for the wickedest of sinners. This last, "the wickedest of sinners," was what my mind came down on, and from that moment on I was the same as sure the old boy had got laid.

There was no more conversation the whole way back, but every side glance at his brooding posture added a little something more to my certainty. And by the time we arrived, I was all bound up in anticipation as to how he would greet Miss Maggie. I'd have bet he was preparing himself.

Right off upon our entering the house, she must have noticed something, because I surely did. It was in character for him on such small occasions to dismiss all formality with a mumbled word or two. But here, in a manner almost tender, he simply called her name. It was a moment when I believed he would have gone on to inquire about her health if prudence had not stopped him. There was a pause. Then, to her question he answered, "Yes, I think. Took some comfort . . . ," and left it at that. I could tell that he thought more was needed but couldn't go on with it. . Whatever Miss Maggie might have thought, she didn't let on, only declaring her certainty that he had been a great spiritual help to the poor sick woman. He took this with a blank expression and went to hang up his coat.

In those first hours I thought the Reverend was on the way to getting himself in hand. He went out with a look of decision and spent some time in the barn busily hammering on something. After that he appeared carrying a bucket of grain to feed the hogs. Next, it was a trip into town to buy more feed, where, being absent at lunchtime, he had stopped to eat at the barbecue place. I saw him when he returned and got out of his truck, and thought he looked almost himself again. In fact he gave me some firm instructions about fixing those bad places in the fence once more, and sent me on my way. I was glad of it.

I didn't hurry at my task, and even after working till almost dusk, I had not quite finished the job. But finally, when thunder and lightning started up, big-time, I headed for shelter.

It was already raining pretty hard when, though still at a little distance, I approached the back of the house and saw the Reverend. He was standing on the steps, just standing there. Then, in a sheet of sustained and brilliant lightning I could see his upturned face and arms outstretched a little, a posture as if to welcome the rain and the thunder and lightning in. When he saw me just steps away he lowered his arms. Water was running down his face. I said, "Let's get inside."

"The Lord is merciful. He sends rain on the just and the unjust alike."

I didn't know why this was so good a thing in his case, but all the same I quickly said, "All right, but let's get inside anyway."

He minded me. He even held the screen door open for me. Inside, with a look that seemed a little demented, he said, "I didn't think of it . . . till a little while ago. It's Wednesday."

So what? I thought, then remembered. Prayer meeting night. Was this a fact that could please him, facing all those people?

"Now it won't be. Because of the storm," he said.

I understood. Saved by the bell. A moment later I also understood that what he had said to me was, consciously or not, something very like a confession. I am not an especially soft-hearted person, but this came straight at me. I found myself thinking, Poor fellow, Poor fellow. And the fault was mine, or partly. From this minute I was on his side.

So what? the thing was done. Confess it all? Urge him to tell Miss Maggie, who surely would forgive him? But what of his church, his "flock," as he called them? These were thoughts I went on mulling till something struck me with a greater weight. Three more days and nights and it would be Sunday. And he with that hard shell broken. He would do it; I knew he would. I pictured him at the pulpit, stiff arms and hands that gripped the pulpit shelf. And that strong voice, shaken now. I doubted that God's own voice could stop him from it.

And she, Miss Maggie Magdalene, secretly looking on with troubled eyes. In my experience, women had usually been quick to attribute errant or perplexing behavior in a man to some suppressed physical ailment. At first this had appeared to be so in Miss Maggie's case. At meals, with a bottle of dark liquid and a spoon in hand, she continued to urge it on him, with no success. Still, his refusals, accompanied by brief displays of joviality that couldn't have fooled her, were not enough to turn her from her purpose . . . or not for a while. But I noticed something. I was all but certain that after the first few tries, her persistence was mere formality, a fiction that was a kind of solace for her. Otherwise there was nothing to do but watch him stumble through the accustomed prayers at meals, mock his own voice in casual brief remarks, and never look directly into her face.

Poor Miss Maggie. I tried to imagine, and could not, the Reverend's hand striking that troubled face. It was impossible. It was a lie. I brooded on it through that first night and came out with a firm decision. I would tell her all.

My decision was not firm enough, however, even though the occasion was perfect. It was she who came to me. She had chosen one of his absences to approach me where I was idling in my hut. She would not sit down. She stood there in her too long blue or bluish dress, aproned, her graying hair not quite in its usual order . . . and tears in her eyes. "Please tell me," she said. "What happened?"

My tongue wouldn't work.

"Please. I've got to know. He's so unhappy."

I fumbled. I said, "I stayed outside . . . while he was in there."

"But you must know something."

I took myself in hand. "He didn't tell me. All I could do was guess." This far and no farther, in spite of my intentions.

Her haggard look diminished in these seconds. "What did you guess? Was it something about the woman? Did he . . . with her?"

Okay. "I just guessed that. He didn't tell me."

She looked away for a second. The haggard look was as before. "I couldn't think of nothing else it could be." Then, "She must be a evil woman."

This, the word "evil," got to me. My feeble "I guess so" was all I could manage.

She stood there for what seemed a long time. Finally she looked back at me and said, "He's a good man. A kind, respons'ble man. He ought to know I'd forgive him."

Smit leaped to mind. Liar. But I wanted it confirmed, and I risked the question, "And he never did harm you any way, did he? I mean . . ."

She was surprised. "Why? Heavens no."

I hastened to say, "He's rude to you sometimes."

"Rude? Oh, little things. It's just his way. He just wasn't brought up too well."

The Adventures of Douglas Bragg

I wanted a way to end this. I finally said, "So maybe you ought to ask him if it's true?"

"He won't lie," she murmured and turned away and left.

Smit. Why hadn't he come last night for the latest news? And more to bring with him: A Whore's Tale of Triumph. Maybe I would break his jaw. But really I hoped that now, his purpose all completed, the son-of-a-bitch would never come again.

— — —

Miss Maggie had already acted on my suggestion. The evidence was clear enough when, at supper, the Reverend did not stumble through his blessing or need to fake his tone of voice or avoid looking straight into her gentle face. There were a couple of moments when I all but expected endearing words to come out of his mouth, but it just wasn't in him to bring it off. Meanwhile I sat there feeling myself more and more in the role of somebody like Judas Iscariot.

It was no better for me when later, to my surprise, he came to my hut for Bible study. Not that it was the usual kind of session. Although, for a little while, he kept choosing passages from the Book to read or quote to me, it was plain that more than this was on his mind. A long pause fell. Across the table from me, defined in the lamplight and hush of chirruping crickets, I could see the unexpected creasing of his brow. His eyelids closed and opened. "Miss Maggie told me you had it figured . . . what I done. The woman put her hands on me. It weren't her fault, though . . . poor woman. All lonesome, and hungry for something . . . no life much in her."

I needed to say something, and couldn't.

"I did it. And now I got to pay for it."

Faintly I said, "You already have . . . confessed it." Then I heard myself saying, preacher-like, "There's forgiveness. You're always saying that."

"It's God's truth. But I ain't earned it yet."

I knew what he meant. I muttered some words about how it ought to be just between him and God, but he shook his head. "I can't live a lie in front of my people."

We both fell silent for a time. He shook his head again and said, "I read a book once't, about a preacher, long time ago, did what I did. Wouldn't confess it till it had about burnt up his soul."

The Adventures of Douglas Bragg

— — —

I knew the book, thinking how unlikely it was, and what a pity, that he had ever read it.

The silence this time seemed final, but he still didn't get up and leave. He was looking at me. Suddenly he said, "I reckon I've been more hard on you than I needed be. I just meant to profit you. Hope I did, some."

It was meant as a question; I nodded vacantly.

"Now on," he said, "I'm going to kind of halfway turn you loose. Going to let you go places, all on your own. Maybe make friends, or something. 'Cause I'm satisfied I can trust you."

I didn't say anything or even look straight at him. Coals of fire on my head, I thought, still thinking preacher-like.

He left, and maybe an hour passed before I put out the lamp. I lay down in a moonless clouded night that extinguished everything, and thought and listened. I listened for Smit, and after a while, sure enough, he came . . . a rustling sound at the door, no silhouette. "You asleep?"

"No," I barely said, trying to think what I would say.

"Couldn't make it last night. Good news, though. He went down like a big old hunk of a schoolboy. Sweet Lola is still laughing."

I was trying to think what to say.

"You ought to be laughing, too," Smit said. "What's the matter with you?"

I couldn't see whether he had sat down or not. I finally said, "It was a mistake."

"Mistake? Lola ain't lying. She's even got his undershorts. And the old crock for sure ain't going to spill it."

"He might."

"Shit. I know him too good. It'd ruin him. That upright 'flock' of his would throw him out like poison. Stop worrying, for Christ's sake."

It was like, in the perfect dark, I could see those greenish eyes scrutinizing my face. I still didn't know what I wanted to say. This went on for an uncomfortable time.

"Unless you gone soft," he said. "You're in it, too. And you better remember he can put you in the jailhouse." He added, almost in a whisper, "And maybe that ain't all."

I nearly let this last go by. "I know."

"Okay. And now it's about time for the clincher."

"'Clincher'?" What do you mean?"

The Adventures of Douglas Bragg

— — —

193

"I mean, a little game of blackmail. I know the old goat's got a stash laid by."

This one came straight at me, but after a pause I only said, "I doubt it," thinking I should have guessed all this from things I had heard him say.

"Believe me. And even if he don't, he'll cough up something. Got to. Anyhow we'll keep him scared."

In this moment, a little late, I felt I had better begin to be wary. I said, "All right. Go ahead, then."

"Okay. Got my letter all wrote. Just keep your eye on the Rev."

He was there for a short space longer, featureless in the dark, before I heard him turn and leave.

It was a hard choice that was waiting for me, one that I kept turning and turning in my mind. Yet, in reason, it was not my choice to make. And either way, public confession or not, the poor man's ruin seemed sure. I thought about Smit's letter and how I might intercept it. But Smit: the bastard leaped to mind on a newborn surge of hate. He would be there still, full of malice, concocting other means. This was enough in itself, but prospects were made even worse by an event that happened the next day.

The Reverend, as a small sign of his trust in me, had sent me alone to the lumber yard for a purchase. I had got the lumber on the truck and was headed for the office building when I came face to face with an old man coming out. At first I didn't recognize him, not until the familiar grin spread across his face. Both of us stopped. Without breaking the grin, he quietly said, sharing a fellowly secret, "That Lola's *somethin,*' ain't she?"

I just stood there with my mouth open.

Still without quite breaking the grin, he said, "Who was that big fellow in there with you? Weren't that that parson . . . Carney? I'd of swore it was."

"No," I quickly said. "Just a friend of mine. Named Miller."

"Yeah." The grin seemed likely to split his face in halves. "Well, tell him Bandy said hello."

Maybe I nodded as I passed him by and went into the office.

Wouldn't he, a customer himself, have to keep it quiet? But I had long since noticed how gossip was just too sweet on the tongue. Another thing, then, to be weighed in the balance . . . if only by myself.

The Adventures of Douglas Bragg

But I changed my mind. The next morning, out in the barn, Miss Maggie came to talk . . . pale, herself, as pale almost as her husband had come to be. In a plaintive voice, she said, "He's going to do it. If it don't kill him, first. He won't even eat. Won't even hardly talk to me. Going to ruin hisself. Then what's he going to do?"

I pondered for a moment, then quietly said, "It might just be for the best."

She couldn't have got much paler, but she looked as if I'd betrayed her. I said, "It's going to get around anyhow, probably. Just by gossip." I told her about Bandy.

For a while she didn't say anything. Then, "But, oh, what'll he do? With his flock all turned against him."

I finally said, "Maybe not. It might not be as bad as you think. If he does it on his own. You know how much they think of him."

She didn't answer, but she seemed not to take any heart in this. Then, just as she was turning away, I had what seemed like a brainstorm. "Wait," I said. She waited. "Look. Think about getting him to resign, go somewhere else way off. Say he's been offered another job. Or maybe just say he's sick or something. Anything they'll believe. Think about it."

I thought maybe she was struck with the idea, but she left without answering.

I held on to the thought, but not entirely for the noblest of reasons. I couldn't overlook the fact that thereby, among other possible benefits, my name would not be mixed up in a scandal. All the same, the benefits would not be only mine. I waited, hoping that my idea might after all win out.

I saw the Reverend only once through the rest of that day. He came out and looked at the lumber on the truck bed, started to unload it, and quit, and went back into the house. He appeared at supper, but stayed just long enough to look at the food in front of him and start on a blessing, which he didn't finish. Then he returned to his room.

Without question he was genuinely sick. As I learned, he spent the night and most of Sunday morning getting out of bed with the dry heaves and in between times lying stretched out and looking something like a corpse that hadn't been treated. In the afternoon, the doctor came, an old man with a black bag full of bottles and instruments. His diagnosis was *flu* and, maybe, a little bit of heart trouble. I guessed that these were his favorite diagnoses, but in a manner of speaking, he was surely right about the second one. Heart trouble? I thought how this might bear on my newly concocted scheme.

Of course, church services, both morning and evening, were out of the question. Miss Maggie had put the word around, mentioning, as she later told me, heart trouble among the causes. Success?

I visited him briefly on Monday, but he was in no mood to talk, and neither was I. He just lay there looking toward a window and hardly once toward me, and I was glad. The coals heaped on my head were hot enough already. And the time would come, no matter for my new scheme, when I would have to tell him.

In fact it came the next morning, sooner than I had expected. Already, yesterday, I had gone to the mailbox early. Clearly Smit's, without return address, was not among the letters. Too soon. But today, there it was. I took it and hurried back to my hut.

It was in red ink, all in capital letters for disguise. "I KNOW ABOUT YOU AND THE HORE. $500 WILL KEEP ME FROM SPREADING THE WORD. IN MAILBOX WHERE THE HORES LIVE. BY NEXT SATARDAY NO LATER."

I stood for several minutes holding the letter, with Smit like a living presence hidden somewhere close. Would he come tonight? Time was needed for my new scheme to work. I would lie to Smit, and hold the letter back. I thought again. There was something ignominious here.

It was up in the morning before I summoned the will. He was better today, alert, propped up on pillows against the head of his bed. A window was open now, and I wondered if the breeze stirring the orange curtain and playing about my face and naked arms seemed as cold to him as it did to me. I guess it was my expression that made him appear to expect some kind of news. There was a chair, and to fill the empty moment I sat down. The letter was folded away in my pocket. He was looking at me, a trustful kind of look. He quietly said, "I've about decided on what you told Maggie. The best thing, I reckon. Just chuck it all." And a little later, "I'm obliged to you."

I drew a breath, then another one. I had to. I reached into my pocket and took the letter out. Looking at it, he said, without much interest, "For me? Who from?"

I couldn't think of a better place to start. In silence I handed him the letter.

It seemed a long time. He read it and, while something like an enflamed stitch took shape in his pale brow, read it again. His eyes on me had come alive. "Who from?"

The Adventures of Douglas Bragg

— — —

My dried-up lips and tongue managed to say, "Smit. Smith. That you used to have here." But I had started and I went on, telling it in fragments, with furtive upward glances that never quite touched on his face. I can say with just a little pride that I didn't too much stress details likely to temper the things I did. I ran out of words and broke off with a dying fall.

He didn't say anything for a time, though once I saw his lips make a silent word. I think it was an oath, a rare thing in the Reverend. He said, with a little shake of the letter in his hand, "I'll see to this."

I couldn't stop myself from saying, "I didn't know he was going to do this. This letter."

Now, instead of through and into a distance, his gaze was on me. It had softened. He finally said, "I reckon I got plenty of blame in this, too." Then, "There ain't a man in this world but's got something he needs to be punished for."

I looked away.

Up in the afternoon, from my hut window, I was all but astonished to see him out there by the truck unloading the lumber I had neglected. I didn't go help him; it would lead to talk. And I already knew that now he would stay and face the music.

— — —

There was supper to be got through that night, mostly without talk, and days yet before "the Sunday." But for now I had more than this on my mind. To my surprise, and also my relief, Smit didn't come that night. On the next one he did, however, and spoke in a voice that somehow struck me as different from in the past. Standing barely silhouetted there, he said, "He's sure got my letter by now. Did, didn't he?"

Carefully I said, "Yeah. I think so."

"Think?"

"I'm pretty sure. There was one yesterday that he looked to be brooding over." The thing not yet clear in my mind was what I wanted Smit to think.

"Did he do anything . . . different? Like, go somewhere?"

Yes, or no? My hesitation lasted longer than I intended. "I just know he put it in his pocket."

Smit fell quiet. He didn't sit down. Though I still couldn't see his face, I had already started to think that his silence had an ominous tone. For the first time, it came to me that I might be in the presence of somebody really dangerous. "He could have gone somewhere and me not know."

Except for the word "Yeah," delivered in an undertone, his silence went on for a space. Finally he said, "It's like I'm starting to get a whiff of something."

I took his meaning. For a disguise I made a stab at humor. "I guess maybe I could use a bath."

"Yeah. A good one. I don't much like the smell."

Sticking to my charade, I lightly said, "I'll see to it."

In a voice gone flatter still he said, "That's sure what I'd advise," and turned away, or vanished, in the dark. The lying son-of-bitch.

My newborn anxiety about him stuck with me for a while, until it became clear that, whatever his feelings toward me, he was helpless. Blackmail was a crime, and in back of that was a criminal record. The Reverend had kept his intentions to himself, but it was possible that even now some kind of legal action was in the works. Meanwhile it was the upcoming Sunday that mainly occupied my thoughts . . . mainly but not completely.

In these days of anxious waiting, I was a sharer, of sorts. I surely had no expectation that I would end up prepared to look on that impending Sunday as a veritable Liberation Day. The application, I'm pretty sure, was first of all to my own case, but in my mind the two came to be like parts of one. The pain would be mostly theirs, but for them and maybe more real than for me, liberation would be the outcome.

It was on Saturday that I received my gift. The Reverend came out to my hut. The haggard and disheveled look was there, but his voice was strong. "I've fixed it for you to go your own way, boy. Any time you want. Now, if you want. Miss Maggie and me might just be leaving, too . . . once it's all over." Forcing my fingers open, he put a bill in my hand. It was for fifty dollars. I made some kind of a protest, but he didn't stay to hear it.

The next morning I watched them drive away, in their regular Sunday-go-to-meeting clothes, he in his tight dark coat and she with the little black ribbon circling under her chin. I was no more willing to go along than they were to have me, and to pass the restless hours I set a task for myself. It didn't help much. At some minutes after eleven I put my hammer down. The service would now be under way, and by the time I arrived it would be half over with. I took the truck.

The Adventures of Douglas Bragg

I had timed it about right. Parked in the lot beside the church I could hear through open windows the hymn they were singing. It was "Farther Along," one I liked, and by my figuring would be the final hymn before the sermon. I was right again; a silence followed. I waited, seeing him in memory, his straightened arms and hands closed on the pulpit's rounded margins, his restless circling gaze, all one with the tireless strength of his voice. I was trying now, but I couldn't hear the voice. Get out of the truck, go nearer? But there were the windows. I listened and listened, and though the silence still prevailed, I heard it once or twice. I thought of, imagined Miss Maggie, up front as always, shrinking in her pew. No; I thought not. I would have bet she sat there like a rock, unshaken through it all. And the rest of them behind her? I envisioned the lot of spellbound faces with mouths hung slightly open.

The organ notes announcing exit did little more than briefly suspend the silence. Out front and nearer to me in the parking lot, clusters gathered: heads leaning one to another and voices thoughtfully hushed. Not all of them, though. I heard, close by, giggles from a couple of boys, and I saw more faces than one with smirks on them. In a hurry now I started the truck and left.

So, at least as far as I knew, it was finished. That silence I had experienced there at the church seemed like it had attached itself to the Reverend and Miss Maggie and, so, had been brought back home with them. In the days before I left, they said nothing in my presence on the subject, and nothing reached me from other sources, either. I did get the impression that they might be thinking about leaving. I never found out.

But if their case was finished as far as I was concerned, my own, arising from theirs, was not. What happened could have cost me my life.

I had learned that Smit was on the run. It was not only the charge of attempted blackmail, there was also the suspicion of drug dealing, which had been around for a while. Anyway, he had got wind of it, and vanished. This suited me perfectly well. It was enough for me to have him permanently removed from the scene. The trouble was that he wasn't. Whether he had been hiding somewhere, or had fled and secretly come back in the night, I have no way of knowing. To say he *appeared* to me is not exactly accurate, because I never literally saw him.

It must have been some good angel who had arranged to have me do what I did on the night before it happened. My cot had been directly

The Adventures of Douglas Bragg

- - -

199

under the window of my hut, but because of a new chill in the night air, I had moved it over against the opposite wall. So Smit had miscalculated. I was sound asleep when a crash, the breaking of my window, waked me violently. The moment's delay that followed was just enough to bring me upright on my cot, already smelling the reek of gasoline. The flash of a struck match was the herald that saved me. My lunge for the shut door, which I crashed right through, was just about simultaneous with the brilliant explosion behind me. I hit the ground and rolled and came up on my feet to see, this quickly, the whole interior a furnace of roiling orange and crimson flame.

I stepped back, circled, scanning for sight of him between my burning hut and the woods beyond. There was nothing to see.

The Reverend was there with me. We watched the fire diminish and settle down at last in a heap of barely throbbing cinders. I heard him more than once mutter the word *evil,* and for the first time the word in its antiquated meaning took on reality for me.

I had lost everything, but the Reverend lent me money enough to get by, accepting my promise that I would pay him back as soon as I was able. I had to return to Boulder Creek to get my impounded car. Somebody must have been fooling with it, because it started right up, and I was on the way out when something occurred to me. I turned around.

It was not too long a drive. There was no car parked in the driveway, and the house itself had a deserted look. To be sure, I climbed the steps onto the gallery and, uneasily, lifted my hand to knock. I did, and nothing happened. I tried the knob. The door came open, and I was facing a room full of silence and nothing else; all the furniture was gone.

At the little store up the road I learned about all I needed to know. From the proprietor's half-amused expression I could tell that he also was acquainted with the ladies and their profession. "Been gone four days," he said. "I reckon they plan on setting up house someplace else." In answer to my question Why, he said, "It weren't the Law told them to. It was just some man plain-dressed. Some says it was a preacher."

I thanked him and got back in my little car and drove away.

6

UNTIL NOW, driving back through Boulder Creek that morning, I had all but forgotten about Buster Bell, and I decided to take a little time out for making inquiries. Supposing that old men would be the ones most likely to know something, I struck up a conversation with several of them. Of these, only one could remember who Buster Bell was, and he had nothing more to contribute. What was I to do, then? . . . take off blind down some country road? I was sick of roads, anyway, and what I finally did was get in my J.T.-mobile and reluctantly head back for Nashville. Then, Birmingham?

At least it was a fine April day for a drive, and I tried to keep my mind on that and the scenery instead of brooding about what I was going to do after I landed. It wasn't very long, though, before I spotted well ahead of me a guy on the road shoulder with his thumb already up. I was determined that this time I was not going to risk picking up anybody, drunk or sober, and I passed him by with hardly a glance. I thought again. My glance had showed me a young-looking fellow, well enough dressed, holding a small grip. Why not? I stopped and even backed up a little way, and he came on at a trot.

He got in with a grateful look on his face and thanked me two or three times. All the way from Knoxville, he told me, two whole days hitchhiking. Hard going in these days, he said, because now just about nobody trusted anybody anymore. Without my asking, he told me he was heading for a place where people did trust each other.

"Where's that?" I said.

"It's a commune. Freedom Earth. Ever heard of it?"

I had barely even heard of communes at all. I glanced at him, noting a kind of pleased expression that looked as if it was not only natural to him but would stay there come what may. I said, "I didn't even know there were any communes in these parts. Thought they were just in California."

"This is the first and only one around here. An early bird. Pretty soon they'll be everywhere, though. Got a friend at this one, wrote me all about it. Sounds like just what I've been needing. More and more. In the kind of world we live in."

Since he seemed ready to open up, I said, "What kind's that?"

He looked at me like he thought I was a rather dim bulb, and finally said, "I'm disappointed you haven't seen it, felt it. Most people haven't, don't want to. Rather not think about it. Just hunker down."

I didn't mind the implication, the truth being that at least up to a point I was likely to be in agreement with him about the world nowadays. Anyway, I was soon feeling disappointment of my own, because what I had taken to be his natural winning expression had now given way to one of Hamlet-like woe. And in fact this expression was preface to a vocal litany of woes he evidently had had to bear in person for some years.

I learned, or was reminded, that a mood of separateness, isolation, and loneliness was everywhere, that our society was structured to alienate people, that we were shut off from our sensory nature and the deep, inner you, that Nature had ceased to speak to us, that true family had ceased to exist, that we were over-intellectualized and other-directed, that we wanted soil, not concrete, under our feet. And the remedy for these things must be a deep-down revolution of consciousness.

And on he went, while I kept thinking that most of what he was saying made pretty good sense. It certainly represented a lot of reading and careful thought by some people with considerable learning. If only it didn't come across to me with a taste of staleness that left me perilously dozing at the wheel. And left him, even well after he had finally shut up, with a fixed, sour expression on his face.

But at last he came back to life. With excitement he said, "This is it, I think. Slow down."

The Adventures of Douglas Bragg

The sign that said "Duncan's Gro" on the wall of a little frame building made him certain, and at his direction, I turned left onto a narrow gravel road. "Hot damn," he said.

It was about a mile, mostly through woods and finally over the top of a hill. "That's it down there," he blurted, and I got a glimpse of open bottomland with some structures roughly gathered in a ring. At the foot of the hill we were stopped by a shut gate, which he (I still didn't know his name) quickly got out and opened, then closed behind me. There was a hard-to-read sign on a tree, but that was all. We passed a grove where four or five cars were parked and stopped well out in front of a hut that put me in mind of an outsize wigwam.

Right at first I didn't see any sign of life except some chickens and three or four goats. One of these, a billy with crooked horns, looked threateningly at me as I got out of the car. My friend (I soon learned that, no doubt because of his nose, he was called Pug) was already prepared to meet the embrace of a lanky young man who, with howls of greeting, was coming on at a trot. Other people appeared. The nearest one, stepping out of a much smaller wigwam, was a fair young thing with a nursing infant at her perfectly bare breast. Seeing me taken aback, she gave a smile fit to knock a weak man flat. I thought that if this was the kind of smile inspired by brotherhood, I should think about staying on for a while.

Her name, she said, was Betsy Lou . . . just that, and as I was soon to learn, there was nobody in this place with a last name. Anyway, after our brief and, on my part, stumbling conversation, I started looking around for other Betsy Lous.

Alas, there were not any. There were women, all young, seven or eight out of a total membership that numbered maybe twenty-five people. But except for a couple of others who also went around bare-breasted, I didn't look twice at any of them. At first, that is, because there was one, not in view till now, who suddenly grabbed, and held, my most rigorous attention. Close-shaved as it was, her head looked to be about the size and shape of a colorless bowling ball balanced on a stalk that grew out of an equally colorless naked torso where large breasts like twin bubbles grew. Somehow she put me in mind of somebody just now arisen from an unquiet grave. It didn't take me long, though, to notice that she was much deferred to here, a charismatic figure. Nevertheless she gave me the creeps.

The Adventures of Douglas Bragg

— — —

203

At least in mild weather like this the men also were not much for wearing clothes. Nearly all of them went shirtless, in shorts, even jockey shorts, or ragged jeans. One, in fact, went buck-naked, evidently supposing that his muscular form was a sight worth seeing. The only one wearing a real shirt was the apparent head man in the company, a tall angular fellow with a persuasive voice, named Buff . . . a Californian, I learned. He, supposing I had come to join up, started out to show me around. Pointing to a large shed with benches inside, the central structure encircled by a dozen knocked-together huts, a couple of trailers, plus a single structure that looked like a real building, he said with a grinding accent, "That one with the benches is where we get together for meditation and prayer. Twice every day. That's just about our main thing, you know. Communion, real communion. With each other and all creation."

I was prepared for something like this, but his pious expression put me off a bit. To show interest I ignorantly said, "Do you have some kind of a 'guru'? Like one of those Hindu 'maharishis'?"

"We will have, by and by." Pointing to the highest of the rich-green wooded hills around us he went on, "But there's our real guru. We all go up there for meditation. To take it all in, breathe it, commune with our deeper selves." (I imagined that hillside spotted here and there with meditators.) He added, "You'll be surprised at the results."

It was at this point that I had to tell him I didn't mean to join, which didn't please him. But after the few moments while I stood there half-expecting him to bid me goodbye, he informed me that I could stay overnight for fifteen dollars. This was a strain on my scant treasure, but I was curious, and I paid him right out of my pocket. I was further advised of my right to attend Meditation Hour, in the shed, if I chose. I did not choose.

That one structure of any real size, which had to have been a barn once upon a time, housed a combination kitchen and mess-hall, with an iron wood stove and a big stone oven, with homemade tables and stools scattered around. The rest of the space inside was taken up with old army cots, some wicker baskets, and several beat-up clothes cabinets. I claimed a cot by putting my handbag on it, but I needn't have. As it turned out, nearly everybody else slept either in the little rough-hewn shacks or in one of the trailers. A few, the more dedicated ones, even slept outside on Mother Earth, for their souls' sake. I guessed that the cots were for new members expected to come in now that spring was here. None showed up while I was there.

When I came out of the building, it was obviously Meditation Time, because everybody was headed for the big shed. Most of the ones that passed close by gave me a brotherly smile or even a handshake, but a couple of them, maybe because I was just an overnighter, looked at me in an unbrotherly way.

In hopes to see Betsy Lou come out of her wigwam, I walked across to other side of the grounds. Alas, too late, already in the shed meditating. But I did see something I hadn't noticed till now. The sun was just about to disappear below the horizon, and against its light, at a distance of maybe three or four hundred yards, a man was plowing behind a single mule. I guessed it was a mule. I could see that the man had already turned up a considerable lot of ground, and it looked like he was going to keep plowing right on into the night. I had supposed that this whole stretch of bottomland was the property of the commune, but it seemed I was wrong. Some poor old dirt farmer out there plowing up ground for the corn he was going to plant. On and on he went, turning a corner now.

Then, a surprise. Betsy Lou emerged, late for Meditation, holding her baby at her breast. This time I didn't have to stumble. I said, "I take it that man out there plowing is no part of all this?"

She looked. "Aw, not really. But he's kind of like one of us. We call him Old Timer. Came looking for a place to live. He went and got him a mule. He's planting corn for us. A nice old man." She smiled and turned and headed on up to the Meditation. I stood watching the man till I saw him, in twilight now, unhitch his mule and lead it off into the dark.

A while later, sitting on a log used for a bench, I listened to them chanting. The words, as best I could hear them, didn't mean anything to me, but the sound, the music, did. It had a pitch, a kind of soaring otherworldly quality, that really did get to me. I was sorry when it stopped, though in the aftermath I kept on hearing it inside my head. Finally I got up and went into the empty building where the kitchen and all were. On the stove there was a big iron pot half full of some kind of vegetable stew (no meat) and some kiwi fruit on the table beside it. I ate a little of the stew and then, suddenly very tired, sought out my cot and lay down.

I must have been asleep for a while before I heard the sound of music, country music. Happy hour now. At first it was live music, the work of somebody not much good at either singing or playing the guitar. This stopped and a little later was replaced by what was obviously recorded music. I recognized the voices of Roy Acuff (singing "Great Speckled Bird"), Little Jimmy Dickens, and a couple of other well-known ones. Then came a voice that actually startled me. It was unmistakable, and the song was "Deep Valley." A miracle, of sorts. I swung my feet to the floor, but I stayed put there on my cot until, only a few minutes later, happy hour came to an end. Then I quickly got up.

The boy I stopped outside the building explained it to me. He remembered, all right, and it certainly didn't matter that he referred to J.T. as J.B. and sometimes as G.T. J.T. had been here and stayed for the best part of a week and had not liked it a bit. "The only thing he liked," the boy told me, "was giving us that record he made. 'Deep Valley.' I don't think it's much, but he was mighty proud of it."

All this sounded exactly like J.T.

The boy went on, "He must have made a lot of money out of it, though . . . or out of something. He had a car bound to cost him a pile."

I left there in the morning pretty early, stopping only in hopes to receive from that sweetly bebosomed young lady another such smile as had almost floored me yesterday. And the smile was there, with the same effect, though the bosom this time was covered. Hanging on, looking at the baby, I said, "He's a fine-looking fellow. What's his name?"

"Beatrice," she mildly said.

"Oh," I murmured, and thought to turn away. But another thought compelled me. "Maybe if you could give me an address . . ."

A gentle movement of her head quite shut me down. Murmuring something in the way of a farewell, I turned to leave, then stopped again. There he was, just as before, though farther out in the field. Plodding behind his mule, on and on as if there never would be an end of it. Outside of time, I was thinking, as I drove away in my car.

– – –

The matter of J.T. was fully, and surprisingly, clarified a few days afterward. Meanwhile, on the drive back to Nashville, I stopped to buy gas, and after paying, discovered that I had exactly seven dollars and fifty-two cents remaining. I thought about the old gas station and whether I might be that lucky still another time. So that was my first stop.

Mr. Cook looked at me with a jaundiced eye, but there was no gainsaying the "Help Wanted" sign once again posted out front. It just wasn't a good place for a gas station, and the job didn't pay enough to keep employees for long. Considering this, I made him an offer I hoped he couldn't refuse. I would stay on the job twenty-four hours a day, at night sleeping or napping on the cot he had in his little office. Also I would draw, daily, just a few dollars from the total salary I would receive at the end of one full week. He grudgingly accepted this, although, as I soon discovered, each evening he left in the cash register barely enough money for me to make change with. But a week should give me money enough, I hoped. And after that . . . ? Back to Birmingham?

It was to be a tiresome week, enlivened only by small interludes of interest. One of these came on my second day when, to my great surprise, I found in the *Nashville Times* a late, months-late, story about Buster and his mysterious disappearance; this and also two letters to the editor on the same subject. Maybe my little private game, that I had given the name 'Goose Chase,' was paying off. At least, as the story mentioned, my cues about where Buster might be found had been taken seriously enough to spur investigation. And there were the letters, both in ardent defense of Buster, along with praise for his "greatness." Even the story in the *Times* spoke of him now as a "notable country music star." So, in addition to the pleasure derived from having kept them all busy, there was my conclusion that I had helped a little to revive his reputation. So, that little trick of mine had borne some good fruit.

Another source of interest was three successive night-visits by a lady of mature years whose hair I took to be dyed blond and whose car, it seemed, required an excessive amount of gas. She had to do so much driving, she said, though the needed quantity of gas on nights two and three came to little more than a gallon per visit. Her name, which she volunteered, was Alice. "This old car just uses so much gas," she said each time, and went on with the likes of "Needs a little tuning up, or something. My husband won't do anything to help, he's so lazy."

I have never considered myself much of a magnet for amorous ladies, but obviously I had made a hit with Alice. I was a little stirred, but mainly for the fun of it, I played along with her, especially on the last of her visits.

"Maybe it's my oil. Maybe it needs checking again," she said with a little sigh.

The Adventures of Douglas Bragg

I did it and afterwards told her it was okay.

"Well," she said resignedly, "Something just doesn't feel right. I don't know what's the matter."

"A sluggish feeling?" I insightfully said.

"Yes. Sort of . . . stiff-like. Like it needs something."

"Maybe it needs a grease job.

"Oh, do you think so?"

"Has it had one recently?"

With a little flash of her eyes, she said, "No, not in a long time. It probably does need one?"

"It wouldn't hurt."

"You could give me one, couldn't you?"

I hesitated. Only to test her, I said, "Yes ma'am. You could get it now if you want."

This time she was the one who hesitated. With lifted brow, "Oh, could I? How long would it take?"

Only a few minutes. You can see I'm not busy now."

"Well," she murmured, hesitated, sighed again, and looked at her wristwatch. It was just as I had come to anticipate. She said, "I'd better wait till another time. I have to go somewhere now." Coyly smiling, she started up her engine and raced it a little before she drove off. This had been her last visit, and I idly wondered if she was now on her way to play footsie with some other gas station attendant. You can see that my days at work were not without their more uplifting interests.

But much more wholesomely interesting was another visit, also at night. The second it turned into the station, I recognized the car. Buster's flaming-red Lincoln convertible, by God, and J.T. driving . . . the car no doubt the one referred to by the boy back there at the commune. J.T.'s grinning face in the window said, "Wondered if I just mightn't find you here. And shore 'nough." He had grown his hair long, and the pale fuzz above his upper lip might yet become a mustache. He was also wearing red suspenders.

"And here you are, too," I said. "What are you doing in Buster's car?"

"Ain't his no more. He give it to me. And that ain't all. Give me a thousand dollars and told me take a nice vacation and then go on back home. Which I ain't goan do."

"Go back home, you mean?"

"Not to no pig farm, I ain't. This here's the place for me. Man, you ought to seen them look when I drove this bugger up where the Opry stars hangs out. One good look and they was looking at *somebody*. I'm going get *in*."

I didn't want to be cruel and I didn't say *baloney*. I said, "I guess you know where Buster is?"

"Yeah, I know. But he told me not tell *nobody*."

"Come on. You know I wouldn't squeal on him."

J.T. firmly shook his head.

I decided to give it a shot. "Back at his old childhood home place, I bet." But even as I said this, there was a thought rising in my mind.

J.T. looked surprised. "How'd you know?" He tried uselessly to correct himself.

"You're just guessing, though."

"You've already let it out."

"Yeah, but you still don't know where it's at," J.T. said defensively.

"Okay. Up there by that commune. How am I doing?"

J.T.'s expression told me I was doing well. I suppose it was no wonder that I had failed to make the connection until now. "I was up there last week . . . just by accident. I picked up a boy who was going there. I saw a man way out in the field plowing, but I never thought about it being Buster."

"All right," J.T. said. "Just don't tell nobody."

"Don't worry." After thinking for a moment, I said, quite innocently, "How much of that thousand dollars have you got left?"

He was a little slow to answer, but he said, "Plenty of it. And which reminds me. Buster said if I saw you again, give you some of it."

"Never mind," I said. "I'm okay. You better hang on to it."

But he already had his wallet in hand and he took a bill from it and held it out to me. It was for a hundred dollars. "Take it," he said.

"I've already been using your car. That's enough."

"Keep it. And take the money, too. I got a-plenty more."

"I hesitated. Then I thought, Why not? It would just go down the drain. And now I would have a enough to pay the Reverend back and plenty left over. I took the money.

"Before you know it," he said, "I'll have a lot more than this coming in. One of them Opry people told me I got what it takes. He's goan set me up."

"Set you up, is right," I said. "Set you up for skinning. He'll end up with your money and your car both. And what he doesn't get, those Opry women will."

The Adventures of Douglas Bragg
— — —
209

"You just wait and see. I ain't no country dummy." He was getting impatient.

"Un-huh," I said. "You better think about it some more. They've got tricks you never heard of."

"I done thought. Anyhow, it's my business."

"All right." I could see it was hopeless. But then, after mulling for a little space, I decided that if anything at all could make an impression, good straight talk would. I thought about reminding him of how he had got hooted down at Buster's party, and what that should have told him. But I didn't . . . a waste of breath. I mumbled something about how farming was a good thing to do, and let it go at that. This didn't even get his attention. He was back in good humor again, and gunning his motor, he left me with a grin on his face and a promise to drop back by.

One more thing happened, on my last night at the station. There had been other times that week when I had thought about that bastard Snipes and imagined he was somewhere out in the dark watching me. And maybe he had been. Anyhow, the way he suddenly showed up in the flesh caught me off balance.

I was casually watching a customer drive away in a brand new Chrysler when I had a sudden intuition that somebody was standing behind me. I was right, and it was Loman Snipes, plain as day in the neon light. "Surprised?" he said.

It took me a moment to gather my wits. "Yeah," I said. "What do you want? But I guess I know, don't I?"

"Yep, you guessed it." His keen black eyes and sharp little snout of a nose were pointed straight up into my face.

"You been watching me?"

"Some. Enough to see if you were ready to bolt on me again."

"Bolt? You think I can't go where and when I please without consulting you?"

He ignored my question, studying me. "Where'd you go?"

"None of your damn business. Anyhow, haven't you got anything else to do but spy on me? Haven't you got a job, for god's sake?"

"Freelance. I follow up my stories."

"Well, you won't get one from me. So, bug off."

He didn't move a muscle. He said, "Wasn't that Buster Bell's little buddy, in that fancy car last night?"

So he had been on watch. "What if it was? All he told me was that Buster had given it to him." I cagily added, "Because it was too easy to spot. After that, he didn't know where Buster went."

"Withholding evidence is a crime," Snipes flatly said.

"Well, it's not my crime." My vexation had turned to anger. With my gaze fixed on that sharp snout of a nose, I thought how much I would like to flatten it across his face.

"Assault's a crime, too," Snipes said, taking me by surprise, causing me to unclench my fist. He added, "But you'll see I'm mighty good at finding things out."

"Not from me. Now get going."

He left me with a nasty smirk on his face and disappeared in the shadows across the street. It was all bluff. And even if he could locate J.T., the boy for sure wouldn't tell him.

I did have one other encounter with Snipes, though not face-to-face. In the morning I settled up with Cook and was a good many miles down the highway to Birmingham before I discovered that the little creep was following me. Recalling what I did next still gives me satisfaction.

I might not ever have realized Snipes was back there except that my J.T.-mobile started giving me trouble and soon threatened to quit on me. Just in time, I came to a turnoff where there was a filling station at the top of the ramp. That was when I saw him. My progress up the ramp was a series of jumps and jerks and allowed time enough for me to recognize him . . . in a vaguely familiar green car driving slowly. For concealment's sake he had to pass on, and by the time I got up to the gas station, his car had disappeared beneath the overpass. But he would come stealing back. Right then my mind started churning.

The good nature, as well as the knowledgeableness, of the station attendant were two more pieces of good luck. It was not only good nature that moved him, but also his interest in my car. Once he had got the hood up and spent a couple of minutes studying the motor, his interest evolved into something like fascination. He said he had never seen anything like it. He said it looked like it had been dreamed up by a gifted maniac or maybe prankster. But he went right at it, chuckling as he worked, while I stood gratefully by.

When he got my car fixed, I was careful to pay him a good deal more than the modest sum he mentioned. It wasn't needed, I could tell, because he seemed more pleased than otherwise to go along with my

The Adventures of Douglas Bragg

little plan. I said, "He'll be in a green car. A little, sharp-nosed man, with lots of black eyebrow. You'll know him right away because you'll want to kill him on sight." A good stroke, that last, I thought, because it added something more to the man's amused expression. I said, "Be sure and tell him I headed for Worthington. That sign over there says eighteen miles, right?"

"Just about. And you'll be heading the other way . . . for Portia, I take it?"

"Well, part of the way."

"A bill collector or something?"

"*Something* is right. *Son-of-a-bitch* is better."

It was done, and I drove across the overpass and parked among trees just beyond the highway signs. I took a concealed position from which I could watch the ramp, and waited. It wasn't a long wait. Snipes had circled back around and, slowly approaching, turned onto the ramp. I moved to where I could see him stop at the gas station and, briefly, his face in the car window speaking to the attendant. Then away he went toward Worthington, in search of me and the much-sought-after Buster Bell. It was small revenge, I thought, but satisfying anyway. I also swore a mighty oath to myself that this would be my last trick ever.

Well before I got to Birmingham, I was thinking hard about my next moves. The thought of confronting my mother, who I had treated shabbily (only two postcards, I think), now presented itself as a bit of an ordeal.

By the time I reached the city limits, I had changed my mind about my agenda. Instead of going directly to her (to my?) home, I would hold off until I could present her, if possible, with the fact that already I had a job. But when and where had I ever had a real job? The Rainbow Paint and Dye Company, Inc.? It was nothing much; none of my jobs were much. The dog pound? I pondered this one. Of all the jobs I had had, this was the only one that had given me any satisfaction, and it was somebody else's fault that I got fired. Law school? I put the thought aside.

At a Toddle House over chili and grilled cheese I thought some more about the dog pound. A lowly job, all right, but like any large establishment it had administrators . . . and I probably could inflate the importance of my position in my mother's eyes. In time, who knew? I might rise to the status of Dog-Warden-in-Chief. So I paid my bill and got under way.

The Adventures of Douglas Bragg

— — —

It was more sightly than I recalled, with brick front freshly scrubbed and much shrubbery and a new addition where happy dogs drowsed or barked or cavorted in open pens. The entrance room, too, was brighter, spanking clean with new paint and practically cleansed of the animal odors I remembered . . . all indicative of the rising status of dogs and cats in our society. Three women at a long table were busily instructing customers who, pens in hand, struggled with intricate forms somehow needed for acquiring or donating animals. To the other side of the room was a large plate-glass window through which I now saw the boss man, Lew Turner, memorable for his shaggy mane. Approaching, I stepped on an escaped puppy, which screamed to high heaven, but it didn't hurt my cause. He remembered me, and after my explanation concerning the fault that had got me fired, he took me on.

Now Mother was on my agenda. Up in the afternoon I turned into the driveway and sat there rather admiring the small neat brick house and the small very green lawn dominated by a single pecan tree. She must have seen me through a window, because when I got there she was standing in the open door. She wasn't a woman much given to crying, but now she had real tears in her eyes. She said, "So you've come back from your travels. I worried, you know." An unfamiliar hollowness of her cheeks was like a small testimonial.

"I'm sorry. I meant to write you more. Things kept happening."

She wiped a tear away. She was looking past me. A smile was forming on her lips. "And I see you've brought a car back with you. I think it's a car. So you haven't come back empty-handed."

"Not quite," I said, responding to her smile. Things were going to be all right.

In the bright little kitchen she made tuna sandwiches and served them to me where I sat at the center table. She wanted to hear my news, but I got in first. "How is Uncle Jack?"

Her face darkened briefly. "He passed on. About two months after you left."

I sat there hushed for a moment. "I bet he went down still talking, telling stories."

"Oh, yes. About old times. Never stopped. He lived back then completely. He was calling for General Forrest when he died."

"I hope the general came." I paused. "It was a world of wonders he lived in."

The Adventures of Douglas Bragg

— — —

213

"Better than ours?"

"From what he told me, I'd say so." I was thinking of my travels and all the things I had seen. I could tell she wanted to hear about them, but then I thought to ask, "Any other news?"

"Yes, sort of." Her face made a little grimace. "Your father. He's in the penitentiary."

"The penitentiary?"

"For two or three years, I think. Some legal matter." She paused, evidently to let it soak in. "He finally outsmarted himself. Now he has all that time to think about how clever he is." With a sort of knowing look at me, and to my surprise, she added, "I hope you'll take warning."

I needed some moments to digest this. My heritage from him. Poor Father.

She insisted on hearing about my travels, and in greatly shortened form and with convenient omissions I proceeded to oblige her. But it was my father I wanted to hear about. When finally the moment seemed right I said, "You mean the Tennessee State Pen . . . where he is?"

"No. In Alabama. It seems he was licensed to practice here, too." She wryly added, "I suppose he saw opportunities here."

I couldn't help but smile a little. "So he's not all that far away."

"No. But far enough, I'm glad to say."

I was thinking that it was not too far, but I let the matter rest for now and went along with subjects more agreeable to her.

But two days later I made up my mind. It was over my mother's quiet protest. "What kind of a father has he been to you? When have you seen him since you were twelve years old? Or heard from him?"

"There were a few times," I feebly said. "Anyway, he's still my father. And being in the pen could change a man."

"In six months? It would more likely take twenty years for him," she said, and shut her mouth tight and turned away.

In her wake I murmured, "Have a little faith," and followed my own counsel.

She did lend me her car, and the trip took barely an hour. I had had visions of talking to my father by microphone through a glass window, as in the TV dramas, but I was surprised. I guessed it was his persuasiveness that had done it. Inside that big, gray, depressing building, all gray inside as out, I was led from the warden's office down a corridor between barred cells where stoical faces, and occasional sly comments,

The Adventures of Douglas Bragg

followed my progress. My armed guide at last opened a door into a room containing only a long table with chairs and that waiting man who was my father. Or was said to be, because on first sight I would not have recognized him. Standing, as he was, he looked much shorter than I remembered. And this was not all. In those first moments I felt almost sure that I was looking at the wrong man. The impression didn't last long, however. The quick black eyes and then the hurried way of speaking brought him back to me all at once.

"Well, son, been a long time. I thought about you, though. Always too busy. Sit down there and talk to me." We sat, facing each other across the table.

I didn't know what to say, but I did feel that maybe this visit was a good thing and that we could get together again in the way I seemed to remember. A long-ago fishing trip came to mind, and I might have brought it up if he hadn't interrupted. "I believe you went to college, didn't you? And graduated?"

"Yes. Didn't you know that?"

"Of course. I just forgot. Certainly."

For a minute I thought he was going to ask me another personal question, but he didn't. All the same I was still thinking that my visit, besides just cheering him up, would have good results for both of us.

"Sorry you had to find me in here," he said. "It's an injustice. Accused me of helping bribe a congressman. Wasn't that way. A crook named Phillips got it put off on me . . . the son-of-a-bitch. I'm not that stupid. All I did was take a few bucks from a fellow said he wanted to support the congressman. I admit I was playing close to the edge, but I never really stepped over. Wouldn't believe me. Brought up against me a couple of little missteps I made a long time ago, didn't have anything to do with the congressman."

I didn't understand it all, but his manner was convincing.

"Won't be in here much longer, though. Got some things working out there for me that are plain sure to fix it."

Somehow the two words *fix it* stuck in my mind . . . for a little while, anyway. It turned out to be more than a little while, however, because, switching the subject, he got off with enthusiasm about a *real deal* he had waiting for him when he got out of here; and *fix it* came up a couple of more times. He left the specifics of his deal pretty cloudy, but from my demeanor he seemed to conclude that I was impressed. In the pause

The Adventures of Douglas Bragg

that followed, his keen black eyes were fixed on me, and I could tell that, for only the second time, something personal was in the works. He said, "Boy, law is the way for you to go. The times are full of opportunities for smart lawyers. Get you a law degree and maybe we could go into partnership."

I sat with my mouth open, not knowing what to say. Fortunately the door was suddenly opened, and our allotted time was up. To my goodbye, all he said was that I should remember his advice. By this time, it did not surprise me that he had made no mention of my mother.

I didn't tell my mother this, or very much of anything else about my visit. But she studied my face and turned away with what looked mighty like a smirk. Without looking back at me, she said only, "Let this be a lesson for you."